DROWNING MY SORROWS

A Cambridgeshire Mystery

Martyn Goodger

This book is a work of fiction. The story and characters are wholly
the product of the author's imagination. Any resemblance to
actual persons, living or dead, businesses or events is entirely
coincidental. For more information about the background
to the book, please see the author's afterword.

To Samuel, my son

1

'If there weren't any students,' I said, 'the University wouldn't be a bad place to work.'

Harriet smiled politely. To be fair to her, I wasn't expecting more. In one form of wording or another, mine was one of the most commonly heard jokes around Senate House.

'In fact,' I went on, 'it would be a perfect place to work if there were neither students nor BDMs.'

I knew, of course, that I was taking a risk with my reference to BDMs. It was less than six weeks since Harriet had split up with Hugh, the business development manager she'd been seeing when I joined the University at the start of July. The relationship had all been very casual, as far as I could tell. However, as Harriet's new line manager, I'd felt it was appropriate for me to sound a note of caution, strictly from a professional perspective, once I got the measure of Hugh. Harriet had a bright future in law and it would have been a shame if this had been put at risk by an unsuitable liaison.

Harriet appeared not to notice the subtext in my remark.

She said, 'There are a couple of things I need to discuss, Alan, before our meeting with Professor Fuller this afternoon. But first let me grab a coffee. I had another date last night and didn't get home until past midnight. I need something to wake me up.'

It sounded like the date hadn't been invited back to hers, which was undoubtedly for the best. We in Legal had a lot on, now the new academic year had started, and it wouldn't be in the team's interests for Harriet to be distracted by an entanglement with some random pickup from Ely or the nearby

1

fenland towns. I watched her walk the short distance to the coffee machine and back. I could see why Hugh had been so keen on her. Although there was no official dress code for professional staff at the University of East Cambridgeshire, she was wearing one of her usual flattering interpretations of smart casual – today a pair of tight-fitting, dark denim jeans with a light blue shirt that accentuated her shoulder-length, dirty-blonde hair.

It was just after 8.30 a.m. and there were still only a handful of people on the second floor of Senate House. It suited us both to arrive early. Harriet liked to be first in the bathroom of her house share near Ely station, and once dressed and ready for work preferred to come in and have a leisurely coffee at her desk rather than hang around at home. I liked the chance to plan my day and spend a bit of time on my own with Harriet. Over the next half hour, the floor would fill up: the University's senior leadership team occupying their individual glass-fronted offices that ran along one side, everyone else taking their places in the pods of desks that were scattered around the open-plan area.

'So will you be seeing this man again?' I asked as casually as I could, when Harriet sat down next to me with her coffee.

She wrinkled her nose. 'I doubt it. He was OK, I suppose. Quite pleasant to look at. But not particularly bright and there were a few red flags. He even called his ex a psycho.'

He didn't sound much of an improvement on any of the men she'd met via the dating app since finishing with Hugh. She'd developed a habit of telling me about them during our early morning chats and I'd been flattered by her trust in me. She never volunteered anything salacious and, needless to say, I never asked. But I got the impression that so far none of the dates had progressed into a full physical relationship. Once, she'd made a laughing comment about a date not allowing her to escape until she'd agreed to a kiss, but she'd looked at me a bit strangely when I suggested she might have been taken advantage of and should consider reporting it to the police.

'Anyway,' she went on, 'enough about my love life, or lack thereof. I need to speak to you about International. Also about

2

some stuff I'm doing for Hugh.'

After certain things that had happened recently, I wasn't surprised to hear her mention International. But I rarely got involved in work she was doing for BDMs.

'What's Hugh's problem?' I asked.

'He's setting up a new KTP,' she said. 'Mostly bog-standard. But he's too impatient to get the contract signed. I've explained it's not so simple, but he's blaming me for slowing things down.'

I'd never heard of KTPs, or Knowledge Transfer Partnerships, before I joined the University, but already I felt I understood them more than most. Essentially, they were government-funded schemes that brought universities and businesses together to work on strategic projects. Businesses liked them because they got access to a university's know-how on the cheap. Universities liked them because they were a source of valuable research income. BDMs liked them because they were a quick and easy way for them to demonstrate to their university that they were actually doing something useful.

'Leave Hugh to me,' I said. 'Let me have a copy of the proposed contract with a note of your reservations. I'll have a read and then speak to him.'

I was already looking forward to putting Hugh in his place. He needed to know that Harriet had moved on. He worked on the first floor of Senate House, along with most of the other staff on the business side of the University. The people there liked to think of themselves as being commercially savvy, but in my opinion few would last long in jobs outside the higher education sector.

'I've also got International on my back,' Harriet went on. 'Mehak said you still haven't provided feedback on those heads of terms she sent you.'

I looked closely at her face in case this was payback for my jibe about BDMs. But she appeared to be in full work mode. That was a relief. I didn't want to have to explain why I'd sat on the heads of terms for as long as I dared, before finally forwarding them to her the previous Friday with a brief *'Please deal when you have time'* instruction.

Mehak was an attractive young woman of Indian heritage, responsible for the University's recruitment of international students. Much of the University's income came from persuading students from all over the world to come to Cambridgeshire's least-known higher education institution. They were then charged around three times as much as home students. However, persuading potential international students to study at the University of East Cambridgeshire rather than at scores of more prestigious UK universities was a tough task. Lots of dark arts were involved, including the use of commission-remunerated agents of various degrees of reputability.

In my first week at the University, Mehak had come up from the first floor to introduce herself to me and to explain how International worked. I'd been eager to show off my knowledge, as I'd already realised that until my arrival there hadn't been a decent practising lawyer anywhere in the institution. Mehak's team had a backlog of legal work to be done and she was clearly grateful for the way I prioritised it, sometimes working late at night or at weekends. She came in early like I did, and once or twice a week she took to inviting me to join her for a coffee first thing at her pod downstairs. We were often the only people on the first floor at that time. We talked about things other than work and occasionally she would reach out and gently touch my knee. It all felt very cosy and intimate, and it was pleasant to be appreciated after everything I'd gone through earlier in the year. After what I thought was an appropriate period, I therefore suggested that she might like to come out for a meal with me one day after work.

'I would love to, Alan,' she replied. 'But I have a boyfriend and I don't think it would go down well with him. He's the jealous type. There's no reason, of course, why we can't continue to have the occasional early morning coffee.'

I had understood, and indeed I had rather liked the idea of being the kind of person to make a boyfriend jealous. I'd taken some pleasure in imagining her boyfriend's reaction if Mehak had announced to him she was going out for a meal with the new solicitor at the University. It would have been my first date since the tragic events concerning Helen earlier in the year that had led to my enforced departure from Doveley's, my previous employer.

I was therefore hurt when, a few weeks later, I overheard on the stairs a fragment of a conversation between two of the administrators in International. 'Mehak's got at least two men on the go,' one woman said. 'I don't know where she gets the energy from.'

It was clear that Mehak's statement about having a boyfriend had been an excuse to reject me. I felt she'd made a fool of me. I pictured people in International laughing at me behind my back. After some thought, I resolved to prioritise other teams' legal work over hers in the future. I am somewhat ashamed to admit that, on occasions, I even thought of other things I might do to make her wish she hadn't deceived me.

But now, if Mehak was obliged to ask Harriet to chase me to get her work done, perhaps she was starting to appreciate the consequences of her behaviour.

'OK, let's have a look at Mehak's heads of terms,' I said.

Harriet wheeled her chair close to mine and placed the document on the desk between us. I scanned it quickly. As no one in International was legally trained, it was as poorly drafted as I expected: full of inconsistencies and in places almost incoherent. In due course, Harriet would turn the heads of terms into a new template contract with the University's overseas agents, being careful to ensure not only that it worked legally but also that it didn't infringe any of the University's policies on the remuneration of third parties. First, though, I would make sure she pointed out to Mehak everything that was wrong with the document. I ran through the key points she should make. I was in my element, with Harriet's full attention on me. I didn't allow myself to be distracted by the closeness of her face to mine or the smell of her perfume.

I must have lost track of the time because it came as a slight shock when Harriet said, 'You may want to finish this later, Alan. The boys are here.'

2

The boys, as Harriet called them, had arrived together as they usually did. They drove to the University on different routes, one from Soham and one from Littleport, but they liked to meet up in the car park for a smoke before coming up to the second floor. I sometimes brooded over how often they talked about me and what they said.

'Good morning, Alan. Good morning, Harriet.'

This was Richard, a weaselly-looking individual in his forties who'd been in Legal for longer than anyone else.

'Hi, Alan and Harriet. How are you both?'

And this was Tom, a much younger sporty type who was every bit as easy-going as he looked.

Richard and Tom were – like Harriet – contracts executives, which meant they were doing legal work for the University without the benefit of a professional legal qualification. From my first days at the University, I'd tried to encourage them all to want to improve the quality of their legal work. When I'd started out in law, I'd been eager to learn from anyone and everyone. However, whilst Harriet had blossomed under my tutelage, I'd soon discovered that I was wasting my time with the other two. Richard simply didn't have the interest or ambition. And Tom ... well, let's just say that while everyone liked him, I'd never heard a word of praise for any work he did.

I sometimes liked to refer to my team as 'Tom, Dick and Harry', although none of them seemed to find this particularly amusing. Before I'd joined the University, they'd reported directly to Lewis. Now they reported to me and I reported to

Lewis. At first, I'd mulled over why Lewis had wanted to recruit as good a lawyer as me, who might be a threat to his position in the longer term. Soon, however, I realised that he simply wanted someone to take over the responsibility for making sure the University's legal work was done correctly, so that he could concentrate on the arse-licking and empire-building he enjoyed most.

Harriet had now rolled her chair back in front of her computer, and Richard and Tom took their normal unhurried time to settle in opposite us on the other side of our four-person pod. I watched as they switched on their computers, shuffled their files on their desks and leant towards each other to continue some conversation. I could see a slight smile on Harriet's face as she noticed my impatience. I banged out a couple of routine e-mails but found it hard to concentrate. Finally, I walked round the pod and took up a position between the two of them.

'Tom,' I said, 'can we have a word please about the NDA you drafted on Friday for the School of Computer Science?'

'No problem, Alan,' he said in his usual laid-back way. 'We were only talking about yesterday's match. Did you see it?'

This was so typical of the man. He knew the NDA (or non-disclosure agreement) was required urgently, and the fact that I was asking him about it first thing on Monday should have indicated there was a problem with what he'd given me to review. But what was his first reaction? Yes, to ask if I'd watched a bloody football match.

'I didn't have time,' I said. 'I had too much work on over the weekend. I didn't even get round to your NDA until last night. And it's not good enough, I'm afraid.'

Tom looked puzzled. 'But I based it on the one which you drafted last month for the School of Engineering. I changed the names but otherwise it was your wording.'

If he'd said this three months earlier, I would have assumed he was taking the piss. But by now I'd concluded that he really didn't know any better.

'In my NDA,' I said, 'the School of Engineering was *disclosing* confidential information to the outside company. So I imposed onerous obligations of confidentiality on the company. But in your NDA it's the other way round. The School of Computer Science is *receiving* the outside company's confidential information. So do you think it's a good idea to impose the same onerous obligations on our School of Computer Science?'

Tom tilted his head slightly to one side, like a garden bird pondering whether some soft soil might contain a juicy worm. I could almost hear him struggling to think it through. I tried not to show my impatience. It's not his fault, I told myself.

'Ah,' he said at last, with the type of smile you'd expect to see on the face of a Nobel Prize winner who has made an earth-shattering discovery. 'You mean the School of Computer Science should only agree to use its reasonable endeavours to keep the company's information confidential?'

It wasn't perfect, and if I'd been drafting the NDA myself, I would have done it differently. But I knew that trying to teach Tom to do it properly would make about as much sense as trying to teach a cat to shut a door after itself. The result would just be that I'd have to redo the whole thing myself. At Doveley's, no trainee solicitor with this slowness of thought would have lasted for more than a couple of weeks. But the University, like many public sector organisations, seemed remarkably loath to deal with under-performance. I supposed that, unlike at Doveley's, the managers weren't paying the salaries of the under-performers out of their own pockets.

I did a quick risk assessment and said, 'It's OK, Tom. Make that amendment and pass it on for signing by Amanda.'

Amanda Middleton was the Secretary and Registrar, the University's principal administrative officer, who worked closely with the Vice-Chancellor and the pro-vice-chancellors. She was one of the University's authorised signatories on documents, and as long as I'd approved a contract she would sign it without bothering to read it – with the unspoken understanding that it was my neck on the block if the contract turned out to be a dud.

But at least Tom was easy enough to handle. Richard was a different matter. He had developed the cunning needed to thrive in a university environment. I didn't trust him an inch.

'I've been looking at the consultancy agreement which you drafted for the School of Social Sciences last week,' I said as I turned my attention to him. 'It's generally fine. But the main terms and conditions say the fee will be paid in three instalments, whereas the appendix says it will be paid in two. They can't both be right. Which is it?'

'Ah, I was going to mention that,' he said. 'The School only provided me with the appendix after I'd sent them the terms and conditions. I spotted the inconsistency, obviously, but I wanted you to check that everything else was OK before I went back to the School.'

I knew that was rubbish, but Richard's invariable response to anything going wrong was to find a way in which he could avoid being blamed. I bit back an angry response. I'd quickly learnt that at the University I had to choose my battles. 'Ask the Dean of School which payment terms he prefers,' I said. 'Tell him it's not a legal issue for us. Then make the relevant amendment. I don't need to see the agreement again after that.'

While I'd been occupied with Tom and Richard, the second floor had gradually been filling up. The big cheeses, including the Vice-Chancellor, had gone into their offices, nodding hellos to various people on the way in an attempt to show that they were still men and women of the people. As I took my seat back on my side of the pod, I noticed a tall, immaculately dressed figure with greying hair striding across the open-plan area towards the office that was closest to me. As I'd often thought, he looked more like an executive from an advertising agency than a manager at a university.

As he passed the pod, he said without slowing down, 'Good morning, Alan. Can you spare me five minutes?'

3

Lewis had already taken his seat behind his desk when I walked into his office. He must have done this deliberately because I'd got up from my chair as soon as I heard his summons. He made me wait just a couple of seconds too long for comfort before inviting me, with a point of a finger, to sit down opposite him. He then turned back to the screen of his laptop and made a pretence of reading something important. I knew he was pretending because his eyes didn't move down the screen.

Lewis Morgan was the Director of Legal Services. Until my arrival, he'd simply been the University Solicitor, but that title had evidently not been sufficiently grand for him. He was the sort of man who would spend more time negotiating an improvement in his job title than he would a complicated royalty clause in a 'bet the business' patent licence. He'd been at the University for about five years, after leaving private practice with the usual excuse of wanting to achieve a work-life balance. More likely, he'd been managed out for incompetence or laziness. Certainly, I'd seen no evidence of him having provided any proper supervision to the contracts executives when this had been his responsibility. I could remember the astonishment on their faces when I first began returning their draft contracts with my red corrections and comments. Lewis, I gathered, would approve their contracts and send them off for signature virtually unread.

Lewis's office wasn't as big as those occupied by the Secretary and Registrar and the pro-vice-chancellors, let alone the Vice-Chancellor, but it still looked very plush and fashionably minimalist: all plastic wood and polished chrome and glass. There wasn't a law book to be seen anywhere. He'd personalised the walls with various abstract artistic prints, all no doubt intended to show that here was a man of culture. In my few months at the University, I couldn't remember Lewis actually doing a scrap of proper legal work. He'd perfected the technique of farming complicated work out to random external law firms, then presenting their advice as if they had simply provided a second opinion which confirmed his own view.

'Thank you for sparing me your time, Alan,' he said eventually in his light, singsong voice. 'I gather you're extremely busy.'

I wasn't sure whether that was a statement or a question, so I said nothing.

'I've heard good things about your work for the School of Engineering,' he went on. 'Simon Fuller says you've been very helpful.'

Harriet and I were going to see Professor Fuller that afternoon. Lewis was letting me know he was on good terms with him.

He continued, 'I wanted a word about Mehak in International. I was speaking to Kate from HR last night at the Vice-Chancellor's drinks reception. She said Mehak had mentioned something about you not being very responsive recently when she'd needed some work doing. Can you reassure me there's nothing in it? International bring in a lot of money for the University, so we in Legal have to support them as much as we can.'

It was going to be the infamous shit sandwich. Praise the work I was doing for Professor Fuller. Have a go at me over Mehak. Then no doubt finish by finding something else to praise me for.

'I don't know what Mehak means,' I said.

'You weren't upset that she didn't want to go out with you?'

For Christ's sake, I thought. Why the hell was Mehak raising this with HR? I knew I had to be careful, though. Although strictly truthful, it wouldn't help if I pointed out that Mehak had lied to me about having a boyfriend. It would make me look like

I couldn't handle rejection.

'Of course not,' I said. 'It's true that I suggested we catch up one evening away from the University. But it was only a suggestion and Mehak was entitled to say yes or no. I don't understand why she thinks I've been unresponsive. Only a few minutes ago, before you got in, I was briefing Harriet on the work she'll be doing for International. That's part of my job – to delegate the less complex work to the contracts executives.'

Lewis fell silent for a few seconds. I knew he didn't much like me. And he wouldn't have missed the dig about me already being hard at work when he got in. But he knew I wasn't foolish enough to say anything which could easily be disproved. He stroked his silvery moustache, which ran in a neat triangular shape right up to his nostrils.

'There is one other thing I wanted to mention,' he said eventually. He'd obviously decided not to pursue the Mehak point. 'The University has, after a thorough due diligence process, appointed new external solicitors on an exclusive basis. For those occasions when we don't have the capacity to do the work ourselves, or when we require input on a specialist area of law.'

I hadn't been told this procurement process was taking place, let alone that an appointment had been made. Even though, as the only decent lawyer in the University, I would have been best placed to advise on how to choose a law firm.

'Fortunately,' he went on, 'it won't take you long to get to know the new firm. It's Doveley's, from Cambridge.'

There was a taste of bile in my mouth. I couldn't believe what he was telling me.

'I must apologise for not bringing you into the loop earlier,' he continued. 'But you might have found it difficult to give an objective opinion on their merits in view of your past association with them.'

Association my arse, I thought. You mean the many years I'd given them, including countless hours of unpaid overtime, and the huge fees I'd generated for them. Only to be chucked out of the door like a piece of dried dog shit when I found out the truth about the death of my former girlfriend, Helen Eccles, also a solicitor at the firm. The truth had been an uncomfortable one for the firm and, in particular, for those involved, but I hadn't deserved to be treated in the way I was. I'd tried to ask the head of HR at Doveley's what I should have done differently, but all she'd said was that it would be easier all round if I accepted the exit terms I was being offered, which included a reference in what would be an agreed form. I hadn't even had the chance to say goodbye to anyone. I heard later from our professional support lawyer, one of my few allies at the firm, that an e-mail had been sent around the firm announcing my departure and offering to pass on any farewell messages that people might have for me. In the circumstances, I shouldn't have been surprised that there weren't any. No one would dare declare an affinity for someone known to be leaving under a cloud.

'You'll have a chance to renew your acquaintance with them very soon,' Lewis continued. 'There's a meeting of the Enterprise Board tomorrow. To discuss various projects that the University is investing in, or which they might want to invest in. They're sending two of their corporate lawyers, a Jeff Parker and his trainee – Lucy something or other. Seems a pleasant bloke, Jeff. I had a chat with him yesterday. He said he's looking forward to catching up with you again.'

4

I'd slunk back to my desk as soon as Lewis had dismissed me. For all the crap I heard spouted within the University about the public sector being better than the private sector, more inclusive and more respectful, the way he treated me felt no different from how I'd been treated by my old boss, Sam Snape, in my time at Doveley's.

The mention of Jeff Parker's name had thrown me into turmoil. My nemesis from Doveley's and the man I still thought of as having stolen Helen from me. My only slight consolation was that in the end he too had lost Helen, and in circumstances which must have made him feel less of a man. I just hoped that when I saw him, I wouldn't have to endure another of the bloody handshakes he was always so keen on.

I wasn't looking forward to seeing Lucy, either. She'd been my last trainee at Doveley's but had totally taken advantage of my good nature. Playing up to me when she wanted something, then going behind my back to snog Nosey Parker when he could be of more use to her. In some ways, she reminded me of Mehak.

Ironically, I hadn't seen anyone from Doveley's in the six months since I'd left the firm. On the rare occasions I went into Cambridge during the week, I steered clear of the streets around Parker's Piece and The Drum pub through fear of coming face-to-face with someone from my old life. And I certainly made sure that I never caught sight of the city centre multi-storey car park where Helen had died and where I had so nearly also lost my own life.

I tried now to distract myself with the work that was at the top of my to-do list for the week. It was mostly a mix of research or commercial contracts with external parties: contracts for me to draft and other people's contracts for me to review and amend. I didn't usually get involved with student, employment or property issues; these were handled by the Student Centre, HR and Estates, respectively.

Around me, most of the forty or fifty people in the open-plan area were at least making a pretence of being hard at work. The senior management's EAs – executive assistants – were typing away at their pods outside the row of glass-fronted offices, trying to make themselves look more important than the glorified secretaries they were. The bean counters who worked for the Director of Finance were doing their perennial number crunching. Next to them were the procurement and insurance teams. When being introduced to the latter on my first day at the University, I'd cracked a joke, which had gone down like a lead balloon, about me only needing a couple of hours once a year to sort out all my insurance requirements. Beyond them were the teams dealing with governance and what was called strategic planning – your guess is as good as mine as to how they filled all the hours of a working day.

I often thought that my work was the most complex – and in many respects some of the most important – of all the work done in the open-plan area of the second floor. Today, I began by marking up my amendments to a clinical trials collaboration agreement between the University, an NHS Trust and a couple of other universities. Next, I finished off a PhD studentship agreement which I'd started drafting the previous Friday. After this, there was a patent licence to work on. Unlike the world-famous University of Cambridge, twenty miles down the A10, the University of East Cambridgeshire was hardly blessed with a portfolio of headline-making patents. But we had a few, and there was always some company wanting to take a punt on bringing a patented invention to market. My job was to make sure that the company took on all the financial and legal responsibilities and that, if the product was successful, the company couldn't wriggle out of paying the agreed royalties.

Meanwhile, Harriet, Richard and Tom got on with their own work without any input from me. Harriet had her mobile phone on her desk as usual, and a couple of times I saw her smiling to herself as she read a new message and then quickly sent a reply. I mulled over whether she was arranging another date, but I couldn't think of a way to ask her without it looking like I was taking an inappropriate interest in her personal affairs.

From around 12 p.m., people began to take their lunch breaks. Small groups of two, three or four people would get up at the same time and head together towards the door that led onto the landing and from there to the main staircase. At 12.30 p.m., I noticed Harriet looking in the direction of Richard and Tom, and there was a mutual nodding of heads. There must have been some kind of prior arrangement because all three then got up. I hadn't been invited to join them and for a moment I felt – however illogically – let down by Harriet. It was usual for Richard and Tom to lunch together, but Harriet seemed to go out for lunch with a whole range of different people from other teams. She was one of the most popular people on the second floor and indeed on the whole professional side of the University – popular with both men and women.

'Have a good lunch hour, Alan,' she said.

I looked for a sign of mockery on her face, but there wasn't one. The truth was that I seldom went out for lunch with anyone. During my first few weeks at the University, a number of people from other teams on the second floor had invited me to join them for lunch, usually in the refectory near the centre of campus. But these had mostly been awkward encounters. My lunch companions hadn't known the answers to the questions I asked about legal issues that affected the University, and I had no particular interest in their areas of work. A couple of times there had been someone who expressed an interest in my two passions outside work: tennis and true crime. But after we swapped a few anecdotes, I got the impression they were ready to talk about something else, whereas I would have preferred a detailed discussion of a subject that appealed to us both. Consequently, I soon got into the habit of spending most lunch hours at my desk, eating whatever I'd brought with me from home. This meant I could get on with my work uninterrupted, so I was not unhappy. And on this occasion, it meant I could prepare for the afternoon's meeting with Professor Fuller.

5

'What do we know about Professor Fuller, then?'

I liked the way Harriet had framed her question. The use of 'we' suggested an intimacy between us.

Harriet and I were on our way to Professor Simon Fuller's office in the School of Engineering, roughly a ten minutes' walk from Senate House. The University campus was on the left-hand side of the old main road as you drove from Ely towards Littleport. Its layout often reminded me of a human body. At the top, closest to Ely, was Senate House, which I thought of as the brain and the eyes and ears of the University. From there, there was a walkway to the central area of the campus where the academic schools were located, most of them reached by two narrower walkways that diverged left and right from the main walkway like two arms. If you kept on the main walkway, however, you would, after a further ten minutes' walk, reach the main domain of the students: the Student Centre and the Students' Union (or the 'cock and balls' of the campus as I termed it). Beyond that, again diverging left and right like two legs, were the routes to the two main campus student living areas, one a large traditional hall of residence and the other a sprawling series of blocks of self-catering flats.

The School of Engineering was one of the schools that the University liked to big up in its promotional materials. And of all the academics at the School of Engineering, Professor Fuller, a specialist in biomedical engineering, was definitely one of the stars. In the old days, he would have increased his reputation outside the University by appearing on some obscure BBC2 programme. Nowadays, it was mostly done via social media.

'Ever since I joined the University,' I said, 'I've had people telling me how loyal Simon Fuller is. How he's altruistically chosen to stay with us rather than jump ship to the University of Cambridge or to any of the other hundred-odd universities which regularly rank higher than us in the league tables.'

'But you're not falling for it?'

I glanced sideways at Harriet to check that she wasn't teasing me. 'I don't think it has anything to do with loyalty,' I said. 'I think he enjoys being the big fish in a small pond.'

Harriet placed a finger theatrically over her lips. 'Be careful who you say that to,' she said. 'I only know him by sight, but the whisper is that he's one of Deborah Jones's favourites.'

'That doesn't surprise me. He must bring in shedloads of money for the University. Not just research income, either. He's the named inventor on a couple of University patents in the field of biomedical engineering which are now being exploited by our commercial partners.'

'And that's why we're meeting him today?'

'Correct. His latest patent is for an invention that, he claims, will revolutionise the market for wearable technology. Smartwatches, fitness trackers, and so on. Most of them now give detailed feedback on a wearer's fitness and health. But Simon's invention takes things a step further. It can apparently flag up warning signs of all sorts of diseases which existing devices can't detect. It won't give you a confirmed diagnosis – you'll still need a doctor for that. But you'll be advised what type of specialist to see and what they should be investigating.'

'Impressive. He can't be all bad if he's helping to save lives?'

At times, Harriet's naivety was touching. It made me realise how important it was that I was there to look after her. Without me, so many men would try to take advantage. As she walked alongside me, her step matching mine, I couldn't help but notice how attractive she looked in the bright autumn sunshine: her hair bouncing gently on the shoulders of the smart black jacket she'd put on over her shirt. I wondered if any of the people who could see us together were assuming that we were a couple.

I said, 'Well, he's certainly no serial killer. But it's a bit like saying that all nurses are angels and all doctors are heroes.' I'd never much cared for members of the medical profession, who often seemed to consider themselves a cut above lawyers. 'I'm sure he's pleased that his inventions do some good,' I continued, 'but remember that he benefits from them personally as well.'

'You mean under the University's intellectual property policy?'

'Precisely. He doesn't own the intellectual property in his inventions. That belongs to the University as his employer. But he gets a percentage of the profits that the University makes. Not a huge amount, granted, but it's free money for him because he doesn't have to take any risks or invest any of his own money.'

'And today we're discussing how his latest invention can be exploited?'

'I've already discussed that with him in general terms. He's got a commercial partner lined up. So today we need to agree with him the main commercial terms of the licence and then you can have a go at producing the first draft.'

'That sounds really interesting, thank you.'

It made me feel good to know that Harriet appreciated the effort I put into my mentoring. Quite unlike some of the ungrateful trainees I'd had at Doveley's. I felt a flash of annoyance at the reminder that I would be seeing Lucy Black, one of my old trainees, at the Enterprise Board meeting tomorrow. I would have to plan carefully how I dealt with this so that it would look to Lucy, and to her colleague Jeff Parker, that I'd moved upwards and not sidewards since my departure from the firm.

*

'It's very good of you to come over, Alan,' Professor Fuller said. 'I do hope it hasn't been a wasted journey for you and your charming colleague.'

I'd been blindsided from the moment we walked into Professor Fuller's office on the first floor of the School of Engineering. On my two previous visits, on my own, I'd sat opposite him across his desk in his comfortable spare office chair, feeling very much that we were professional equals, albeit in different fields of expertise. I'd noted at the time that, near the door, there were two cheap plastic chairs that I assumed were for use by students. Today, the Professor was seated in the same office chair, but seated opposite him, in what had been my chair, was another man I hadn't seen before. Although Harriet and I were expected, the impression I had was that we were interrupting a cosy tête-à-tête.

Both men were about the same age: late forties or early fifties. But there the resemblance ended. The Professor had a bony, almost entirely bald head, and he didn't seem to be carrying an ounce of spare flesh. He looked like a stereotypical Yorkshireman – the type who would nut you with his head as soon as punch you with his fist – except for the fact that his lips were unusually fleshy, almost feminine-looking. In contrast, the man opposite him looked like nothing so much as a massive egg. His neck was so fleshy that his small, round head seemed to merge into his body.

'Alan, this is Ian Davey,' Simon said as both men stood up to shake our hands. 'He's the founder and MD of the company which is the School's main commercial partner. Ian, this is Alan Gadd, the new solicitor at the University, who is here to make sure I don't do anything foolish. And this is his colleague, Harriet Wells, who I understand from Alan isn't yet a qualified lawyer but who hopes to be one in the future.'

I looked sideways at Harriet, worried that she might feel I'd been underselling her on my previous visits, but she seemed not to have noticed what I was sure was a deliberate slight by Simon.

There were then a few minutes of the usual small talk. Ian Davey had walked up from the student end of the campus, and he made an admiring comment about the new swimming pool which had been built down there next to the leisure centre.

Harriet laughed and said she was tempted to use it to finally learn how to swim. Harriet and I then sat down on the cheap plastic chairs like a pair of naughty schoolchildren, and Simon launched into what sounded like a prepared speech.

'Alan, your advice last time was very helpful. Lots of food for thought. I looked through the licensing models you left with me. I can see how in theory they would be the most suitable way for the University to exploit my new wearable technology.' He paused, manifestly only for effect; he knew what he was going to say next. 'However,' he went on, 'things are not so simple in practice. There is massive competition from some of the world's biggest companies. They won't just roll over and let Ian's company become a market leader. They are likely to challenge the validity of the patents. Or find ways to invent around them.' He paused again.

But this time, as if responding to some non-verbal cue, Ian Davey took over: 'That means, Alan, that my company will have to invest a huge amount of money in the further development of the technology and the manufacture of the devices, with no guarantee of success.' Although Ian was still sitting opposite Simon across the desk, he had turned his chair to face me and Harriet. It felt very much like them against us. 'I can't sell this investment to the Board if we're only a licensee of the patent,' he continued. 'It's too much of a risk.'

I said, 'What are you suggesting then, Simon?' It annoyed me that Ian Davey was even at this meeting and I wasn't going to debate with him directly. 'Do you want to look for another licensee?'

Simon shook his head as if dealing with a delinquent child. 'Not at all. Ian's company is best placed to take the technology forward. And we have a long-term relationship with them on a number of other projects too, as you will be aware. It's the licensing model which isn't appropriate, as Ian indicated. Ian is concerned that they may invest a lot of money and time and then end up being ditched by the University.'

'But we covered all this last time,' I said. 'We can draft the

23

licence in such a way that Ian's company has all the long-term protection it needs. The University wouldn't be able to terminate the licence early unless the company breached the terms of the licence.'

'I hear what you're saying, Alan. But you have to understand things from Ian's point of view. He believes he can only justify the investment to his Board if the company's going to own the technology outright. He has consequently made an offer, which I feel is a generous one, to buy all the intellectual property rights in the technology in return for a one-off lump sum payment.'

I couldn't believe what I was hearing. It wasn't the principle – everything has a price, after all. Rather, it was the fact that this had been discussed and agreed behind my back.

'How much?' I asked.

Simon and Ian exchanged brief glances. It was as if they were deciding who was to go first.

'We've agreed that one hundred thousand pounds would be a fair price,' Simon said. 'Plus full reimbursement of our patent costs to date. On top of that, Ian's company has kindly agreed to provide some ongoing benefits in kind. Things like an internship for one of our students.'

I was nonplussed. At our last meeting, without Ian Davey being present, Simon had been talking about the University getting hundreds of thousands of pounds a year in royalties if the technology proved only to be a modest success. And millions of pounds a year if it really took off. Compared with this, a one-off payment of £100,000 – even with the promised add-ons – was peanuts. OK, with the licensing model there was a risk of the University getting nothing if the technology flopped or if Ian's company couldn't bring it to market, but that kind of risk was routine for a big institution like the University with its fingers in many pies.

'That seems incredibly low,' I said. 'You said last time that if the technology was as successful as you hoped, then—'

'Alan,' Simon interrupted. He had the cheek to raise the palm of his hand in my direction as if to tell me to shut up. 'You've been good enough to give us the benefit of your advice. I'm grateful for that, I truly am. At the end of the day, though, you are only a lawyer. One who, dare I say, is still relatively new to the University. You advise on legal issues and very authoritatively so. However, you – and by you I mean the Legal team, not you personally – don't make commercial decisions for the University.'

I suddenly saw a way forward. 'Exactly,' I said. 'But with the greatest of respect, Simon, neither do you. Decisions of this importance need to be made at Senate House, by the—'

'By the Pro-Vice-Chancellor for Enterprise and Innovation.' Simon completed my sentence for me. 'Yes, I've already discussed the proposal with the PVC, who knows more about the commercial realities facing the University than either you or me. Taking everything into consideration, she agrees that the offer of one hundred thousand pounds, plus the reimbursement of our patent costs, plus all the benefits in kind, is a fair price and one which the University should accept.'

6

Harriet remained silent for most of our walk back to Senate House. She could see the mood I was in. I was annoyed with Simon Fuller for striking a deal with Ian Davey behind my back. I was also annoyed with the PVC for, apparently, supporting the deal without seeking my opinion first. But I was probably most annoyed about being outmanoeuvred in front of Harriet.

Since my arrival at the University, I'd done my best to show her how an experienced solicitor such as myself deals with a varied and complex workload. I wanted her to unlearn all the bad habits she'd undoubtedly picked up when being supervised by Lewis. Yet here I was having been completely wrong-footed by some head-in-the-clouds academic in the arse end of the Fens.

Deep down, I knew I'd handled the meeting badly. Other solicitors at Doveley's, even those not technically as good as me, would have torn Simon Fuller's head off – PVC or no PVC – for negotiating a deal of this magnitude without the prior involvement of Legal. But I'd bottled it. I'd backed down from confrontation, as I often did, and I felt sick as I remembered the triumphal smile on Ian Davey's face when I'd simply said that I would discuss things further with the PVC. I knew from past experience that, once I got home that night, I would spend ages running over the meeting again in my head, coming up with all sorts of better responses that I could have made to Simon Fuller's bombshell.

For the umpteenth time since leaving Simon's office, I threw Harriet a sideways glance. She had the feline half-smile on her face that made her look so attractive, even though objectively her nose and mouth were slightly too large to make her conventionally beautiful. I couldn't help but wonder what she was thinking. However, she was clearly waiting for me to break the silence. It wasn't one of those occasions when she was going to gush spontaneously about how well I had performed.

'That was very disappointing,' I said eventually. 'Professor Fuller has no authority to enter into agreements with commercial partners. He's … he's …' It was on the tip of my tongue to say that he'd 'gone native', but it occurred to me that this term might nowadays be considered unacceptable in the higher education sector.

'I think he treated you very unfairly,' Harriet said straightaway. 'Springing the deal on you without warning. Having Ian Davey in the room. Not telling you beforehand that the PVC had given the deal her blessing. I thought you handled it very well considering.'

I hadn't expected that at all.

'It did occur to me,' she went on, 'that the PVC might not have been told the whole story. If Simon simply passed on what Ian Davey told him, perhaps the PVC felt she had no choice. Are you going to find out how exactly the deal was spun to her?'

Perhaps, after all, I had painted too pessimistic a picture to myself of how the meeting had gone. It was typical of Harriet that she could spot things that others missed. How lucky I was that we'd found each other.

'Yes, I'm most assuredly going to find out,' I said.

To tell the truth, I wasn't yet sure how to approach this. But I had plenty of time and planning was my forte.

As we approached Senate House, walking companionably side by side, I realised Harriet had changed the subject and was asking me a question: 'Do you know anything about gas safety checks in rental properties?'

'A bit. I rent out my old flat south of Cambridge. And I'm renting now myself, as you know. Why do you ask?'

'Well, it's the house I rent with Kat. We had a gas safety check done last week. We'd both been feeling under the weather. A bit flu-like, headaches and so on, usually after we'd been cooking. I looked it up on the NHS website and they mentioned carbon monoxide poisoning as a possible cause. So I messaged our landlord and a few days later a gas engineer turned up. He found a small gas leak in the kitchen and was surprised it hadn't been picked up on the previous check. He asked to see the previous gas safety certificate, but I'm pretty sure we never got a copy. Is that normal?'

'No, it's not. The landlord is supposed to give you a copy. Otherwise, how would you know everything is safe? Just ask him for a copy now.'

*

As we started to walk up the stairs at Senate House, I noticed Mehak coming down from the first floor. I certainly hadn't forgotten her comment to HR about me being unresponsive. She'd known damn well that this would get back to Lewis, but it had meant that she hadn't had to raise it formally with him herself.

I'd always felt that she had a haughty air about her, and this was now accentuated by the way she was looking straight ahead rather than downwards as she descended the stairs. Once she spotted me, I was expecting her to stop and ask about the work we were doing for her. I was looking forward to telling her that Harriet was fully briefed on what she had to do. I thought I might also try to embarrass her by letting her know I was aware of her comment to HR and that Lewis had agreed with me it had been completely unnecessary.

Instead, as we approached each other, she still didn't look in my direction. She gave a slight nod to Harriet without slowing down, then passed us both so closely that I caught a whiff of her perfume – one that I knew well from those cosy mornings when she'd invited me to come and talk to her at her desk. I was tempted, just for a moment, to turn on my heels and go down the stairs after her. But Harriet must have seen the look on my face because she gave a quick shake of her head and half-raised her hand as if to grip my sleeve.

The moment passed, and Harriet and I continued on our way up to the second floor. I was, as always, struck by how quiet the floor was even though most desks were occupied. At Doveley's, there was invariably some noise and often a sense of urgency on the floor where I worked. Here, people mostly sat quietly at their computers and the atmosphere felt much like a library. Or rather, like an old-fashioned library before they started showing how 'down with the kids' they were by introducing all sorts of interactive activities.

Richard and Tom were working on the type of standard contracts that were their bread and butter. They would have seen me coming, but rather than acknowledge my arrival they both seemed to stare even harder at their screens. In his office, Lewis was similarly absorbed in whatever was in front of him. Pound to a penny, it wouldn't be anything to do with the law.

I was most interested, though, in the office next to Lewis's. This was the office of Deborah Jones, the Pro-Vice-Chancellor for Enterprise and Innovation: the person who had apparently blessed Professor Fuller's agreement with Ian Davey without involving me. I was itching to find out what cock-and-bull story Simon had spun her so that I could get her authority to stop what he was doing. He might be one of her favourites, if what Harriet had said was right, but she would surely listen to Legal.

However, Deborah had Amanda Middleton, the Secretary and Registrar, in with her. The two women were notoriously as thick as thieves even though they were quite different in looks and, on the face of it, personality. Amanda seemed to be doing most of the talking, so there was a sporting chance that they were discussing university rankings or student satisfaction surveys – two of her pet obsessions.

After waiting for about twenty minutes, I was losing patience. I walked over to Deborah's office and hovered outside the door, directly in her line of sight. She must have seen me, so I was slightly surprised when she made no attempt to pause her conversation with Amanda. I did a little jiggle to show that I was trying to catch her eye, but I could swear that she actually diverted her gaze from me. Irritated, I gave a gentle rap on the glass with my knuckles and opened the door a couple of inches.

'Sorry to trouble you, Deborah,' I said, peering through the gap, 'but I was wondering how long you were likely to be?'

I noticed that Amanda, who was sitting with her back to the door, didn't even bother to turn her face in my direction. I'd expected Deborah at least to apologise for not being able to see me straightaway and to give me a rough idea of when she would be free. So I was taken aback when she simply shook her head and waved her hand a couple of times from side to side. I felt like a bloody waiter being told not to disturb a couple of diners enjoying a romantic moment. The blood rushed to my face and I muttered some kind of garbled apology. As I walked back to my desk, I half-wished that I'd gone to announce that one of the University's buildings was burning down with a risk of a great loss of life. I would love to have seen how horsey-faced Deborah would, in the subsequent full glare of publicity, have explained away her dismissal of me.

As I sat down, I noticed a very definite grin on Richard's face. I made a mental note to pay particular attention to the next piece of work he gave me to check. I tried to do my best by people, but if they didn't reciprocate they could expect no further favours from me.

7

As it happened, I didn't get a chance to speak to Deborah that afternoon. She left her office, accompanied by Amanda, about twenty minutes after I'd been dismissed, both women heading off downstairs together. Deborah didn't even bother to make the small detour to my desk to apologise for not being able to see me.

As usual, I was one of the last on the second floor to leave. When I'd been in private practice at Doveley's, fee earners would at least make a pretence of not bolting for the exit on the dot of their official finishing time. But this was the public sector, and at 5 p.m. almost everyone in the open-plan area leapt to their feet and skedaddled for the door as if a fire alarm had gone off. In my early days at the University, Tom and Richard had done the same, but after I'd made a few sarcastic remarks at their expense, they did now make a point of not immediately joining the exodus. Regular as clockwork, though, they were both on their feet, nodding a goodbye to me and Harriet, by 5.10 p.m.

'No need for you to stay, Harriet,' I said. This was a little charade I liked to indulge in. Harriet had never shown any particular desire to stay late, but by giving her permission to leave I felt I was underlining that my relationship with her was different from the one I had with Richard and Tom. As she shut down her computer, I resisted the temptation to ask if she had another date that evening.

Just like at Doveley's, the hour after most other people had left was normally a sweet spot for getting work done. Tonight, though, I felt unsettled, as if something of importance had happened during the day that I couldn't yet put a finger on. I ended up only filing the e-mails in my inbox and leaving the building just after 5.30 p.m.

*

The drive home in my Toyota Aygo took its usual ten minutes. I turned right out of the car park onto the main road towards Ely, went past the old RAF hospital on the left and shortly afterwards turned off towards the modern estate where my rental property was. It had been too far to commute to the University from the flat I owned south of Cambridge, so after getting the boot from Doveley's I'd rented the flat out and taken a six-month initial tenancy on the first low-maintenance house I could find in Ely. With my new job likely to involve less driving, I'd also traded in my Toyota Prius for a three-year-old Aygo with less than 8,000 miles on the clock. The showroom salesman said it had been owned by an elderly couple who only used it for supermarket shopping, so I'd been amused to see that it had one of those emergency escape tools mounted in the driver's footwell, as if they'd seriously believed they would ever have to use it. Although some people might have thought it a backward step going from hybrid to petrol, I'd never been able to shake off the associations in my mind between the Prius and the car park where I'd nearly lost my life earlier in the year.

My property was one of half a dozen terraced houses in a detached squarish block: two at the front, two at the back, and one on either side. None of the houses therefore had a back door or back garden, but mine had a small lawn outside my front door that I shared with the house next door. The landlords came as a double act: a cheery middle-aged woman who did most of the talking, and her husband, apparently a former lawyer, who always turned up to do maintenance jobs – however minor – with a massive two-storey toolbox on wheels. Once, during the summer school holidays, they'd brought their eleven-year-old son with them, and to my mild irritation he'd plonked himself down without asking on my sofa and spent the entire visit playing computer games on his tablet.

I noted with satisfaction that my allocated parking spot in the communal car park was free. When I'd moved in, one of the families in the block had a habit of parking their second car in my spot, forcing me to park my Aygo on the road. I'd got quite worked up over this, especially after my landlords told me to sort it out myself, and had even toyed with letting the air out of their tyres one night so they would be late for work the next day. In the end, I'd settled for leaving a mildly sarcastic note under their windscreen. This had resulted in the man of their house – some sort of tradesman judging by his grubby workwear – banging on my front door, wanting to know what had rattled my cage (as he put it) and why I hadn't simply come round to explain that I'd moved into the property and would be using what had, during the previous tenancy, been an unused spot. We hadn't spoken since, although my approach had manifestly been vindicated because they hadn't parked in my spot again.

Inside, the ground floor of my house looked more like a flat. There was a combined kitchen, dining and living area, the former two differentiated from the latter only by having tiles rather than carpet on the floor. Upstairs, there was my bedroom and a poky second bedroom that I thought of as my office even though when I brought work home I invariably did it downstairs on the sofa.

The first thing I did when I got inside was to feed my cat. I say 'my' cat, but I had inherited her from the previous tenant whose children had moved him into a care home without bothering to rehome his pet. I've never been one for cats, but this one had a deformed front paw and was ravenously hungry when she pushed open the cat flat on my first evening in the house. So I'd given her a few scraps, and then one thing had led to another, and although I would never show weakness by admitting it at work, I did now look forward to her companionship each night when I got home.

Tonight, I cooked a ham and cheese pizza with a couple of handfuls of oven chips and half a stick of garlic bread. I washed it down with half a bottle of chilled Villa Maria Sauvignon Blanc. While I ate, I re-watched one of my favourite episodes of the BBC's *Murder, Mystery and My Family* true crime series, which declared unsafe the 1951 conviction of two Northern petty criminals for a brutal murder in Liverpool. I had a book about this case in my true crime collection, and I always felt a shiver down my spine when I read the men's final letters from their condemned cells at Walton Prison before they were hanged side by side early one April morning.

I was proud of my interest in historical true crime. I could honestly say that, without this interest, I would never have worked out the solution earlier in the year to the death of my former girlfriend, Helen, and her killer would never have been caught. The fact that I, too, had been so close to death in that frightening confrontation in the centre of Cambridge only validated my interest. In some ways, I felt I was now a professional in my understanding of the world of crime.

With my meal over, I switched off the TV and sat back on my sofa, mulling over the events of the day. I couldn't help but feel resentful about how certain people were treating me at the University. I'd put a lot of effort into bringing Richard and Tom up to scratch, but they slowed down the moment I took my foot off the pedal. My line manager, Lewis, seemed to be taking the side of Mehak against me. Simon Fuller had treated me like a lackey, as if my job was just to produce legal contracts to order. And Deborah seemed to think I was a nuisance.

And tomorrow I had to face two of the people who had contributed to making my life so unpleasant at Doveley's: Jeff Parker and Lucy Black.

The only positive I could take from today was the trust that Harriet felt she could put in me. She was prepared to share her dating experiences with me even though they were with people who were patently unsuitable for her. And she'd asked me for help on a matter which had nothing to do with work.

Thinking about Harriet reminded me that I had to deal with that oily oaf, Hugh, tomorrow morning. The fact that he'd had

Harriet in his bed didn't give him the right to criticise the work she was doing for him professionally. I preferred not to picture what they had been like as sexual partners. I was sure, though, that Harriet would have sensitivities that a self-centred man like Hugh could never respond to, and needs that he could never satisfy.

I spent a long time planning how I was going to tackle Hugh. Just like a barrister preparing a cross-examination, I drew a little chart with my opening remarks in a bubble, with a number of arrows pointing off to other bubbles, each of which contained a different follow-up remark depending on his initial response. By the time I'd finished, I was feeling a lot better. I would show Hugh what was what.

The wine was having its usual effect on me and I went to bed shortly after 10.30 p.m. I listened to Times Radio while I drifted off to sleep. As often happened, I woke up again in the small hours. But at least this time it wasn't after a nightmare in which I was dragged screaming up the stairs of that multi-storey car park in Cambridge by my enemies at Doveley's before being tossed over the parapet of the top floor. That was a nightmare which, in one form or another, I had endured many times over the preceding months. Tonight, however, all the horrors on which my nightmares were based seemed to be in the distant past, and soon I was asleep again.

8

I had decided to catch Hugh unawares. If I'd tried to make an appointment, I wouldn't have put it past him to make an excuse to avoid me. He knew he wasn't a match for me intellectually.

Harriet was due in late that morning because of a doctor's appointment. So I worked quietly at my desk until 9.30 a.m. when I headed down the stairs to the first floor. In size and general layout, the first floor was little different to the second. The main distinction was that it had no glass-fronted offices running down one side. No one who worked there was important enough to merit one.

The first floor was the lair of the business development managers (or BDMs) and everyone else below the senior management level who was involved in the University's commercial work. Their job descriptions said things like they were responsible for identifying, developing and implementing new business opportunities across the University. In practice, this meant finding any organisations, from the government through to private companies, who could be persuaded to give money to the University.

The International team was also based on the first floor, as befitted their purpose of bringing money into the University from overseas students who were desperate to have a degree from an English university on their CV. I was relieved to see that today Mehak was not among them.

Hugh occupied a pod with three of his cronies in the far corner. I marched as confidently as I could towards him. Although I wasn't directly in his line of sight, I could sense that he'd seen me. That showed just how little proper work he and his ilk did; most of the time when I was at my pod, the King of England could have walked past without me knowing anything about it. I tried to control my breathing as I got near, as I knew I had to stay calm. It wasn't easy, though, given the effect he'd had on Harriet when they were seeing each other. On the occasions that she'd said she was going to 'stay the night' at his house, I'd always felt frustration because I knew that the next morning she would show signs of not having slept much the night before: yawning, or with dark rings around her eyes. Naturally, she had a right to a sex life with whoever she wanted, but I had to deal with the aftermath. And I wouldn't have been human if I hadn't imagined all the sexual things they might have been doing to each other while I lay on my own in bed at home.

Nevertheless, I can honestly say that, even without his connection with Harriet, I would still have disliked Hugh. He was invariably dressed and groomed as if he thought he was a young corporate partner in a cutting-edge city law firm rather than a low-level BDM in a university near the bottom of all the ranking tables. His dark brown hair always had that tousled and slick look which you get from spending too long in front of a mirror with various expensive potions to hand. His eyebrows were carefully trimmed and his skin was clean-shaven and healthily pink with not a stray hair or spot anywhere. As a modern, well-educated professional, it goes without saying that I don't like to form stereotypical views about people, but he really did look the archetypal Italian gigolo.

As I came to a stop by his pod, he very deliberately looked me up and down. Not for the first time, I was uncomfortably aware that I was still in the habit of wearing the suits, shirts and polished black shoes from my time at Doveley's. I'd once overheard someone at the University saying that I looked like a lawyer who'd taken his tie off to go into the pub.

'Hugh,' I began, 'may I have a word?'

He stretched in his chair and yawned. 'OK, if you must, Alan. But I am rather busy.' He had the kind of soft southern Irish accent that, unaccountably, women rave about.

'It is important, Hugh,' I said. 'It's about the KTP that Harriet is helping you with.'

He shook his head in amusement. 'How did I guess? Go on, what do you want to say?'

I glanced at the other members of his pod. They were trying just that little bit too hard to pretend they were engrossed in their work; clearly, they were all listening. I wondered what things Hugh had said about me previously.

'Can we speak in private, please?' I was determined to keep things civil.

He shrugged but got up from his chair and led me over to a table and two chairs that stood in a corner of the room, presumably intended for conversations where the participants didn't want to be interrupted or overheard. Once we'd sat down, he raised an eyebrow at me. His hands were resting on the table between us. His nails were neatly manicured: not a bitten nail to be seen, and the cuticles were smooth and even. I tried to keep my mind off what those hands had been up to when he'd been seeing Harriet.

'As I was saying, Hugh, it's about the KTP with the company on the Business Park. Harriet's concerned that you want to get the contract signed too quickly. In particular, she's worried that the company is being given all the intellectual property that may come out of the KTP without any of the usual benefits being retained by the University. She—'

'So she's come running to you?' He said this in such a calm, almost pleasant voice that he might have been talking about Harriet's coffee preference.

'She's come to me as her line manager. And as the qualified solicitor who heads up the team. It's my job to look into her concerns.' I knew my voice was sounding slightly strained.

'Which I'm sure you love doing, Alan. You always have her concerns at heart, don't you?'

There was no justification for him to adopt that manner with me. OK, I'd made some mildly disparaging remarks about

38

him to Harriet when they were together, intended just for her ears. But even if she'd repeated them to him, this didn't affect their validity. I'd also felt obliged to mention to Harriet the times when I'd seen him being over-familiar with other women around campus. Hugh was a player, and Harriet had a promising future in the legal world. The last thing I'd wanted was to have to recommend against her progressing to qualification as a solicitor because of distractions in her personal life. On a number of occasions at Doveley's, I'd seen attractive female trainees lose their focus after becoming involved with brainless oiks from the Cambridgeshire badlands: men who would know what to do with weights in a gym, but who wouldn't be able to satisfy an intelligent woman intellectually once the initial physical passion had blown itself out.

'I have the University's best interests at heart,' I said. 'I know you want to get the KTP signed off. But we in Legal can't do that until we're sure the University's position is sufficiently protected.'

'Until you came along, Alan, we never had problems like this. Correct me if I'm wrong, but didn't Harriet say once that you didn't even know what a KTP was before you started here? I've been doing KTPs for three years now and there's never been a problem. Doesn't that tell you something?'

I felt the blood rush to my face. It was difficult to stay polite under this sort of provocation. 'I don't know what sort of bad habits went on before I started, but that's irrelevant. What matters is what's going on now.'

Hugh gave me what I can only describe as a sly, knowing smile. 'I'm sure you'd feel differently about a few things if you were aware of everything that had gone on before you joined. Take Lewis. He was Harriet's line manager before you. They worked, how can I put this, extremely closely together. But tell me, when did you last see Harriet pop into Lewis's office for anything other than work purposes, or see him stop by her desk for a friendly chat? Have you ever thought about that?'

It was obvious what the fucker was hinting at. He was trying to rile me, being for some reason under the misapprehension that I had some kind of personal interest in Harriet. I wouldn't give him the gratification of falling for it.

I went on the counter-attack. 'I know you're probably still upset, Hugh, about Harriet ending her relationship with you. It can't have been easy. Not the kind of thing that normally happens to you, I would guess. But you can't start spreading lies about her and Lewis. He's married, remember. His wife works here.'

Hugh smiled, like a crocodile spotting its prey on the riverbank. 'He wasn't quite so openly married in January,' he said. 'His wife didn't work here then either. I hear he'd even been saying that he and his wife were leading separate lives. It was only when his wife started at the University in March that people realised they were still together. It's not for me to tell tales out of school. But you might ask Richard or Tom about a shouting match between a certain woman and a certain man that took place, also in March, in Lewis's office. An office where the door was slammed shut but bounced open a few inches. A shouting match where the woman was heard to threaten to tell a certain truth to the man's wife ...'

9

I have no clear recollection of how my meeting with Hugh ended.

I can remember feeling sick and worrying that I was going to throw up. And I can remember that bloody man calmly spreading the proposed KTP contract on the table between us and asking me to identify which clauses I had concerns about. I don't have a clue what I said, except that I know I backed down and didn't insist on any changes. I suspect I just wanted to get away from Hugh as quickly as possible. Anyway, my next distinct memory is of walking back to my pod on the second floor and seeing Harriet, fresh from her doctor's appointment, working at her desk next to mine.

'Hello, Alan,' she said, looking up, 'how did it go with Hugh?'

Before getting up that morning, I'd enjoyed a few pleasant minutes thinking about this moment in advance. I'd imagined laying down the law, literally, to Hugh, and coming back upstairs in triumph to tell Harriet that I'd dealt with him. I'd toyed with a few different forms of wording but decided that 'dealt' would make me sound the most authoritative. I'd envisaged Harriet gushing with gratitude, perhaps even suggesting that we have lunch together in order to celebrate.

Now I had to think on my feet.

'I took a view,' I said. 'It wasn't worth a row. The contract isn't perfect, but in practice the KTP partner won't get anything which is likely to prejudice the University.'

'Hugh can get the contract signed then? But I thought—'

'Leave it, Harriet, please.'

Harriet looked like a child who'd just had a birthday present snatched back by their parent. I had educated her about legal risk during my short time at the University and explained how it wasn't our job in Legal to be popular; we had to do what was necessary to protect the University's interests. Now here I was, backing down in precisely the kind of situation I'd warned her about. I knew I'd let her down.

However, I don't think I can be blamed too much after the shock I had experienced. There was a horrible ring of truth in what Hugh had said. Lewis had for almost a year worked as closely with Harriet as I was now doing. Yet it was undeniable that, although I'd never paid attention to it before, the two never spoke unless they had to. Had they really been having an affair before she took up with Hugh?

I looked at Harriet's face and imagined what those full lips and wide mouth might have done with Lewis. For the second time that morning, I felt like I was going to vomit. If they'd been having sex, where had they done it? Since Lewis was married, had they gone to Harriet's shared rental property near the station, or had they paid for a hotel room?

If what Hugh had hinted at was true, Lewis's behaviour was unforgivable. He'd been Harriet's line manager. No matter the temptation, it was an abuse of his position. He might well have pressurised her into having sex. Or even if he hadn't, she probably hadn't enjoyed it much anyway. You only had to look at Lewis with all his plastered-on suavity to know that no sensible woman would willingly go to bed with him. OK, he had a wife – whom he had betrayed – so he must know the basics of what was what sexually. But she was probably either frigid, or bored with whatever routine marital sex Lewis had accustomed her to.

I wasn't forgetting the hypocrisy of the man, either. He'd had a go at me over Mehak when all I'd done was – arguably – misread the signals she'd been giving me. Part of me wished I had the courage to burst into his office and bang his head against his desk until he told me exactly what had been going on with Harriet.

I genuinely believe my anger at Lewis was justified. I was briefly angry with Harriet too, although with hindsight I know this was wrong of me. However, if she'd been having an affair with Lewis, she'd kept that from me the whole time I'd been at the University. She'd been open enough about her relationship with Hugh and her subsequent dating catastrophes, so why the secrecy over Lewis? I could have comforted her and, perhaps, helped her get her own back. What things had they done that she didn't want me to find out about? It wasn't as if it might have tempted me, as her new line manager, to do something which I knew I mustn't. I had been scrupulous about not hinting at anything improper and about not touching her unnecessarily.

All these thoughts flooded through my mind – although not as coherently as I describe them above – while Harriet sat looking at me.

Eventually, I said, 'Sorry to have a go at you, Harriet. I didn't sleep well last night. Maybe I'm wrong about the contract, but I've made the call so don't worry about it. I might just mention it to Lewis, though, unless you've already done so?'

I couldn't resist that question. I wanted to see what effect his name had on her.

She didn't turn a hair. 'No, I haven't mentioned it to him. I discuss all these things with you now. To be honest, even before you joined, Lewis wouldn't have been particularly interested. He's not as diligent as you.'

But you still bloody jumped into bed with him, I wanted to say. He undoubtedly showed you some interest then. Instead, I said, 'Funnily enough, I hadn't realised his wife only started here earlier this year. Have you met her?'

This time I got a reaction. There was a definite flush on Harriet's cheeks. 'What's Hugh been saying?' she asked, looking straight at me.

I had to admire her. In her position, I would have avoided asking the direct question. I didn't have the courage to give her a direct answer. 'Nothing much,' I said. 'It's just that until she joined, I believe many people didn't realise they were still a couple.'

It sounded lame, and I looked down at my hands as I spoke. There was a long silence. When I looked up, I was surprised to see a slight glistening in Harriet's eyes, as if she was on the verge of tears.

'Yes,' she said, 'they are very much still a couple.'

I don't know what we would have said next because Tom came round to our side of the pod with a draft contract for me to review. As usual, he'd made a pig's ear of what had started off as a standard template. By the time I'd put things right, Harriet had gone off somewhere.

*

I spent the rest of the morning buried in work at my desk. Fortunately, I've always been able to rely on legal work to distract myself from personal worries. There's something about drafting a contract that I find comforting. Everything is under my control and I know I won't be thrown a googly.

I still hadn't seen Deborah, but I wasn't too bothered because she was due to attend that afternoon's Enterprise Board meeting.

Towards lunchtime, Lewis came out of his office and approached my desk. We hadn't yet spoken that day. Not for the first time, I was reminded of the twentieth-century prime minister, Lloyd George, another promiscuous Welshman who'd been known to some of his rivals as 'the Goat'. And Lewis really did look a bit like a randy bloody goat, I thought. I was curious about what he wanted. Normally, he summoned me to his office if there was some wisdom he wished to impart.

'Hello, Alan,' he said. 'How are you today?'

Now he sounded like a supermarket check-out girl, using the prescribed form of wording laid down by customer services. It was always the 'today' that irritated me. I toyed with asking him how he'd been 'yesterday' or how he was going to be 'tomorrow'.

Instead, I said, 'I'm fine, Lewis, thank you. I'll be doing my prep soon for the Enterprise Board meeting. Is there anything in particular you want me to contribute?'

'That's what I wanted to mention. Since we have the Doveley's duo coming, I won't stay for the meeting. I'm happy to leave the internal legal input in your hands. However, Jeff Parker and Lucy Black will be arriving early. A chance for them to meet me and Amanda before everyone else turns up. Two o'clock, in the main conference room. We thought, as you know them, you might like to come down to do the introductions. You may as well bring Harriet. It will do her good to gain some exposure to external legal advisers.'

10

In the aftermath of Helen's death, I had always seemed to be shaking Jeff Parker's bloody hand.

After I'd left Doveley's, I'd hoped never to see the man again. I loathed him for all sorts of reasons to do with Helen, even though I grudgingly had to admit to myself that he wasn't as bad a lawyer as I would have preferred to think. Now here he was again like the proverbial bad penny. And, worse, he had my former trainee, Lucy, in tow. She'd made it quite clear what she thought about me before I left the firm.

Amanda, Lewis and I had assembled in the ground-floor conference room after lunch. Harriet had joined us a few minutes later; it was the first I'd seen of her since she shot off in the morning. The four of us sat at one end of a huge polished oval table which could easily sit twenty. Amanda was a small woman with a pixie-like face, short-cropped blonde hair and a pair of large black-framed glasses that were, I suspect, intended to lend her some gravitas. I quickly gathered that she, as the Secretary and Registrar, had been primarily responsible for the appointment of Doveley's as the University's preferred firm of solicitors.

'As you would expect, we undertook a rigorous procurement exercise,' she said. 'But we must have solicitors we can trust even if they aren't necessarily the cheapest. And Lewis agreed with me that Doveley's was the right choice. Alan, tell me what I need to know about Jeff Parker and Lucy Black. They aren't partners at Doveley's, but I was keen for the firm to send along two of the lawyers who will actually be doing work for us rather than just fronting it.'

'Jeff's a very experienced corporate lawyer,' I said. 'He's done a lot of work in the higher education sector. He's popular with clients because he can talk their language.' *Meaning he can bullshit with the best of them.* 'Lucy's still only a trainee,' I went on, 'but she was very efficient when she was working for me.' *Particularly bloody efficient at sticking her tongue down Jeff's throat when she thought it might give her a leg-up into his team.*

I was having to be cautious. I knew how plausible Jeff and Lucy could be. So even though I couldn't bring myself to say anything positive about their technical abilities, I prattled on a bit about them having a reputation for being 'client-friendly'.

'Speak of the devil.' Lewis interrupted me mid-sentence.

The door had opened and a man and a woman, both smartly dressed and in their late and early twenties respectively, were being shepherded into the room by the receptionist. The man had that fresh, boyish look I remembered so well; the woman was as immaculately made-up and groomed as ever.

'Jeff and Lucy, I presume?' This was Lewis again. Already he and Amanda were on their feet and heading towards the new arrivals, leaving me and Harriet sitting at the table like lemons.

'It is indeed,' Jeff replied. 'Lewis and Amanda, I believe?' If anything, he was emphasising the West Country accent that seemed to go down so well with women.

The four of them went through the usual rigmarole of shaking hands. Such was the mutual excitement that I half-expected Lewis and Amanda also to shake each other's hands, and Jeff and Lucy to do likewise with each other.

'And Alan, of course,' Jeff said, looking at last in my direction. 'I don't think we need any introductions. It's great to see you again. How are you?'

This was so typical of the bloody man. He always had the right small talk for the right occasion. I had no choice but to get up and shake the little shit's hand again.

'Hello, Alan.' Now it was Lucy's turn. 'How lovely to see you again. I hope you've settled into your new job?'

A job I wouldn't have had to take if you, Jeff and every-bloody-one else at Doveley's had behaved like decent human beings, I thought. Instead, I said, 'I'm well, thank you, Lucy. I'm pleased to see that you seem to have settled so well into the Corporate team. How much longer are you going to be with them?'

'Actually, Alan, I'll be staying a long time, I hope. I qualify soon as a solicitor and I've accepted an offer of a permanent job in Corporate.'

I didn't have time to ask a follow-up question because Jeff's eyes had lit upon Harriet. 'And you must be Harriet, Alan's new assistant?' he said, offering her his hand. 'Let me tell you now, Harriet, how lucky you are to have Alan as your line manager. I was a humble trainee in his team many years ago ... and look at me now.'

Everyone laughed. Apart from me, that is. This was so typical of Jeff. On the face of it, he was paying me a compliment. But everyone knew it was done with a nod and a wink as to what he really thought about me. I was the private practice has-been who had gone in-house. He was still on the escalator to partnership.

I noted how Jeff held Harriet's hand just that little bit longer than was necessary, and how there was a very definite flush to her cheek when she turned to shake hands with Lucy. The two women exchanged a girls-together smile, and I decided it would be better if they didn't get a chance to chat together on their own.

'And now to business.' This was Amanda. 'We've got a few minutes before everyone else arrives. Let me explain for Jeff and Lucy's benefit what we are doing and why they are here.'

Jeff and Lucy adopted their best listening mode while I asked myself why I'd even been invited to the meeting.

'Today is the monthly meeting of the Enterprise Board,' Amanda continued. 'This is the committee which oversees the commercial projects in which the University invests. The money comes from a variety of sources and includes our own income as well as funding from government and other public bodies. As you'd expect, we only invest in projects that we consider to be of public benefit. However, we won't invest in a project unless we believe there is a realistic chance of generating a positive return. A return which we can then use for the greater benefit of the University.'

'Is it just University people on the Board?' This was Jeff, showing that he was paying attention.

'Yes. But remember that we aren't all ivory tower academics. We have accountants from Finance, lawyers such as Alan from Legal, and some of the Board also have outside business experience.'

'And how can Lucy and I help with today's meeting?'

'To be honest, you probably can't do much today. Don't worry, you won't have to advise us on whether to invest a million pounds in some academic school's latest folly.' Jeff and Lucy laughed dutifully. 'But we will definitely need your legal input going forward on some of the bigger projects in which the Board invests, so I thought it would be useful for you to see how all the projects originate.'

'That's very good of you, Amanda.'

I was fed up already with all this brown-nosing. I wasn't going to sit on the sidelines like a spare prick at a wedding. This wasn't my first Enterprise Board meeting, but it was the first one on which I was leading from Legal. I'd show Jeff and Lucy how much the University valued my opinion.

*

'Finally, let's discuss the Landlord Relax spin-out. We've provisionally allocated fifty thousand pounds to the new company we plan to set up, and we just need to get everyone's agreement to go ahead.'

The meeting had now lasted for nearly two hours. Lewis had, true to his word, shot off before the meeting started, and the other five of us had been joined by Deborah, as the Pro-Vice-Chancellor of Enterprise and Innovation, two other pro-vice-chancellors, two University governors and the Director of

Finance. It was pretty clear that Amanda and Deborah were calling the shots. The others were there to bless the process and make it look like the decisions were taken by a consensus of the University's great and the good. Jeff and Lucy were sensible enough to keep their heads down and ostentatiously make notes from time to time. Most of the discussion was about projects that had been running for quite a while, with either Deborah or Amanda reporting on progress and the other then adding her praise.

Landlord Relax was the last item on the agenda.

'Just to recap,' Amanda continued. 'This project will commercialise a new software package which should make landlords' and letting agents' businesses more efficient. At first sight, that doesn't seem like a very ethical investment. But we're satisfied that if the businesses are more efficient, they will have more time and money to spend on looking after their properties, many of which are occupied by some of the poorest and most vulnerable people in society.'

I pricked up my ears. Even Amanda didn't normally bullshit quite so much.

'We've already spent ten thousand pounds on seed funding,' she went on. 'This has enabled the founders, both academics in the School of Computer Science, to produce beta versions of the software package and trial it with a selection of local letting agents. The agents have found it extremely useful and we expect demand for the package to be very high. Our recommendation is that the University invests a further fifty thousand pounds in the new company in order to roll out the software package nationally. In return, the University will take a forty per cent stake in the company's share capital and the two founders will each take thirty per cent.'

Amanda paused for the first time, and I saw my chance.

'Excuse me for interrupting, Amanda,' I said, 'but is there really a gap in the market for this package? A sufficiently large gap, I mean, to justify this level of investment? Don't letting agents and landlords already have various packages which perform this function?'

Amanda's pixie-like face took on the look of a schoolteacher explaining to a delinquent child that two plus two really does equal four. 'Alan,' she said, 'you surely don't think the founders would have recommended the investment without doing all the necessary research, do you? Yes, there are software solutions out there already. But none, I am assured, that perform as well as ours.'

'But what's the actual business model?' In for a penny, in for a pound, I thought. 'If we set up a company ourselves, the implication is that the founders will have to devote much, if not most, of their time to supporting the software. How are they going to do this at the same time as they fulfil their academic duties? Or are we suggesting they take a sabbatical, in which case don't we have to factor in a cost for replacement staff? Wouldn't a better business model be to license the software to an established independent company which is experienced in rolling out and supporting these types of packages? Jeff, don't you agree?'

With the benefit of hindsight, I should have realised that calling on Jeff, the representative of the law firm just appointed to advise the University, wasn't the wisest of moves. But I was annoyed by what seemed to be the complete short-sightedness of Amanda and Deborah, and by the unwillingness of the rest of the Board even to question what was being proposed.

'I'm sure Amanda and Deborah are best placed to advise on the most appropriate business model,' Jeff said, flashing a practised smile around the table. 'And if anyone's concerned about the amount of legal work involved, this is something that Doveley's can help with. We can provide all the paperwork very quickly. It's the kind of thing that Lucy has been doing a lot of recently.'

It wasn't the amount of legal work needed that was bothering me. I was frustrated because it made no business sense to pour this amount of money into a spin-out company for this type of product.

'Thank you, Jeff,' Amanda said. 'It's refreshing when a lawyer understands which decisions fall within the remit of the legal function and which don't. Perhaps you and I can catch up separately afterwards to scope out the extent of the legal work you think will be needed? In the meantime, are we all agreed to go ahead with this investment?'

There was a succession of nods around the table. No one else wanted to risk having their head bitten off. I watched Harriet out of the corner of my eye, and to her credit she was the only other person not to join in the nodding. I couldn't fault her for her loyalty.

*

'Were you wanting a word about something else, Alan?' Deborah asked.

The Enterprise Board meeting had ended, and Amanda had taken Jeff and Lucy off to the School of Computer Science to introduce them to the two Landlord Relax founders, asking Harriet to accompany them for some reason.

Deborah had noticed me trying to attract her attention and she waited for me at the door. She really did have a face like a horse: significantly longer than it was wide, with a prominent chin and a mouth full of teeth. I wondered if she had found a husband or a boyfriend. Well, if not, I certainly wasn't going to make a fool of myself, like I had done once at Doveley's with our professional support lawyer, by offering to make myself available to her. I had learnt the hard way that less attractive middle-aged women don't usually appreciate men who are deliberately aiming low.

'Yes, please,' I said. 'It's about Professor Fuller. Harriet and I went to see him yesterday, and he said that you'd approved the sale of the intellectual property rights in his wearable technology for just one hundred thousand pounds. Surely—'

'That's right,' she said. 'I've read his and Ian Davey's feasibility report. I've also had one of the BDMs – Hugh, in fact – do some independent research. The commercial risks for Ian's company are very high and the chances of them hitting the jackpot are pretty low. One hundred thousand pounds, plus the various add-ons being offered, is therefore a fair price. A bird in the hand and all that.'

'But I'm not sure how much weight you can attach to the feasibility report. And Hugh isn't any kind of specialist in the valuation of intellectual property. I would suggest that—'

'Alan, I don't mean to be rude, but I presume you heard what Amanda has just been saying? About the value of lawyers who understand the remit of the legal function? The decision has been made. So please can you get on with producing the legal paperwork to assign the intellectual property to Ian Davey's company.'

I had never really cared for Deborah, but until now I hadn't realised how much I disliked her. She liked to cultivate a slightly jolly public persona, no doubt realising that she wouldn't bowl anyone over with her looks. But, like Amanda, she seemed to want to make a point of – as she would no doubt see it – putting me in my place. Well, I thought as she stalked off, two can play at that game.

11

After the Enterprise Board meeting, I couldn't face going back upstairs. I'd been belittled by both Amanda and Deborah; worst of all, the belittling by Amanda had taken place in front of Jeff Parker and Harriet, my nemesis and my new protégé, respectively.

I needed some time on my own to recover my equilibrium.

I left Senate House with the vague idea of heading into the centre of campus and grabbing a coffee at the refectory. I was lost in my own thoughts, so it took me a few minutes to realise that I was walking a short distance behind Mehak. She was accompanied by a gangling, scruffily dressed young man of about her own age whom I hadn't seen before. I wondered if he was one of the two boyfriends I'd heard about. From my view of him from the rear, he looked more like a student than an academic member of staff, not that it was always easy to tell the difference. If he was a student, I couldn't understand what on earth an attractive, going-places woman such as Mehak could see in him. The appeal couldn't be money, status or even – if he was at the University of East Cambridgeshire – intellectual ability. Was it just physical? Was he able to do things she didn't think she'd have got from me? Did he know about Mehak's other boyfriend and, if so, did he care?

As we neared the centre of campus, I expected them either to go to the refectory or to veer off left or right onto one of the walkways which led to the various academic schools. Instead, they continued straight on the main walkway, heading towards the student area of campus. I kept walking in the same direction but slowed down slightly so that a few people could overtake me. If Mehak and her companion turned around, I wouldn't want them to think I was spying on them. I was interested to know where they were going, though, and the longer-than-expected walk would do me good.

I don't know what I would have done if they had continued on to one of the student residences. As a professional member of staff, Mehak should have been working at that time of the afternoon, and however elastic her job description was it wouldn't include taking her clothes off in a student bedroom. However, I was realistic enough to know that I could hardly either intervene personally to enforce compliance with her contract of employment, or complain to someone more senior.

Accordingly, I was relieved – and surprised – when they turned left at the Students' Union and made for the nearby Student Centre. They ignored the Student Centre's ostentatious big front entrance and disappeared instead inside a smaller side entrance. Although I'd never been inside the building, I knew that the front entrance was for students and front-office staff: those staff, mostly junior and poorly paid, who had the job of hand-holding students through all sorts of issues, from personal and medical crises through to the provision of financial and careers advice. The side entrance was used by the back-office staff: the managers who dealt with all aspects of getting a couple of thousand domestic students onto campus each year.

For a minute or so, I kicked my heels outside the Student Centre. I didn't really want to hang about waiting for Mehak and the man to come out, but I did want to know what they were up to.

Then I had an idea. I could kill two birds with one stone.

I went through the same entrance as Mehak had done and asked a question of the young woman to whom I showed my staff pass at the small reception desk. I then went through into the large, brightly lit open-plan room where the back-office staff worked. Mehak and her companion were talking to a couple of people at a pod in the far right-hand corner. This seemed to indicate that they were together for some kind of work meeting, which was a relief. I could, I suppose, now have turned on my heels and left; no one was paying me the slightest bit of attention. However, I headed towards a different pod to which I had been directed by the woman at reception.

'Hello,' I said to the middle-aged woman who was sitting at the pod on her own. 'Do you have a copy of the latest UCAS Adviser Guide?'

'I've got loads,' she said with a friendly smile. 'Is it just one copy you want?'

'Yes, perfect, thank you.'

I'd never spoken to Lewis's wife before or, as far as I was aware, even seen her. This wasn't too surprising – regardless of the state of her and Lewis's marriage – given that she worked at the opposite end of the campus to him. Fortunately, I'd remembered just a few minutes earlier that she was based at the Student Centre. Lewis had once made a comment about them both still needing their own cars to travel to work even though they shared the same employer.

If Ruth had asked me why I wanted a copy of the Adviser Guide, I wasn't, of course, going to say that it was just an excuse to see what she was like. I was going to come up with a story about needing to check that the terms and conditions in our student contracts were consistent with what UCAS (the national admissions service for universities) was telling applicants. But my approach had raised no red flags and she clearly didn't recognise me. I wondered if Lewis had ever mentioned me by name and, if so, what he'd said about me. She seemed a pleasant enough woman, albeit a little plump and not particularly attractive, and I was curious about what had attracted her to a lazy slimeball such as Lewis. Did she even know that Lewis had done the dirty on her? If not, it seemed a shame that – for her own self-respect and peace of mind – no one had told her.

Lewis didn't deserve to get away with what he'd done to Harriet.

I didn't return to Senate House after leaving the Student Centre. I had no idea if Amanda and Deborah had gone back to their offices, and I didn't want to take the risk of bumping into them, or indeed into Jeff and Lucy if they were still around after their visit to the School of Computer Science. I also hadn't decided yet what I was going to say to Harriet about what Hugh had been insinuating.

As it was nearly 5 p.m., I therefore left for home.

I spent a lot of time that evening analysing the events of the day. I needed to speak properly to Harriet and not rely on our normal casual tête-à-tête before the 'boys' arrived. I booked one of the meeting rooms in Senate House and sent her a meeting request for 9 a.m. the following day.

Although I went to bed fairly early, I didn't sleep well, and I spent a couple of hours in the middle of the night reading my latest true crime purchase. It was about a notorious London criminal kingpin in the days when the old-fashioned underworld still existed. He seemed to spend most of his 'professional' life fearing a pair of handcuffs from the police or a bullet in the back from one of the rivals he'd double-crossed, but he still appeared to live life for the moment and to take pleasure from it. In contrast, however much I tried not to, I seemed to spend much of my life worrying about work or my personal life. There was a lesson to be learnt, but I wasn't sure if I was capable of learning it.

12

'It must be important, Alan, for you to have sent the meeting request so late last night.'

I'd noticed, when I got up that morning, that Harriet had accepted the request at around 11 p.m. She couldn't therefore have brought a date back home. She wouldn't have been checking her work e-mails if she'd had male company.

We were in a meeting room on the ground floor of Senate House. I'd come in later than normal and met Harriet there. It was smaller than the room we'd used for the Enterprise Board meeting the day before, but it could still easily have accommodated a dozen people around its polished oval table. One thing I'd had to get used to in the higher education sector was how many people turned up at meetings and how the University had to create room space accordingly. Unlike fee earners in private legal practice, staff at the University didn't have to record billable time in order to justify their value to the institution. So by attending run-of-the-mill meetings, even if they contributed nothing, they could make sure that their faces were seen, that they looked as if they were doing something productive, and that they weren't being complained about behind their backs.

Harriet was leaning back in her chair, enjoying the bright autumn sunshine that flooded through the window. Her white shirt stretched tight across her chest and I could see the outline of her bra. I was careful not to look too closely for fear of appearing inappropriate.

'It's nothing especially important,' I said. 'I just didn't get a chance to arrange the meeting with you yesterday because Amanda took you off with the two people from Doveley's.' I couldn't bring myself to mention Jeff and Lucy by name.

'Jeff's so charming,' she said. 'I really felt he had time for me even though I'm not yet qualified. And Lucy's sweet too.'

It really pissed me off to hear, yet again, how Jeff had got a woman eating out of his hand. Didn't Harriet realise he was only after one thing where women were concerned? And as for Lucy, she was ambitious, and Harriet would be a key client contact for her, so she was undoubtedly going to have her tongue up her arse.

I said, 'I want your help on a couple of things. Not so much the legal side, I can deal with that. It's more the background. The first is Simon Fuller's deal with Ian Davey's company. It doesn't smell right to me. I can see how Ian might have persuaded Simon to sell the technology to his company for a hundred thousand pounds. Simon's an academic, not a businessman. What I don't understand is why Deborah is in favour too. She's experienced enough to know that it can't be in the University's best interests.'

'I saw Deborah speaking to you yesterday after the Enterprise Board meeting. What did she say?'

'To stick to being a lawyer and get on with the paperwork.' I felt embarrassed having to admit this because I knew it made me look weak, but I had no choice if I wanted Harriet's assistance.

'She shouldn't say things like that, Alan. Not when you're only trying to do your job. What do you want me to do?' Harriet looked genuinely concerned. I was uncomfortably aware that, in her position, I would get a secret pleasure in seeing my boss cut down to size.

'If you can,' I said, 'try to find out why Deborah and Simon – particularly Deborah – are so keen on the deal. The licensing model I recommended instead would be more lucrative for the University, but only in the longer term. For all I know, Deborah may be thinking of moving on to another university and needs some good short-term figures to show what she's capable of. I'll be honest with you, Harriet. I'm a good lawyer, but I've not been here very long and I don't know people well enough to gain their confidence and ask the right questions. You can do that better than me.' Again, I was having to be unusually frank.

'No problem,' she said. 'Leave it with me. I know people in both Simon's and Deborah's teams. I'll ask around.'

This didn't surprise me. Harriet seemed to have friends all over the University. Sometimes, I found myself reflecting on why she made friends so easily and why I didn't.

'Thank you,' I said. 'The other thing was Landlord Relax. You heard Amanda biting my head off yesterday. All I did was point out why the business model makes little sense. If there's a good reason for making the investment, it will help me at future Enterprise Board meetings if I know what it is.'

I wasn't being entirely honest here. I wasn't really interested in evidence which would support the correctness of Amanda's decision. I wanted evidence which undermined it. But I would look less of a man if I confessed I was itching to get my own back on Amanda.

'I'll see what I can find out,' Harriet said. 'But remember, Alan, it's not their own money which the Board hands out. If it was, well, I don't think they would make half the investment decisions that they do.'

That was unusually cynical for Harriet. I was usually careful about making caustic comparisons between the private and public sectors. Even some of the brightest people at the University got defensive when I pointed out things which I thought could be done better.

I hadn't been intending to mention Lewis, but the affinity between me and Harriet emboldened me. If Lewis and Harriet had been in a relationship, it could only have been because Lewis had abused his position of seniority over her. It wouldn't be right for him to get away with it. 'How did Lewis deal with things like this?' I asked. 'He must have come up against similar issues. Did he discuss them much with you?'

For a moment, Harriet looked slightly wistful. 'Not really,' she said. 'To be honest, he was never as conscientious as you. If this sort of thing with Deborah and Amanda had cropped up, he'd just have shrugged his shoulders and done what they'd said.'

If that's your opinion of him, I thought, why did you jump into bed with him? I didn't say that, of course. Harriet might have thought I was jealous, rather than angry on her behalf. 'He must have shared some private thoughts with you, though,' I said instead, 'when it was just the two of you together?'

I had to admire Harriet. If I'd been her, I would have lied without hesitation. I would have said something like I could never stand the man or bear to spend any time with him. But I could see she was trying to be truthful without giving too much away.

'Lewis avoids making difficult decisions,' she said eventually. 'He'll say what he thinks you want to hear, even if it means storing up problems for later. But if you don't mind, Alan, I'd rather not talk about Lewis any more.'

Well, that was that, I thought. He had bloody shagged her. God, I remembered the last time I'd been in his office; how he'd run that wet tongue of his around his lips, carefully avoiding the hair of his moustache. I couldn't stop myself picturing him using that same tongue for other purposes. I didn't know which would be worse: Harriet being coerced into letting him do things like that to her, or Harriet actually enjoying them. I felt sick and angry. But I also felt let down.

*

I realised Harriet had moved on to something else.

'Two things, Alan, if that's OK. One work, one personal. I feel awful about the first, but Finance said I had to tell you ASAP. They were looking for you late yesterday afternoon and there was only me left. They'd been trying to determine if VAT was payable on one of Richard's contracts.'

'And?' I didn't see the problem. This was routine stuff.

'Look at the contract.'

I picked up the document she'd laid in front of me. There was a standard front sheet with the names of the University and the outside company we'd contracted with. There was a one-page appendix containing the various milestones and the amounts we were being paid. And there was a standard back sheet showing the University's and the company's signatures.

'Where's the rest of it?' I asked.

'That's the point. There is no rest of it.'

'But I saw this contract in draft before Richard sent it to the School of Performing and Creative Arts. There were also three pages of our standard terms and conditions. They must have fallen out after the contract was signed.'

'They didn't fall out. Finance checked with Amanda's EA. She makes a scan of every contract that's signed. That's what Richard took over to the EA and that's what Amanda signed.'

'Fuck,' I said. 'Amanda wouldn't have looked at anything other than where she had to put her signature. What the hell was Richard playing at? I assume he doesn't know yet that Finance spoke to you?'

'No. I didn't see him last night because he was going home straight from a meeting, and he hadn't got in this morning when I came down here to meet you. I'd like to have had the chance to warn him before telling you, if I'm honest. I feel like I'm dobbing him in with you even though I didn't have any choice.'

It sounded like this was bothering her more than what Richad had actually done. 'Don't worry,' I said, 'you've done the right thing. I'll speak to him this afternoon.'

'Thank you.' She still looked shame-faced, though.

'You said there was something else? Something personal?'

'Yes. It's that gas safety issue I mentioned on Monday. I asked the landlord for the previous certificate. He put a copy through our letterbox last night. There's still something not quite right, but I can't put my finger on it. I could have brought the certificate in today, but I hoped you might have time to pop round to ours one day on your way home from work. That way, you can see what the engineer checked. Would that be OK?'

Is the Pope a Catholic? I knew where Harriet lived, and out of curiosity I had once found a reason to drive past the house she shared with Kat. But I'd never been invited to visit her there. It would be interesting to see how she had personalised the house and what sort of clothes she changed into after finishing work.

'Yes, of course,' I said. 'I can call tonight.'

I was glad of the opportunity to do Harriet a favour. But I was also flattered that she'd come to me for advice. I would try to make the most of it.

But first I had to deal with Richard.

13

I don't mind admitting that I had never taken to Richard.

I could cope with Tom, who meant well even though he wasn't the sharpest knife in the drawer. Richard's deviousness, on the other hand, always grated on me. His priorities were steering clear of hard work and avoiding taking responsibility if things went wrong. I was pretty sure too that my dislike for him was reciprocated; I hadn't forgotten the grin on his face when I'd been sent packing by Deborah after the meeting with Simon Fuller. For that reason, although it was my duty to raise with him what Harriet had told me, I won't deny that I'd summoned him to a meeting that afternoon with a certain relish.

It was time for him to realise that actions have consequences.

'This is what Harriet gave me this morning,' I began, after we'd taken our seats in the same room that she and I had used earlier. 'Finance had flagged it with her, so naturally she felt she had to tell me straightaway.' I'd chosen my words carefully. I wanted to underline to Richard that Harriet was in my camp and not his. 'The contract's looking rather different from the one I approved, isn't it?'

I tried, not altogether successfully, to raise an eyebrow with quizzical effect. I could almost hear the wheels whirring inside Richard's head. I was certain he wouldn't be plucking up the courage to confess all. He'd be trying to work out how much I knew and how he could best limit the damage to himself. I noticed with satisfaction that a red flush had appeared on his neck, just above the collar of his open-neck shirt.

'That's odd,' he said eventually.

He'd managed to force a look of earnest surprise on his face. He really did look like a weasel or a stoat, and for a moment I racked my brain as to what the difference between these two creatures was.

'Odd?' I asked.

Less is more, I had decided. I wouldn't make it easy for him. After all, he hadn't made my early days at the University easy. I'd often had the impression that he resented my arrival, especially when I began picking him up on his mistakes.

There were a few seconds of silence. I was content to wait, as I was rather enjoying his discomfort. If he'd been in private legal practice, he would have known the mantra that applies to all junior lawyers. If you've screwed up, fess up. Don't cover up; it's the cover-up that kills you.

'I can see the contract isn't exactly the same as what you saw,' he said at last. His eyes weren't meeting mine.

'So it would appear. In what way isn't it exactly the same?' I was playing him like a cat does a mouse.

'The middle bit isn't, er, there.'

'The middle bit?'

'The terms and conditions.'

'Ah, you mean the *legal* terms and conditions?' I emphasised the word 'legal'.

'Yes.'

The thought crossed my mind that if this was a Victorian drama, I would use the word 'pray' in my next question. Something like: 'Pray tell me, Richard, how the middle bit managed to disappear?'

Instead, I said, 'So we have the front sheet. We have the appendix. And we have the back sheet that both parties have signed to confirm their agreement to be bound by the legal terms and conditions of the contract. Except there are no terms and conditions. Genius.'

With my use of that last word, I had an uncomfortable feeling that I was quoting either Basil Fawlty in *Fawlty Towers* or Mark Corrigan in *Peep Show*. I therefore decided against picking up the document and ostentatiously pretending to search for the missing terms and conditions. I feared this would be over the top. So I remained silent. I'd read in my true crime books that this was often the best interrogative technique.

'It's what the School wanted,' Richard said in the end. 'They said the terms and conditions would put the client off.'

'Put them off? You mean the client wouldn't want to agree to certain basic legal terms such as promising to do what they had, er, promised to do?'

'Sort of.'

'And what did you say?'

I wasn't intending to be completely unsympathetic. If he'd said that the School had insisted and that he'd wrongly accepted responsibility to save overburdening me, I would have bollocked him anyway. But afterwards I would probably have helped him to fix the problem. However, that wasn't how Richard operated. It was invariably everyone's fault but his own.

'You were always saying how busy you were,' he said in almost a whine. 'And how hard you find it to get your own work done, let alone find time to check ours. I didn't think you'd want to help me.'

You utter bastard. It was my fault now, was it? Yes, I was busy. And yes, I let my team know I was busy, not least because they needed to understand that I wasn't an idle waster like Lewis. But I had never, in my entire career, been unwilling to help a junior in need. Even Sam Snape, my old boss at Doveley's, had never found an excuse to pull me up for that. And now I could see Richard spinning this line to Lewis or, worse, Amanda, making it look like I was to blame for what he'd done. I was furious. I actually felt my hands tremble as I leant forward towards him.

'Just listen to me, Richard. You've let a project go ahead without the protection of a proper legal contract. You've exposed the University to potentially unlimited liability. You've allowed the School to believe they don't have to heed what Legal says. And you've risked making us the laughing stock of the University. Imagine what Amanda's going to say when she finds out that she's signed a contract which isn't worth the paper it's written on.' I wasn't entirely sure of the validity of this metaphor, but I didn't care. 'As far as I'm concerned,' I went on, 'you're not fit to work at the University.'

I paused, not because my fury was abating, but because I couldn't think of a logical follow-up. I could hardly say that he deserved to be thrown off the top of Senate House. But a threat of referring him to the University's notoriously inefficient HR team would appear laughably weak.

Again there was a silence. Richard looked down at the table, still avoiding my eyes. Then, bugger me, but he looked up and I could see wetness in his eyes. As I watched, a tear ran down each of his cheeks. The man was older than me – he'd been at the University for years – and here he was starting to cry. It was probably the first time he'd ever been spoken to in this way. And I didn't know what to do next. If, hypothetically, it had been Harriet across the table from me, I could anticipate the warm feeling that would have swept over me, and I could imagine how it might have helped her were I to put a comradely arm around her shoulders and give her a comforting hug. But I certainly wasn't going to put my arm around Richard.

'I ... I ... I'm sorry, Alan. I ... I just ...' And he broke down completely.

I'd never seen this happen in the workplace before. He was actually sobbing. Air escaped from his mouth in little gasps while his shoulders heaved. I didn't know where to look. I was just glad that no one else was in the room to see my predicament.

It was probably only a couple of minutes before Richard pulled himself together even though it felt much longer. He looked up at me as if he was in physical pain. He hadn't wiped his cheeks, so they were still wet with tears.

'I'm sorry,' he said again.

I wasn't sure if he was apologising for his tears or for his screw-up on the contract. Either way, it was excruciatingly embarrassing. I elected to be magnanimous. He'd had his rollicking and, however much I disliked the man, I still had to work with him. It would be impossible for me to get rid of him. The most that line managers at the University could normally achieve was to move incompetents onto another team. But as there was only one legal team at the University, Richard wasn't going anywhere.

'Let me decide what to do,' I said. 'Most mistakes are fixable. Just please make sure you do nothing like this again. You can, er, go now.'

I'd been expecting some gesture of appreciation for my kindness, but evidently I'd had all that Richard was going to give. He got up and headed towards the door without another word. The room felt deathly quiet after he'd gone out. I looked again at his so-called contract. For all his incompetence, I knew his mistake would probably never matter. It was a low-value project where not a huge amount could go wrong. Even if it did, the company wouldn't want to get into a legal wrangle with the University. We were too good a long-term client and had too much money.

Then, strangely, I started to feel guilty. I remembered my last meeting with Sam Snape at Doveley's when it had become clear that I had no future at the firm. I'd been close to tears on that occasion; I hadn't been able to speak through fear I would break down. All right, I'd had reason to feel mistreated, whereas Richard had just been a fool. But I had an uncomfortable feeling all the same that I could have handled the meeting with Richard better. Undoubtedly, I shouldn't have lost my temper. Perhaps I'd been prejudiced against him because he wasn't as good as Harriet. Perhaps, even, because he wasn't Harriet.

I felt ashamed.

I wished Harriet was with me now. I felt she was the one person at the University to whom I could unburden myself. I remembered the early days of my relationship with Helen when we were both working at Doveley's. How she'd been willing to listen for hours while I shared my worries with her. It was at times like this that I missed her the most. If she hadn't ended our relationship, she would still be alive and we might even have been together. It was different with Harriet, of course, because I was her line manager and not her lover. Nevertheless, there was a definite empathy between us which was surely only going to get stronger. And I was seeing her tonight, at her house; that was something I was really looking forward to.

14

I had great difficulty in concentrating on my work for the rest of the day. I kept looking at my watch to see how much longer there was until I had to leave for Harriet's house.

I hadn't seen Harriet since my meeting with Richard. She'd been due to see Mehak to discuss the work she was doing for International, and she was then in meetings elsewhere on campus for the rest of the day. Accordingly, we'd arranged to meet outside her house at 6 p.m. I was a bit concerned that she and Mehak might have talked about me and that Mehak might have mentioned the misunderstanding – as I preferred to see it – that had occurred between us. Realistically, though, there was nothing I could do about that.

I hadn't spoken to Richard since his bollocking. He and Tom made a big show of concentrating on their work whenever I looked in their direction. I assumed he'd told Tom what had happened, or at least his version of it.

I'd sent an e-mail to the Dean of the School of Performing and Creative Arts, saying that 'regrettably' an incomplete version of the contract had been signed, but that in my opinion it was unlikely to have any adverse consequences for the School. I'd copied in Lewis and then sent him a separate e-mail summary of what Richard had done. I'd deliberately chosen not to tell Lewis about it face-to-face. Partly because I wanted a written record both of what Richard had done and of the fact that I had informed Lewis. But partly also because I couldn't stomach being physically close to the man, given my strong suspicions of what he'd been up to with Harriet before I joined the University.

Deborah and Amanda were in and out of their offices for much of the day, ostentatiously making themselves look busy.

As usual, Richard and Tom left for home shortly after 5 p.m. I allowed them ten minutes to get clear before I left. I didn't want to give them the chance to think that I'd joined the University's legion of clock-watchers.

The first stage of my trip to Harriet's house followed my usual route home. However, instead of turning off the main road shortly after the hospital, I continued into the centre of Ely and straight through the traffic lights. I had to stop at a pedestrian crossing outside an entrance to the famous independent school in the centre of Ely, and I silently cursed the small mixed-sex group of senior pupils who dawdled past in front of my car, seemingly more interested in chatting each other up than allowing traffic to flow freely. Shortly afterwards, I turned off the road which went down the hill towards the station, took a few more turns and drew up under a streetlight close to Harriet's house.

Her house looked no different to any other of the modern two-bedroom houses on the street, but I felt a tingle in my spine at the thought of being so close to where she spent so much of her time. I couldn't see her car anywhere, so I waited outside her front door in her small front garden. A youngish woman came out of the house next door, carrying a bag of rubbish for her bin, and she gave me a smile which seemed to contain a hint of curiosity. I wondered if she was used to seeing different men arriving at Harriet's house, but I knew better than to ask.

Within about five minutes, I saw Harriet parking her car on a paved area opposite in what I assumed was an allocated spot for her house. She'd only recently bought the car, a brand-new Toyota Aygo X. It had irritated me slightly that she'd chosen a newer and slightly better version of my car; I'd ruminated for days over whether she'd done this deliberately. As she walked towards me, she raised one of her arms, and for a heart-stopping moment I thought she was going to give me a hug. It was the first time we'd met outside work and I wasn't entirely sure of the etiquette for a greeting in these circumstances.

'That's the box for the gas meter, Alan,' she said, as she pointed with the arm that she'd raised. 'The engineer did something there to shut off the gas while he was doing his repair.'

We went inside. There was a small entrance hall, with a door to the left leading to the kitchen and a door to the right leading to the lounge. The paintwork was a faded magnolia, so the landlord evidently hadn't decorated for a while. The carpeting was a cheap-looking synthetic grey. However, I could see through the open door to the lounge that Harriet and her housemate had done a lot to personalise the room and make it look less 'rental'. The soft furnishings were covered in multi-coloured throws and there were various floor cushions and interesting-looking girly knick-knacks lying around.

Harriet must have noticed me peering into her lounge because, presumably misunderstanding my interest, she said, 'Don't worry, Kat's at her boyfriend's. She won't be back until late.'

I was slightly curious about the relationship between the two women. Since I'd left home to go to university, I'd always lived on my own. I hadn't been invited to share a house with other students, and my relationships with women had never lasted long enough for us to move in together. I wondered how much information Harriet and Kat shared about their lives and, in particular, their boyfriends, and whether Harriet ever mentioned me.

I'd hoped to be invited to sit down in the lounge so we could have a chat about things, but Harriet led me straight into the kitchen. 'This is what the landlord put through our letterbox last night,' she said, handing me an A4 size sheet of paper. 'It's a copy of the original gas safety certificate that was done before we moved in.' She then handed me a second sheet. 'And this is the new certificate that last week's engineer gave us. They were different engineers. What do you think?'

I studied both documents carefully. At first sight, they seemed perfectly normal. They both contained the name and address of the landlord, the address of the rental property, the details of the gas engineer and their business, and the details of the appliances checked. They were both signed and dated at the bottom. But something Harriet had said niggled at me.

'Is that the hob which was faulty?' I asked, pointing to the appliance at the back of the kitchen.

'Yes. The second engineer was surprised that it passed the original gas safety test. But I checked the first certificate and it definitely says it was safe.'

I went over and peered at the hob even though to me one hob – broken or working – looks much like another. Then I looked again at the first certificate. I held it up to the kitchen light. I felt a wave of understanding.

'I know what's going on,' I said, holding out the first certificate so Harriet could read it. 'Look at the box that says "Appliance Details".'

'Yes?'

'There are two appliances listed,' I said, 'the boiler and the hob. Each gas appliance should be tested and listed on the certificate. But look at the handwriting in the row where the hob is listed. It's not the same as the handwriting elsewhere on the certificate. Also, there's an empty box where the model of the hob should be included.'

'So?' Harriet still hadn't made the connection.

'I don't think the first engineer ever checked the hob. He might have forgotten, or not even seen that you had a gas hob. Either way, there was originally no mention of the hob on the certificate. Your landlord wouldn't have noticed. He was only interested in getting a piece of paper to say the gas at the house was safe. But when the second engineer found a fault with the hob, your landlord would have looked at the first certificate and spotted the omission. He must have panicked. He hadn't given you a copy of the first certificate as he was supposed to. He therefore filled in the details of the hob himself retrospectively, to try to show that the hob had been safe at the time of the first test.'

Harriet looked more closely at the sheet. 'You're right,' she said. 'The handwriting is different. And,' she added with a hint of triumph in her voice, 'my landlord wouldn't have a clue as to what the model of the hob was, which must be why he left that box blank.'

'Exactly.' I felt very pleased with myself. I'd never received the praise I deserved for bringing Helen's killer to book, and I suspected the police believed that I'd simply blundered upon the truth. I didn't claim to have all the same skills as a seasoned police investigator – I hadn't been trained in how to fill out the necessary paperwork, for a start – but I certainly knew what was what. After all, within a few minutes of arriving at Harriet's house, I had spotted a clever forgery.

'What do you think I should do?' Harriet asked. 'Should I report him and, if so, to whom?'

I thought quickly. 'I wouldn't rush into reporting him. Yes, he will be in trouble, but you still have to get on with him as your landlord. Instead, why not just mention to him casually that you know what he's done? That way, you have something to hold over him which might be of use in the future. For example, if he wants to increase your rent or even evict you.'

Harriet's smile made me feel warm all over. 'I like that idea, Alan,' she said. 'He owns a shop in town, so I'll pop in there tomorrow lunchtime. I'll thank him for the copy of the old certificate and say just enough to let him know I've worked out what he did. One thing occurs to me though. How could we ever prove that he forged the certificate?'

I was on firm ground here. Out of a lawyerly force of habit, I'd looked up the rules when I was given the gas safety certificate for my rental property. 'That's easy,' I said. 'The original engineer will have produced three copies of the certificate. One for you – although you didn't receive it. One for your landlord. And one for his own records. He's required by law to keep his copy for a specified period. That being so, all you'd have to do is report it to the Health and Safety Executive. They would ask the engineer for his copy, then compare it with the one that your landlord pushed through your letterbox ... and bingo. I have to say your landlord has been very stupid. Although, strictly, it's his responsibility to get all the appliances tested, I don't think he'd have been in too much trouble if he'd simply fessed up and blamed the original engineer. No one died and the hob is now safe.'

'Ah,' Harriet said, 'I can explain that. The first engineer said he was the brother-in-law of my landlord. So the landlord probably didn't want to grass up a member of his own family.'

'That will be it.'

'I can't wait to tell Kat. She's never much cared for our landlord either.'

'Actually,' I said, 'you might want to keep this to yourself. I know the two of you get on well, but you never know when it might be to your advantage to have a bit of private information that could be to your benefit. You might not always be friends.'

It may sound surprising that I didn't want my skills praised to Harriet's housemate, but I preferred the idea of Harriet and me sharing our own little secret.

For a moment, a strange look appeared on Harriet's face as if she'd smelt something unpleasant. But then she gave me her usual friendly smile. 'I'm really grateful for your help, Alan,' she said. 'But if you don't mind, I will have to get on because I'm going out tonight.'

That was a real disappointment to me, as I'd hoped she would invite me to have a drink in her lounge now that we'd got the main purpose of my visit out of the way. However, the tone of her voice didn't invite questions about where she was going or with whom.

'Of course not,' I said. 'I'm going out too.' I hadn't been intending to go out, but I didn't want her to think I had nothing better to do than go back to my house and sit there on my own. 'Could I just use your loo before I go?' I asked. The cold evening air and the coffee I'd drunk during the afternoon had exerted their usual effect on my bladder.

'By all means. It's the first right at the top of the stairs.'

As I went up the stairs, Harriet was already walking into her lounge and picking up some things that I assumed she was taking out with her. After I'd finished in the bathroom, I paused a second on the landing. I knew which of the two bedrooms was Harriet's because she'd mentioned once that sometimes the streetlights at the front of the house kept her awake. Her bedroom door was wide open and I could see the corner of a double bed. I couldn't help but wonder if Hugh or, worse, Lewis had spent time in, or on, that bed. The wall between her bedroom and Kat's was only plasterboard, and it occurred to me that if Hugh or Lewis had spent a night in Harriet's room, Kat would have heard the sounds of their sexual congress. I felt sick as I pictured what Harriet might have done in that bed with them. Both men really had taken advantage of her. Hugh, with his oily ways, had smooth-talked her into bed with promises of God knows what. And Lewis, her then line manager, had done still worse, using his power over her to coerce her into an unequal relationship even though he was married. How wrong it was that Lewis, in particular, should get away with this. For just an instant, I was tempted to peep further around the door of her bedroom in case there were any clues as to what she'd done with Hugh and Lewis. But common sense prevailed. I went hot and cold at the thought of Harriet hearing a creak from upstairs and realising where I must be.

Quickly I went downstairs, hoping the guilt I was feeling didn't show. Harriet, however, didn't seem to be giving me a moment's thought. She plainly had something more important than me planned for the evening.

'Thanks again, Alan, for coming round,' she said, as she locked the door behind us. 'I'll let you know what my landlord's reaction is. Have a good evening.'

76

15

I wasn't in the mood to go straight home after leaving Harriet's house. I'd been so much looking forward to spending some time with her in her home environment, and now I was feeling rather flat.

I therefore dropped in at my tennis club, in a small village between Ely and one of the surrounding towns. I hadn't arranged a game, but there was a practice session for current and potential men's team players on Wednesday evenings and, as always, I had my kit in the boot of my car.

By the time I was changed, three courts were in use under the floodlights. There were two games of normal doubles, and a third game of American doubles with three players, where one player was taking on the other two but only defending the singles court. I stood watching the American doubles from outside the wire fence for a few minutes, swinging my new yellow and black Babolat racket to show that I was warming up and calling out 'good shot' at appropriate times. I was expecting them to invite me to join them but they seemed to have eyes only for their own game.

I'd almost given up hope when, at the end of one rally, the player on his own looked over in my direction. 'Are you going to give me a hand or not?' he shouted.

I cursed myself for not taking the initiative sooner and knelt down to check that the laces on my tennis shoes were tight enough. I was just getting back up when a stocky man with greying hair in probably his late forties or early fifties walked briskly past me onto the court.

'I was here first,' I called out when I recovered from my surprise.

But the man was already shaking hands with the player who had summoned him and a normal game of doubles quickly began. For a few seconds, I was again the small boy at school who was always chosen last for the football team. I felt a prickle of a tear in the corner of my eye. I couldn't make myself disappear into the ground, but I did the next best thing, bending down to my tennis bag and sorting through my kit as if checking that everything was there. I was worried that everyone might be watching me, but when I raised my eyes to look cautiously around, I might as well have been invisible for all anyone cared.

It quickly became apparent that the player who had stolen my place wasn't as good a player as me. If he couldn't reach a ball within a stride or two, he rarely bothered to chase it down, and he seemed incapable of killing an overhead smash at the first attempt. However, to my surprise, this didn't seem to upset his partner. Once, when the player gave up on a cross-court shot that he could have easily retrieved, I was sure his partner would make a critical comment. Instead, the partner made some jolly little remark and both men burst out laughing. I could expect this sort of thing in a social session for elderly ladies, but these were men who wanted to represent the club in the local league and it all seemed so amateurish.

Eventually, I was invited at a changeover to make up a four, and I set out to impress. I was clearly stronger than my partner, but I'd learnt from my experiences at my previous tennis club near Cambridge and I deliberately let him return some shots down the middle of the court that I could easily have got to myself. I tried not to show my annoyance when he put a few balls into the net, but he still must have picked up on something because he started to mutter a 'sorry' after each of his mistakes. Once, when we swapped ends, I tried to be helpful and gave him a few tips on how he could improve his game. If I'd been in his position, I would have been delighted that a stronger player was trying to help me get better, but my partner didn't even pretend to be paying attention and just continued to swig from his water bottle. Not surprisingly, we lost the set 6-2. I normally try to keep my temper on court, but after one of our opponents hit the winning shot, I smashed the ball as hard as I could into the wire fence behind me. When I turned around, everyone was looking at me.

*

I had heard that, after the practice session, it was customary for most of the players to go for a drink at a pub in the same village. As everyone towelled down and put their kit back in their bags, I listened out for a general summons. None came, and no one seemed to be seeking me out to invite me, so I latched onto a small group of men of my age who'd been playing in one of the other doubles games. They'd been talking quite animatedly when I joined them, but they now fell silent.

'Who's going for a drink?' I asked. Normally, in these kinds of situations, I waited for people to speak to me first, but for once I'd taken the initiative.

'I might stay for a quick one,' one of them said after a brief silence.

'How about the rest of you?' I asked. 'It sounds like a really good way to finish off a practice. A chance to discuss what you've learnt and what you can do to improve.'

I had the impression that each of the other three men was waiting for someone else to speak.

'I'll come for one as well,' one of them said eventually. 'You're welcome to join us, if you like.'

'I'd love to,' I said. 'Thank you.'

The pub was just a short walk away; it was one of those refurbished places where the owners had patently spent a lot of money trying to create an old-fashioned look. Almost everyone who had attended the practice session seemed to be there, so I was a bit surprised no one had asked me earlier if I wanted to come along. I would have been happy to buy a round for the four people I'd joined, but I didn't get a chance. One of them pointedly asked the other three if they wanted their usual and disappeared off to the bar to get their drinks in. I went to the bar to get a pint of lager for myself. Next to me was the stocky man with greying hair who had pinched my place in the American doubles game. But I was prepared to let bygones be bygones.

'Can I get you a drink?' I asked.

'It's very kind of you,' he said, 'but I'm in a mini-round already. You'll find that most of us are.'

The way he said this made me feel like an outsider. Nevertheless, I followed him back to where he was sitting, which was with the three men from the American doubles game. I found it annoying that they'd used the session to play what looked like their regular 'four'. Surely the whole point of the session was to play with different partners and to spot players who had the potential to turn out for the teams? I had sense enough not to say this directly, but I did want to find out how the sessions worked.

'How do they choose who plays for the teams?' I asked. 'I didn't see anyone going around watching all the games.'

'We mostly all know each other already,' said the stocky man. 'Most of us have been playing for the teams for years.'

'So how does a new player get onto a team?' I persisted. 'Is it possible to play a challenge match against one of the existing team members? I wouldn't want to boast, but I did think I might have an edge over some people I played with tonight.'

'It's Alan, isn't it?' This was the man who, at the start of the session, had ignored my presence at the fence and had instead beckoned the stocky guy onto the court.

'Yes, Alan Gadd,' I said, 'I'm still quite new here. I'm a solicitor at the University.'

'The thing is, Alan,' he said slowly as if talking to a small child, 'there is such a thing as loyalty. People here have turned out for the teams year in, year out, in all sorts of weather. It wouldn't be fair to ask someone to step down just because some johnny-come-lately might beat them in a "challenge" match.' He said the word 'challenge' almost as if he was spitting it out. 'Besides,' he went on, 'we don't normally talk much about tennis when we're in the pub. We've done our bit on court and now we want to chew the fat with our mates.'

I don't think I am especially sensitive, but even I could tell that I was being excluded. It just wasn't fair. I knew someone at the University who played squash, and he'd said that team selection at the local squash club was much more meritocratic. If you could show that you were better than an existing team player, you were in. It was on occasions like this that I sometimes wished I'd chosen a sport other than tennis as my speciality.

*

I got back to my house at about 9.30 p.m. I would have left the pub sooner, but I was worried that everyone might start talking about me. So I'd sat, mostly silent, in my chair around the little circular table until the small group I was with finished their drinks and got up to go. I had the impression from the surprised look on some other faces that they were leaving sooner than usual.

I put a Charlie Bigham macaroni cheese into the oven while I had a shower, then I added half a stick of garlic bread for the final 15 minutes' cooking time. I was only wearing a dressing gown, but the house was as beautifully warm as ever even though it was a chilly October evening. I opened a bottle of one of my favourite Californian Zinfandel red wines, a 2019 Bedrock, and finished my first glass while my meal was still cooking. It was a beautifully smooth wine, with a powerful black fruit taste, and I made a mental note that I would soon need to buy another case from my usual wine merchant in Cambridge.

While I ate my meal, I watched a reality TV show hoping it would distract me from the disappointments of the day. But I got increasingly irritated by the participants, and particularly by the women whose main criterion for choosing a man seemed to be whether he looked 'hot'. I doubted that any of these men actually knew how to please a woman physically, judging by the gormless look on most of their faces. I couldn't imagine any of them reading a book on how to be good in bed.

Normally, I tried to make a bottle of wine last two nights. But tonight, once I'd drunk two-thirds of the bottle, I decided it was too late to save the rest. I switched off the TV and lay down on the sofa with a cushion behind my head and the last of the wine in a glass in my hand. I ran over the events of the day and mulled over what I could have done differently. I remembered the sight of Harriet's bed and pictured that sleazebag Lewis naked on it with her. I was angrier with Lewis than I'd ever been with Hugh. For a start, he'd been Harriet's line manager, and he'd crossed the professional line with her in a way that I'd been careful never to do. But, worse, he'd betrayed two women: his wife, Ruth, and Harriet. He was undoubtedly the sort of man who would relish having two parallel relationships and being able to compare one woman's sexual performance with the other's.

It just wasn't right that he should get away with it.

After a while, I picked up my phone and switched on my VPN. I was used to doing this when carrying out research, as occasionally I stumbled across websites which would cause me some professional embarrassment if it ever came out that I had accessed them. I hadn't forgotten having had to hand over my phone to the police when they were investigating Helen's death.

I then went onto the website of one of the companies which allows you to set up an anonymous e-mail account without having to supply any other contact details such as a phone number. I was an old hand at getting these accounts, and within a minute or two I had a completely anonymous e-mail address. I'd never had to send an e-mail to Lewis's wife at work, but e-mail addresses at the University were all in a standard format of first and last name separated by a full stop and followed by the University's generic e-mail address, so I knew what hers would be.

I quickly tapped out a message:

Dear Ruth

I've never done anything like this before, but I think you need to know the truth about your husband. He's had an affair with a girl called Harriet Wells who works in the Legal team.

Please don't blame her, as I'm sure she didn't know Lewis was still with you.

I thought this was something you ought to know. Your husband is a rat.

A Friend

I read it through once and pressed the 'send' icon.

*

I woke up later in bed, as I often did, after about an hour's sleep. For a moment, I thought I'd only dreamt about sending the e-mail. Then I remembered that I really had sent it. I could feel the muscles stretch around my eyes and mouth as I grimaced with horror and embarrassment. I imagined people's reactions if they knew what I'd done. I pictured, in particular, the look on Harriet's face. She'd shown me nothing but respect and kindness since I'd joined the University, and she'd demonstrated on a number of occasions how much she trusted me. And this was how I repaid her. God, I could be such a fucking shit. It was no excuse that I'd had too much to drink.

Ruth wasn't likely to read the e-mail until she logged on at work in the morning. Unlike in private legal practice, few people at the University bothered to check their work e-mails out of hours. Unfortunately, my anonymous account didn't provide for the recall of e-mails.

My mind turned to whether anyone would know that I was the person responsible. I'd covered my tracks from a technical perspective and I hadn't been stupid enough to sign my name. But I wondered if I'd revealed too much information in my e-

83

mail. If Harriet ever saw it, she would ask herself who knew about her and Lewis. Lewis obviously did, but he wouldn't be stupid enough to send the e-mail to his own wife. And Hugh evidently did, but if he was going to send an e-mail like that he would have done so a long time before. However, if Harriet saw the e-mail and asked Hugh about it, he was just the spiteful sod to say that he'd recently dropped a broad hint to me about her and Lewis. It wouldn't take her long then to work out that I must be the culprit. I was such a fool, such a bloody stupid fool. How I wished I could go back in time and not send that damn e-mail.

I had one of my worst night's sleep since leaving Doveley's. I kept dropping off to sleep and then waking up again shortly afterwards, each time telling myself what a dumb thing I'd done. But there was nothing I could do about it now. I would just have to be prepared to face the music.

16

I hadn't chosen to do so deliberately, but the next morning I found myself going out of my way to be agreeable to everyone, beginning with the Senate House receptionist. Subconsciously, I suppose, I was trying to get people on my side before what I'd done came to light.

As soon as Richard and Tom arrived, I walked round our pod to spend a few minutes with each of them, making sure they were on top of their work and knew that I was available if they needed any help. Tom seemed grateful enough, even if I had to bite my tongue when I saw some of his most recent drafting. Richard, however, was quite surly. He evidently hadn't forgotten, or forgiven, the bollocking I'd given him. He also ignored a couple of Harriet's attempts to start some idle chit-chat; undoubtedly he was indulging in a game of shoot the messenger. Normally, I wouldn't have been unhappy about this – I felt the two had become too close for Harriet's good – but today it didn't help with the positive team spirit I was trying to foster.

Harriet wanted to discuss with me the work she was doing for International. Mehak apparently wanted to pay agents a higher rate of commission than seemed justifiable. But as I looked into her warm, trusting eyes, all I could think about was how she would react if she found out how I'd betrayed her.

The thread holding the sword of Damocles over my head broke at around 10 a.m. I was staring into the middle distance, trying to think of a better way to draft a complicated royalty payment clause in a patent licence, when I saw Ruth come through the door from the staircase. If someone was telling a story, they would probably say something like she was white-faced or trembling with rage. But in fact, other than for a certain determination in her step, she could have been any other middle-aged female employee at the University coming up to the second floor for a routine conversation about work. She was plumper than I remembered her, now that she wasn't behind her desk, but she was more apple-shaped than pear-shaped and it didn't slow her down.

I watched with a dry mouth as she marched down the aisle that ran down the centre of the floor. I didn't know if she was coming to see me, or Harriet, or Lewis. I had no idea what I was going to say if it was me. Would I be able to deny convincingly all knowledge of the e-mail? Or would I be better off trying to blame someone else and, if so, whom? Fortunately, when she reached the end of the aisle, she turned left and headed straight for Lewis's office. She didn't bother to knock on his door, simply flinging it open and then closing it firmly after herself.

Harriet must have spotted Ruth at about the same time as me. If I'd had any doubts about what had gone on between her and Lewis, they would have been dispelled by the haunted look on her face, as if she'd seen someone whom she thought was long dead. Now, like me, she turned to watch the scene in Lewis's office through the glass wall. It was like a silent movie; we could hear nothing but see everything.

Ruth was standing in front of Lewis's desk. She had a sheet of paper in her hand that she flung down on the desk. She then crossed her arms and stood there, mouth closed, plainly waiting for him to say something. After a few seconds, Lewis made a gesture of helplessness, as if to indicate that there was nothing useful he could say. Ruth began alternately to speak and fall silent, as though she was asking questions and waiting for a response. Each silence lasted until Lewis said something, usually very brief, following which Ruth again started speaking. Once, I glanced quickly around the second floor, but no one other than me and Harriet appeared to be paying any attention to what was going on.

After about five minutes, Ruth wheeled on her heels and marched towards the door. She opened it normally but slammed it behind herself so violently that I feared the glass would shatter. Heads now turned. Instead of going straight back to the central aisle, she diverted towards our pod. For a moment, I was terrified that she was going to confront me in front of everyone. But she had a different target. She stopped a couple of yards short of Harriet and mouthed a single word:

'Bitch.'

Then she turned away and headed quickly for the exit, watched by most of the people on the floor.

I was drenched in sweat and realised I'd dug one of my fingernails into my thumb so hard that it was bleeding. I turned my head to my left and saw Harriet sitting motionless in her chair, looking a bit like a puppy which has been kicked.

I had mixed feelings. Part of me wanted to get up out of my chair and give her a comforting hug. But another part of me was angry that she could be so upset by something to do with Lewis. I don't think she was even aware of my presence, let alone that I'd seen everything. Richard and Tom had bent their heads to their screens and were pretending not to have noticed that anything was amiss.

'Harriet,' I said at last, 'shall we continue our discussion of what you are doing for International?'

I'd like to think I said that to take her mind off what had happened. But if I am truthful, there was an element too of wanting to remind her that there were more important things in her life than Lewis.

She replied, 'Not now, Alan, please,' and continued to stare at nothing in particular.

'Harriet. A word, please.' Lewis had approached unnoticed. It was the first time I'd ever seen him flustered. His face was flushed; the redness stood out in bright contrast to his greying hair.

He couldn't leave her alone even now. I hoped she was going to tell him to fuck off. Instead, she got up and followed him into his office like an obedient poodle. Again the glass door closed, and again I tried to follow a silent conversation as they stood facing each other. This time, it appeared to be Lewis who was angry. He kept gesticulating at Harriet. She stood there like a punch-drunk boxer, shaking her head from time to time. I was sorely tempted to burst into the office and punch Lewis hard in the face. He had no right to punish Harriet for the consequences of his own treachery.

After about five minutes, Harriet came out of the office and back to our pod. To my slight disappointment, she didn't slam the door behind her like Ruth had done. Richard and Tom were still making a show of being engrossed in their work. Now that she was closer to me, I could see that Harriet had been crying. I wondered what exactly she and Lewis had been saying to each other and whether they'd worked out that I might have sent the e-mail which had triggered off the morning's events. I decided I was better off not saying anything to her and bent my head to the paper draft of my patent licence.

A few minutes later, Harriet got up without a word and headed towards the door to downstairs. I prayed she wasn't going to tackle Hugh. If this was her intention, though, there was nothing realistically I could do to stop her.

I didn't have a clue about what I would say to Lewis if he came out of his office to confront me, but he wasn't moving from behind his desk.

I wasn't sure what I'd been trying to achieve when I sent that e-mail to Ruth, but whatever it was it didn't seem to have worked. Harriet hadn't even turned to me for comfort in her distress. And now I had the ongoing worry about the truth emerging. Lewis could make my professional life a misery if he found out what I'd done. And if Harriet found out … well, I wasn't sure that I could cope with that either professionally or personally.

Everything was going wrong for me at the moment. I knew I wasn't perfect, but surely I didn't deserve this.

17

I spent most of the next hour keeping a close watch on the door to the second floor. I was dreading seeing Harriet and Hugh come storming up together from the first floor to berate me for having sent that bloody e-mail to Ruth. I daren't ask anyone if they knew where Harriet had gone in case they were curious about why I was showing so much interest.

Tom and Richard were continually whispering to each other, and from time to time some other random person from our floor would come over and join in. Although they wouldn't have admitted it, they were all plainly enjoying the morning's excitement. I tried, with little success, to listen to what they were saying. The only good thing from my point of view was that no one as yet seemed to be pointing a finger of blame at me.

I tried to crack on with my clinical trials collaboration agreement. A contracts manager at the NHS Trust – who had no legal qualifications, as far as I could tell – was being a complete pain, sending snippy comments on my amendments and copying in everyone else on the e-mail circulation list. Needless to say, she hadn't a clue about what I was trying to achieve and didn't appreciate that my amendments reflected what had been agreed upon at the highest levels between the parties. However, as always when dealing with the NHS, I had to treat her like a saint and not tell her the home truths that I would have done at Doveley's if faced with a tiresome private practice lawyer on the other side of a deal.

'Alan, what's your timeline please on the contract for Professor Fuller?'

I hadn't heard Deborah approach. She looked like a horse and trod like an elephant, so she must have deliberately crept up on me to catch me unawares.

'It's all in hand,' I replied. 'But I still need to bottom out the exact intellectual property rights being assigned to Ian Davey's company. While it's easy enough to identify the registered intellectual property rights such as the patent, it's not so easy to identify all the unregistered ones such as the confidential know-how.'

Deborah's eyes narrowed. She thought I was bullshitting. And, of course, she was right; I was bullshitting. I could have knocked out an assignment of the intellectual property rights, in consideration of the payment of £100,000, in a couple of hours. But she wasn't a lawyer – her degree was in some useless social sciences subject – and she was savvy enough to know not to dictate what went into a contract.

'Understood,' she said. 'But if you could please prioritise this work, I would be grateful. Ian Davey's company has been very good to us and I wouldn't want any delay to jeopardise our future working relationship with them. I'm sure Simon will give you any input you need on the technical side.'

'I'll be in touch with Simon as soon as I need to,' I said. 'Don't worry, Deborah, I appreciate the importance of getting this over the line.'

I was such an arse-licker. How I wished I had the courage to say to her face that this deal wasn't in the best interests of the University. But my fear of another dressing-down, this time in front of Richard and Tom, made this impossible. In theory, I could appeal over Deborah's head to Amanda, but the two women were always so palsy-walsy that this would only have one outcome. And not a good one for me.

*

'Alan, can I have a word please about Landlord Relax?'

Ten minutes had passed and now it was Amanda's turn. She

and Deborah were like a double act. It was as if they'd tossed a coin to decide the order in which they were going to pester me. She was looking down at me with a tight smile in which there wasn't a scrap of humour.

'Yes, of course, Amanda,' I said, swivelling in my chair to face her and trying to look like I was pleased to be interrupted. 'How can I help? I thought Doveley's were leading on the Landlord Relax spin-out?'

'They're doing most of the paperwork, certainly.' She had a sheet of paper in her hand, from which she now read out a long list of the legal documents that Doveley's must have said would be needed. I chuckled to myself; Doveley's were bigging up their role all right. 'But I want you to oversee all this,' Amanda concluded. 'Make sure it works legally and reflects the University's and the founders' interests. Can you do that?'

I wasn't keen to be involved. Partly because of how Amanda had humiliated me in the Enterprise Board meeting. And partly because it would mean liaising with Jeff Parker and Lucy Black and putting up with their insufferable ways. However, I had no real choice. 'I'd be delighted to,' I said. 'I'll touch base with Jeff Parker. I can then brief you at key stages on where we are.'

'Actually, can you please make sure I'm copied in on all e-mails. I'd like to stay closely involved.'

That was unusual. Amanda was going to have a lot of e-mails landing in her inbox, most of which she didn't need to see. It would also make a difference to how Jeff and I corresponded with each other. Rather than concentrating on the issues, both of our priorities would be to portray ourselves in a good light to Amanda. Jeff would want to demonstrate how much value he was adding to the in-house legal function. Whereas I would want to show that there were nuances of the legal issues that an external lawyer could never understand.

'Absolutely fine, Amanda,' I said. 'I'll let Jeff know.'

*

Lewis didn't emerge from his office all morning. I speculated about what he'd do if he needed a pee. Perhaps he used one of the plant pots in his office.

I ate lunch at my desk as usual, hoping Harriet would be back soon. While I munched down my sandwiches, I browsed the 'People' section of the Doveley's website. There were pages of head-and-shoulders photographs in identikit style. All the faces showed a typical 'How may I help you?' smile. All the shoulders were slightly turned away from the photographer to give a more casual effect. The bios were all full of quotes from selected clients saying how 'commercial' and 'pragmatic' the lawyers were. For a while, I avoided looking at Jeff's picture and bio, but I couldn't resist for ever. And there he was, with that earnest fresh-faced look that women inexplicably went for. I read his bio. Bugger me, a client was quoted as saying what an 'absolute star' he was. It was enough to make anyone sick. More of an 'absolute shit' is how I'd have described him. If it hadn't been for Sam Snape and those who had fallen into line behind him in the aftermath of Helen's death, it would still have been me on that website, probably with the 'Partner' designation next to my name that I'd always craved.

When, around 2 p.m., Harriet still hadn't made an appearance, I went for a wander. I wouldn't say that I was actively looking for her, but I couldn't face spending all afternoon not knowing where she was. As I went down the stairs and approached the door to the first floor, my first instinct was to scurry past. But then I told myself that even if Hugh had been informed about my e-mail to Ruth, he couldn't have worked out that I was the sender or he would have come upstairs hunting me down. And I had to check that Harriet wasn't in there. I therefore took a deep breath and went through the door, intending to scan the room quickly before continuing downstairs.

Hugh, inevitably, was there, holding forth at his pod on the far side of the room, with his three cronies hanging on his every word. Unfortunately, just at that moment, they all turned their heads in my direction and burst out laughing, though whether at the sight of me or because Hugh had said something funny, I couldn't tell. Desperately, I racked my brain for a reason for having come into the room. I daren't just turn on my heels and go out in case it looked like I was running away. Then I spotted Mehak at her desk in the International section. I could use her as my excuse.

'Hello, Mehak,' I said as I approached her desk. 'How are things in International?'

Mehak looked slightly wary as she raised her face. She was alone at her pod, so no one would be able to overhear our conversation, and there was nothing unusual about someone from Legal dropping in on an internal client.

'All fine, thank you, Alan,' she said. Her body language was all 'keep away from me': she sat back in her chair with her arms folded and her body turned slightly away from me. It seemed a long time ago that we'd had those early morning one-on-ones.

'And how are things with you personally?' I asked.

'Fine too, thank you. And with you?'

'All good, thank you,' I said.

Bloody hell, we could be foreign school kids being taught our first polite phrases in English. I remembered how Mehak had ignored me when I was coming up the stairs with Harriet earlier in the week. I also remembered how Lewis had torn a strip off me for not being, as he put it, responsive to Mehak's requests for help with legal work. Mehak hadn't thought or cared about the effect of these incidents on me. I decided to see how she liked a taste of her own medicine.

I said, 'And how are your boyfriends ... er, sorry, your boyfriend? You obviously wouldn't have more than one at the same time, would you?' I finished with what I hoped came out as a light-hearted laugh.

I'd expected her to blush or at least look embarrassed. She must realise that I knew her excuse for turning me down – of already having a boyfriend – was just that: an excuse. Instead, she gave me a look of what I can only describe as mixed disbelief and dislike. I'd been prepared to be forgiving if she'd been suitably apologetic, but now I felt annoyance. I wasn't the sort of man to be toyed with and tossed aside without consideration of the consequences.

'That reminds me, Mehak,' I went on, remembering what Harriet had been concerned about earlier that morning. 'I've been helping Harriet with your agency contracts. She said we pay a higher rate of commission to certain agents than any other university she knows about. Can you explain how that is in the University's interests please?'

I will give Mehak her due. She breathed a slight sigh of impatience. It was as if she was relieved that our conversation had moved onto professional matters. She unfolded her arms and leant forward. I could smell the scent that she always splashed so generously upon her slim, soft-skinned neck.

'Alan,' she said, 'I'm very grateful to you and Harriet for the work you're doing. I'm sorry if anything I said to anyone was misconstrued. But what you have to understand is that we are – and please don't quote me on this – a third-rate university trying to compete for international students with some of the best-known universities in the world. Some of the agents we use act for other universities as well. That being so, we have to give them something to encourage them to work that little bit harder for us. Do you understand what I mean?'

I don't like being made to feel foolish, but that's exactly how I felt now. Mehak was implying I was naïve, and I couldn't immediately think of a retort which would put me back in the driving seat. 'I understand,' I said. 'But all the same ... well, it seemed excessive to Harriet.' I tried to deflect some of the criticism away from myself, to make it look like I'd only been passing on something which had occurred to Harriet. 'I'll mention to her what you said.'

'Is there anything else I can help you with today?' There it was again, that use of the superfluous 'today' which had so irritated me when used by Lewis.

'No, thank you,' was all I said though. 'It's, er, been good to catch up.'

As I headed towards the door leading back onto the staircase, I felt incredibly self-conscious. I was imagining Mehak's eyes, and those of Hugh and his crew, watching me go. I wondered what they were thinking and what they might all say about me after I'd gone. There was a glass panel in the door and, after closing it behind me, I was tempted for a moment to stop and look through the glass to see what was going on. But if I did this, people might think I was behaving in a paranoid way. I continued downstairs, therefore, not quite knowing where I was going but hoping to find out where Harriet was.

18

'I'm sorry for disappearing yesterday, Alan, but it was an awful day.'

Despite my wandering around, I hadn't come across Harriet the previous afternoon. This morning, however, she arrived at her normal time, looking a bit tired but otherwise her usual calm and collected self. I'd decided not to broach the subject of Ruth's visit, hoping it might arise naturally in the course of our early morning coffees at our desks, but the first thing she asked me was whether I fancied a coffee together in the main refectory for a change.

Do bears shit in the woods? I said I thought I could spare the time.

We slipped out of Senate House before any of Lewis, Richard or Tom arrived, and strolled companionably along the walkway towards the centre of the campus, talking about this and that while studiously ignoring the events of yesterday. There were very few other people around. The University had learnt from bitter experience that it was a waste of time scheduling teaching sessions for 9 a.m. when most students were still in bed. Academics also seemed to find it hard to turn up for work at what was a normal clocking-in time for people outside the ivory towers of higher education.

The refectory was a large single-storey building next to the School of Law. Ironically, given my role at the University, I hadn't yet had to set foot inside this School, and I had no particular wish to do so. My opinion of academic lawyers was one held by quite a few people in legal practice: namely that they were obsessed with theoretical issues that had no relevance in everyday legal work, writing articles that were only read by other academic lawyers, and lacking the balls to go out and earn a proper living in the profession.

The refectory was even quieter than the walkway. I bought the coffees: a cappuccino for Harriet and a large americano for myself. I would have preferred an espresso, but I thought a longer drink would give me a better chance to have a gulp and a think if it looked like Harriet was getting close to working out who had tipped off Ruth.

It was only when we were seated at an isolated table in the corner of the refectory that Harriet made her apology for having disappeared the day before.

'You looked upset,' I said. 'But you shot out of the door before I had a chance to ask if I could help. What was it all about?'

'Lewis had a go at me. He blamed me for something that happened. I told him I'd done nothing wrong, but he didn't believe me.'

She paused, and I had a quick think about how best to respond. I didn't want to show too much knowledge in case she got suspicious, but I could hardly pretend that I hadn't heard what Ruth had said to her.

'That's terrible,' I said. 'What did he think you'd done? Was it anything to do with Ruth coming up to the second floor?'

She nodded. 'I wasn't going to say anything to you. It was before your time and it was all a stupid mistake. But me and Lewis, well, we had a fling.'

Even though her words weren't a surprise, they still caused a rush of blood to my head. I felt as if I'd downed a glass of wine in one big gulp. 'But he's married,' I said. I didn't trust myself to say more.

'I know. But I thought he and his wife were living separate lives. He told me they hadn't slept together for ages. I believed him. More fool me.'

Now I felt anger. Anger with Harriet as well as with Lewis. I couldn't believe she'd fallen for that old line. Anyone could have told her that Lewis was the sort of man who would say anything to get a woman into bed. I tried in vain to stop myself from thinking about what the sex had been like. Had he told her it was the best sex he'd had for years? Had she offered him things that Ruth would never have consented to? I flinched in pain as my fingernails dug into the fleshy part of my hands.

'Don't blame yourself,' I said, trying to pull myself together. I made an effort to say something that I thought she would want to hear. 'He was totally in the wrong.'

'Do you really think so? Don't you think I was too naïve?'

Yes, of course you bloody were, I thought. 'No, not at all,' I said. 'Men like that tell lies as routinely as they breathe. You could hardly ask Ruth if he was telling the truth.' There was something I had to know the answer to. 'Er, I guess if he was still sharing a house with his wife, you must have been limited as to when and where you could meet away from work?'

'He told me that his divorce would be more unpleasant if Ruth knew he was seeing someone else. That meant I couldn't risk spending the nights at his even when Ruth wasn't there. And he couldn't spend them at mine either. Kat's a good sort, but she's got a big mouth and knows a lot of people in Ely. So we used to slip away to mine at lunchtimes when Kat was at work. We would go in separate cars just in case we were seen.'

I felt sick. I imagined Harriet and Lewis leaving Senate House a short time apart, both having spent the morning knowing that they would soon be having sex with each other. I hated the idea of Lewis being any good at sex, but I couldn't imagine Harriet wanting repeat performances unless he was able to deliver.

'The thing is, Alan,' she went on, 'I honestly would never have done it if I'd known that he and Ruth were still together. I've always thought badly of people who have affairs. I wouldn't want someone to hurt me that way, so I wouldn't intentionally do it to someone else. I ended it when I found out the truth, as you would expect.'

I knew Harriet wouldn't lie over something like that. But I couldn't tell if she'd just been naïve or had deliberately done the equivalent of sticking her fingers in her ears to avoid hearing something unpleasant. I stayed silent for a few seconds, scared that I might say something I would regret.

'What exactly happened yesterday?' I eventually asked. 'I saw Ruth go into his office, and she had a go at you when she left. Had he told her about you?'

'No. Someone else tipped her off. I don't know who. Lewis doesn't know either, although at first he thought it must have been me. I assumed it was Hugh. I told him about Lewis when we started seeing each other. So when Lewis finished having a go at me, I went straight downstairs to see Hugh. But I could tell straightaway that it wasn't him. He looked genuinely shocked at the idea. I know you never liked him, but he's a decent enough guy and whoever told Ruth must be an absolute shit. I mean, why do something like that and cause so much pain?'

Harriet was looking straight into my eyes and I cursed myself for having been so stupid. Why the hell had I sent that bloody e-mail? All she had to do was go back and ask Hugh who else he'd told, and she would know from his reply who the culprit was. Or even if she didn't ask Hugh, he might put two and two together himself and tell her. Harriet would never speak to me again. She was right; I really was a shit, even if I had only behaved like that under provocation.

But there was no point confessing. In for a penny, in for a pound. 'Perhaps she was only pretending to have been tipped off,' I said. 'Perhaps she had her suspicions and decided that was the best way to find out the truth.' I was careful not to mention an e-mail. Harriet hadn't said anything about the tip-off being by anonymous e-mail, so if I revealed this information it would be obvious even to her how I knew. This was the type of mistake made by many of the murderers in my true crime books.

'She'd received an e-mail,' Harriet said. 'She showed it to Lewis. It was from an anonymous account, though, so she doesn't know who sent it.'

'Ah,' I said, 'perhaps a friend of hers who felt she deserved to know the truth but who didn't want to tell her face-to-face.

Perhaps even someone who works in IT if they know how to set up an untraceable e-mail account.' I was pleased with that last suggestion as it would hopefully deflect attention from me. 'But why didn't you contact me last night to tell me all this? I can understand you wanting to get away from Senate House, but you know my personal mobile number and you could have phoned me at home in the evening.'

Harriet looked slightly shame-faced. 'That's very kind of you. But I was out last night until late. I went for a drink with that solicitor you know. Jeff Parker.'

I have occasionally wondered what is meant when someone is said to have almost fallen off a chair in surprise. Now I knew. I actually felt the room begin to spin. If someone had given me the faintest of touches with their finger, I'm sure I would have toppled onto the floor of the refectory.

'Parker?' I croaked. 'From Doveley's?'

'Yes, who else?' Harriet looked puzzled by my reaction. 'We had a lovely chat after that Enterprise Board meeting, and I must have said something about hoping we could continue the conversation on another occasion. And then the next day he phoned when you were off somewhere and asked if I would like to meet up for a drink. I must admit,' she laughed, 'he's a quick worker.'

I really didn't know where to look. Parker. The man who'd stolen Helen from me. OK, not literally stolen. But the man with whom she'd taken up after dumping me. The man at Doveley's whom everyone seemed to like. The man who'd snogged Lucy when she was my trainee. The man who couldn't avoid his share of the responsibility for Helen's death. Whatever else may have happened, it was as sure as night follows day that Helen wouldn't have died if she'd still been with me.

I thought I'd seen the end of Jeff Parker when I left Doveley's. It had been enough of a shock to find out that Doveley's had been appointed as the University's preferred solicitors and that Jeff Parker was leading for the firm on their first big piece of work for us. But then to find out that the man had taken Harriet out for a drink, after only one meeting, was almost more than I could bear. I'd been working alongside Harriet for months. We'd shared many companionable moments. And yet I'd never once asked her out for a drink. It wouldn't have been professional. And it most assuredly wasn't bloody professional for Jeff 'Nosey' Parker to be asking Harriet out for a drink when she was a client. I wasn't falling for this 'I must have said something' crap from Harriet, either. She would have known exactly what she was saying and what effect it would have on a shit like Parker.

I would have to think very hard about what I was going to do.

*

'He's actually quite sweet,' Harriet was going on, a slightly dreamy look on her face. 'I was worried that I might have been boring him, rambling on about all my stuff, but he listened very attentively and seemed really sympathetic.'

I'd never got my head around how stupid some women could be. Harriet had been around the block a few times, to put it bluntly. And yet here she was, falling for Parker's sleazy charm just as I'd seen many other women do in the past. What the hell was it about him that made him so attractive to women? He wasn't even a particularly good lawyer. Although he was sharp enough to know most of what mattered within his area of practice, he was hardly blessed with great intellectual ability. And I was convinced he emphasised that West Country burr when trying to pull a woman. I'd lost most of my northern accent within a few years of living in Cambridge, whereas his accent sometimes seemed to be even stronger than when he arrived. I'd once read somewhere that the West Country accent had been named the least sexy in Britain, yet here were women who seemed to think it promised all sorts of delights. It was ridiculous.

I knew from experience that it was no good telling Harriet directly what a con man he was. However, I felt it was my duty at least to warn her, as I had done regarding Hugh.

'I've known Parker for years,' I said. 'I can understand why some people like him, but I'm not sure he can be relied upon as regards his … his personal behaviour. I've seen him say anything to get a woman to, er, do what he wants.' I couldn't quite bring myself to be more explicit. 'And, believe me, there have been quite a few women.'

To my surprise, Harriet burst out laughing. 'He's obviously slowing down, then. He didn't make a move on me all evening. There must be something wrong with me. Perhaps I'll have to drop a few hints next time.'

I couldn't believe what I was hearing. Not only had my comments not put her off Parker, but she seemed to be saying that she planned to see him again. She was even hinting that she wouldn't be averse to him taking things further. What had I done to deserve this? Parker had been shagging Helen after she'd dumped me, and now he'd followed me to Ely and was planning to shag Harriet too. I'd half-forgotten how much I loathed the man. But – my God – I could certainly remember now.

'He's asked to see you again?' I asked as mildly as I could.

'Yes. He's away next week, like you. But he suggested a drink and a meal down by the riverside when he gets back. I said yes. He's an interesting guy. He was telling me how Doveley's got appointed by the University. They'd apparently made a big play for Amanda and Lewis over the summer. You know the sort of thing – invites to posh garden parties in Cambridge, meals at expensive restaurants, and so on. I got the impression that Amanda and Lewis were quite bowled over. They've not had that kind of attention before.'

In different circumstances, I would have been very interested in how Doveley's had been appointed. But I was struggling to contain my rage at the prospect of Harriet and Jeff meeting again. I was worried that I'd made things worse by telling Harriet what Jeff was like. Might she be angling now for him to do to her what he'd done with so many other women before? Why was it that Jeff could carry off this kind of thing so successfully, whereas when I tried to do the same everything came crashing down around my ears?

'Are you OK, Alan?' Harriet was still speaking. 'I get the impression you don't much like Jeff. Why's that? He said some very complimentary things about you.'

Well, that was Parker all over. He wouldn't want to come over as bitter and twisted by saying what he really thought about me. He'd be worried that he might lose some of his appeal in Harriet's eyes. I was curious, though, about what he'd said about me. I hadn't breathed a word to Harriet about Helen. No doubt she'd heard about Helen's death and the subsequent arrest of her killer; it had been one of the main news stories in Cambridgeshire earlier in the year. But my name had fortunately barely been mentioned anywhere.

I tried to get a grip on myself. I wouldn't let Parker get to me. But I was still angry and wanted to take it out on someone. And who better than the people at the University who'd been annoying me recently. I wouldn't put myself in the firing line. However, everyone at the University – Ruth excepted – seemed to like Harriet. So she could risk taking some of the flak for once. And if she did piss some people off, well, it might teach her something too.

'Well remembered, Harriet, about me being away next week,' I said. 'Can I rely on you to continue looking into those various things for me? Don't be frightened of making waves. Sometimes you have to give an apple tree a good shake for the fruit to fall off.'

'No problem. I'm already trying to find out what Professor Fuller is up to regarding the deal with Ian Davey's company. And why Deborah is backing him up. I'm also trying to find out why Amanda is so keen on the Landlord Relax spin-out. Was there anything else?'

There wasn't really. But if it hadn't been for the appointment of Doveley's, Jeff Parker wouldn't have come into Harriet's life. It was a long shot, but maybe there was a way of getting back at him as well.

'Can you also speak to Procurement?' I asked. 'Check that all

103

the proper processes were followed regarding the appointment of Doveley's as the University's preferred solicitors. I'm sure they were – we both know how careful Lewis is over things like this. But it's important for us in Legal to be seen to be squeaky clean. So don't forget to mention the wining and dining of Lewis and Amanda to Procurement. No need to refer to our discussion, though, just keep it very low-key.'

I was pleased with that last bit. I didn't want my interest to become known to Lewis and Amanda. If Procurement were to disclose Harriet's enquiries to them, she would get the blame and not me. But if it turned out that any corners had been cut, it wasn't impossible that Doveley's could find their appointment revoked. I pictured Jeff in a meeting at the University when this happened – just think, I might even have to call security to have him physically removed from the premises. And if Doveley's found out that Jeff had been blabbing to Harriet about how they were appointed, well, he might even get told by Doveley's that he must never see her again.

I was pleased with the way I'd managed to control my temper and possibly even turn it to my advantage. Harriet was making a note of my instructions in that big notebook that she always carried around with her. As I watched, the tip of her tongue crept out of the side of her mouth like a little pink rosebud. I couldn't stop myself from thinking about what else that tongue might have done, and with whom. Yet Harriet clearly wasn't thinking about those sorts of things at all. Her mind was solely on her job. I reminded myself what a promising future she had in the legal profession and how important it was for me to protect her from things that could go wrong. It would be a disaster for her if she was to become entangled with someone like Jeff Parker.

It was a shame that I was on leave the following week, but at least Jeff was apparently away too – there was nothing he could get up to while I was absent.

19

It had seemed such a good idea at the time.

Some of my happiest memories are of winning tennis matches. I find the game a way to channel my frustrations into something demanding and creative. The only thing I don't like about tennis is the way so many people take it less seriously than me. The worst offenders seem to be the groups of middle-aged and elderly women who have populated the courts at every club I've played at. Sometimes, while waiting for a court to become free, I've watched them chattering away in groups between sets as if their social lives were more important than the result of their matches. At times, I've had to resist the temptation to tell them that if they want to talk, they should come off court and let other people play.

My only regret over tennis was that I didn't start playing earlier. How I wished I could have played more as a junior, travelling around the country and competing in official tournaments. I would have been surrounded by players who took the game as seriously as me and who would have respected me. For this reason, I was very much a cheerleader for the promotion and development of junior tennis.

When I'd been at Doveley's, I'd been tempted once to offer some free tennis lessons to the children of our professional support lawyer, as a way of saying thank you for the help she'd given me in the aftermath of Helen's death and in the hope that her children would fall in love with the game too. But I hadn't had the courage to do so, cringing internally at the thought of them asking their mother how they could politely say no.

I'd therefore been delighted to see my new club advertising some half-term tennis camps for children. They were being run by our resident professional, but the chairman had sent out an e-mail to all members asking for a second person to help out as a volunteer. I offered my services straightaway, so I was slightly surprised when a week later there was another message from the chairman, this time on the club WhatsApp group, asking anyone interested in volunteering to let him know. I wondered if my initial response had been overlooked and sent it again just to be sure. After another lengthy delay, I received an e-mail thanking me for my interest and setting out the procedural steps that needed to be completed in order for me to help out at the camp, including the requirement for me to have an enhanced DBS check.

I was a bit worried in case my involvement with the police following Helen's death might be an issue. From my online research, I gathered the police were entitled to disclose information if they considered it relevant. And although I'd done nothing illegal in connection with Helen, I had done a couple of things that I could envisage a malicious person misinterpreting as casting a shadow over my good character. However, I got the 'all clear' within the standard timescale, so all seemed in hand.

I applied for the week off from work in the normal way, and I sent a courtesy e-mail to Lewis explaining that I was volunteering at a children's tennis camp. While I hadn't expected to be rewarded with a bottle of champagne and flowers, I was still disappointed that my willingness to give up my time to help others didn't even merit a congratulatory acknowledgement from him.

*

The club's resident professional was a man of about my age, in his early thirties. Tony liked to boast of the countries to which he'd travelled to play tennis, name-dropping a few opponents whom some of us had heard of. I had, on an idle evening, once looked up some of these opponents, and it was clear that Tony had either played them early in their careers when they were on their way up or at the end of their careers when they were on their way back down. While, naturally, I had more sense than to disclose this within earshot of him, I had mentioned to a few people at the club that he seemed to have opted for coaching as a last resort after failing as a professional player rather than as his preferred metier.

Although I had no formal tennis coaching qualifications, I was sure that the skills I'd gained from supervising trainee solicitors at Doveley's would be easily transferable. I'd therefore sent Tony a friendly e-mail over the weekend:

Hi Tony

Alan Gadd here, I've volunteered to run next week's junior tennis camp with you. Perhaps we should put our heads together beforehand to decide which of us does what? I'm happy to do anything, but I'm probably most suited to looking after the older and better players.

Best wishes
Alan

Tony's reply had been succinct:

Hey Alan, thanks for your message but I'll let you know on Monday what I want you to do if that's OK, cheers Tony

I won't deny that I was a bit put out by the tone of his e-mail. His LinkedIn profile indicated that all he'd ever done was play and coach tennis. He seemed also to have been subsidised by his parents if the impression given by his other social media footprints was correct. However, I decided to wait and see how events unfolded during the week rather than start off under a grudge.

Twelve children had enrolled in the camp. It was a bit chilly on the Monday morning, but there was hardly any wind and no sign of rain. We put all the children on one court to begin with, asking them to hit a few balls so that we could gauge their standard. They were a complete mix, ranging from those who clearly already played regularly through to those who looked like they'd never hit a tennis ball before. Tony divided them into three groups: the stronger and older children, who would play with adult yellow balls; the younger children who had some hand-eye coordination, who would play with softer orange balls; and the complete beginners, who would play with the slowest and softest red balls.

It was odd. Beforehand, I'd thought that I would want to teach the yellow ball children, who were mostly in their teens. But I found their social confidence a bit off-putting, and I don't mind admitting that Tony's laddish banter probably went down better with them than anything I would say. For that reason, he took it upon himself to look after the two stronger groups, leaving me with the four red ball children. Three of them had at least some degree of athleticism, but one little lad was almost as wide as he was tall and didn't have a clue about how to connect a racket with a ball. I set up a miniature game of doubles, with me joining the two weaker children to keep the rally going against the other two, and I have to say that my heart warmed to the little fat kid who was doing his absolute best to contribute. I felt sorry for him because, judging by the look of his watching parents on the other side of the wire fence, I guessed he hardly got any encouragement at home to exercise. Although it was only mid-morning, the parents were already chomping away on snacks as if they'd never seen food before.

'Don't worry, Danny,' I said as he completely missed a ball for the umpteenth time. 'Let me throw the ball for you, and you can have another go.'

I picked up the ball and bounced it as carefully as I could in front of him. Danny swiped and again missed completely. His eyes filled with tears. I was taken back to my days at primary school and my ineptitude at football. I could remember not just the laughing children but also the PE teacher who seemed to write me off completely rather than try to encourage me.

'It happens to us all,' I said, bending down so our faces were at the same level. 'I've played years longer than you, and you should see some of the balls I still miss. Remember to keep your eye on the ball the whole time and then gently stroke it with the centre of your racket.'

But Danny missed again. I was picking up the ball to give him another go when I heard a burst of laughter from the other side of the fence. It came from the father of one of the yellow ball children. I felt a surge of anger and walked over to the fence.

'Just shut up,' I snapped at the man, who was dressed in the kind of smart casual, branded clothing that you see on middle-class rugby fans at Twickenham. 'The kid's trying his best.'

And that was all I said. Other parents must have overheard me, and the man went bright red, turned on his heels and went off to the clubhouse. At the lunchtime break, I saw him speaking to Tony. I had the impression that they already knew each other. I assumed the man's son was one of Tony's regular pupils.

*

At the end of the day, Tony stopped me in the car park after the children had all gone. He looked first at his feet and then slightly to one side of my face, as if he'd spotted something of interest just behind me.

'Thanks for your help today, Alan,' he said. 'Now that I know all the kids, I won't actually be needing your help for the rest of the week. But, er, thank you anyway.'

It took me a few seconds to process what he was saying. 'But I've taken the week off work,' I said, 'to help out each day. The club said you needed someone all week.'

'As I said, I don't need your help any more, thanks.' Still, he wouldn't look me in the eye.

Then I got it. 'It's that business over Danny, isn't it? It's because I told the other boy's dad where to get off. He deserved it.

Poor Danny was in tears.'

'Look, Alan,' Tony said. 'Toby's one of my best private pupils. His dad's very supportive of his tennis. You humiliated him in front of the other parents. And let's face it, Danny won't be at the club after the camp finishes. He's crap at tennis. To be honest, I'll be surprised if he even turns up tomorrow. So, well, that's how it is, I'm afraid. I'm sorry.'

*

As I mulled over the day's events at home that night, I wondered how I was going to fill the rest of the week. I had nothing but an empty schedule and an empty house to look forward to. Several times, I drafted and discarded an e-mail to the club chairman, complaining about Tony and the parent I had tackled. But in the end I did nothing, knowing that the club would close ranks and that I would be the one getting his marching orders.

I seriously contemplated cutting my holiday short and going into work the next morning. But I couldn't face dealing with all the likely questions, even if I could avoid saying that I'd been sacked as a volunteer at a children's tennis camp.

I stayed up late that first night, drinking a complete bottle of Zinfandel red and reading one of my new true crime purchases. It was an in-depth investigation into one of my favourite murder cases: that of the young judge's daughter, Patricia Curran, who was found stabbed to death in the grounds of her family's house in Northern Ireland in the early 1950s. A Scottish national serviceman had been tried for the murder and found guilty but insane, thereby avoiding the gallows, and it was only in 2000 that his conviction was overturned by the Court of Appeal. I'd previously read everything I could find about this case, and like most people who took an interest I had my own theory as to who the real killer was, while recognising that the truth would almost certainly never now come out. As often happened, the troubles of others helped to put my own problems into perspective, and when eventually I went to bed I slept deeply and dreamlessly.

I'm not totally sure I could give a detailed description of how I spent the rest of the week and the following weekend. I have memories of a train trip to Cambridge, spending most of my time hoping not to bump into anyone I knew from Doveley's; of driving one day to the north Norfolk coast and walking along the beach at Wells-next-the-Sea and eating fish and chips in the restaurant overlooking the harbour; and of spending a few hours one day in the centre of Ely, browsing in the independent book shop, having lunch at one of the upmarket chain restaurants in the High Street, and flicking through more books in the library near the supermarket where I did most of my shopping. But mostly I moped around my house watching trashy TV or browsing online, and looking forward to my evening meal when I could open a bottle of wine without worrying that I was behaving like an alcoholic. Sometimes I caught myself eyeing my cat, wishing I could achieve her level of contentment in her own company. She was happy as long as I was there each day to give her food and an occasional stroke.

I tried hard not to think of Jeff Parker and Harriet. My only comfort was that he, too, was having a week off and couldn't pester her in my absence. I didn't know or care what he was doing. I just wished – I once thought viciously – that whatever he was doing, it was something dangerous.

20

'I've made a list of things to report back to you on, Alan,' Harriet said.

It was 9.30 a.m. on Monday, on my first day back at work after my week off. Harriet and I were sitting, side by side, at the polished oval table in the same meeting room on the ground floor of Senate House that we'd used after the Enterprise Board meeting. She'd made today's booking so we could catch up undisturbed, first allowing me half an hour in which to find out what sort of mess Richard and Tom had made of things while I'd been away.

We had exchanged small talk on our way down to the meeting room. Harriet asked how my week off had gone, and I tried to make it sound as if I'd enjoyed it. Naturally, I didn't mention what had happened regarding the tennis camp. She volunteered nothing about her romantic life and I didn't ask.

Harriet usually wore trousers at work, but today she had on a tight black knee-length skirt that highlighted the narrowness of her waist and the curves of her buttocks. Her dirty-blonde hair hung loose on the shoulders of her denim jacket, looking as if it had only just been washed and dried.

'What do you want to start with?' I asked.

She puckered her lips in thought, and I wondered who was the last man to whom she had offered those lips to kiss.

'Maybe Simon Fuller,' she said. 'I found out something intriguing. I got nowhere with his social media accounts because they're either private or only used for professional purposes. But his commercial partner, Ian Davey, isn't so

112

discreet. I found some photos he'd posted on Facebook of him on holiday in Cyprus with his good friend Simon.' She did a pair of air quotes with her fingers when she said 'good friend' to show she was being ironic. 'It looked like they were staying at Ian's *very* nice private villa with a pool,' she added.

'Are you sure it was Simon?'

'One hundred per cent. I'd recognise that bony head with the girlish lips anywhere.'

'You'd better check if Simon declared the hospitality. We'd look fools if we said something and it turned out that Amanda or Deborah were already aware of it.'

'He didn't declare it. I checked the register of interests which all academics have to fill in when partnering with outside companies. In relation to any interests with Ian's company, Simon just wrote "None".'

'Wow.' I was impressed, so I could forgive myself for sounding like a student. 'No wonder he's willing to sell the University's technology so cheaply. Do you think there's more to it than just the holiday?'

'I'm not sure. I have a few more things to check. I'll let you know if I find something.' She gave one of her feline half-smiles. 'I'm quite enjoying this. It would be nice to take Simon down a peg or two after how he's treated you.'

'You've done really well. Thank you. What about the Landlord Relax spin-out? Have you got any idea why Amanda is pushing it so hard?'

'As it happens, I might have.' Again, there was the slightly mischievous smile on her face. 'I looked everyone up on LinkedIn. I found out that Amanda was at the same university, at the same time, as the two founders of the spin-out. I know that means nothing on its own, but it's worth me doing some more digging just in case.'

This all sounded very promising. An image came into my mind of me asking Amanda at the next Enterprise Board meeting if she knew the founders. Of her side-stepping the question. Of me pursuing my line of questioning with forensic skill. Of Amanda eventually breaking down and having to confess all in front of the other Board members. Of me being praised by the Vice-Chancellor himself for having exposed unethical practices at the highest level of the University. I rubbed my hands together in pleasurable anticipation. Of course, I would make sure that Harriet got her fair share of the plaudits for having investigated matters in accordance with my directions.

'What about Mehak?' I asked. 'She told me we had to pay higher than normal rates of commission to our overseas agents. Otherwise, they would steer international students towards other UK universities.'

'I've got something for you here as well.'

She was plainly on a roll. We were like a conjuring double act – with me the feed and Harriet the conjurer pulling white rabbit after white rabbit out of her hat.

'I'm mates with someone who used to work in International before Mehak joined,' she went on. 'We had a chat and it turns out that my mate is a good friend of the University's agent in Malaysia. They used to work together a lot, and I gather they partied hard when my mate went out to Malaysia on University business.'

She was taking her time getting there, and I was curious about whether this 'mate' was male or female, but I could already sense where this might be going.

'Anyway, to cut a long story short,' she continued, 'I got my mate to speak to the Malaysian agent. And it all came out. Mehak is arranging for some agents to get a higher commission, and in return they're paying her what they call "reward money". Basically, they're sharing the excess commission.'

'So Mehak is defrauding the University?' This was potentially dynamite. I had to be sure about what Harriet was saying.

'Yes. No doubt about it.'

I was struggling to conceal my delight, remembering how Mehak had treated me. How she instigated those cosy one-on-ones at her desk early in the morning when no one else was around. How she cast me aside when I'd served my purpose without troubling to spare my feelings. How she later complained about me to HR, knowing that it would get back to Lewis. And how she'd given me haughty looks, as if I wasn't worthy of her attention, when our paths subsequently crossed.

Well, what was sauce for the goose was certainly going to be sauce for the gander. 'Have you said anything to Mehak yet?' I asked. I was really hoping Harriet would say that she hadn't.

'No, I wanted to tell you first. Shall I say something to her or do we need to go to Lewis or Amanda straightaway?'

I thought for a few seconds. 'I'll tell you what,' I said. 'Let her know what you've found out in very general terms. Don't give her the names of your contact from International or of the agent in Malaysia. Just say that a particular agent, whose name you won't reveal to her at this stage, has made certain allegations – but only to you. Say that you are going to have to tell me, but that first you want to give her the chance to tell you her side of the story.'

Harriet looked slightly uneasy. 'What will we gain from that?'

The truth, although I hardly dared admit it even to myself, was that I was hoping Mehak would come to me begging for forgiveness, asking me not to report her. I would listen to what she had to say, as was only fair. And then I would say that, regrettably, my professional responsibilities meant I had to escalate things to the highest level. She might, I speculated, break down in tears and perhaps even touch me on the knee again, to try to persuade me that we still had a personal bond. However, tempting as it might be to show kindness, I would unfortunately for her have no choice but to make a formal report of her wrongdoing to Amanda. I reminded myself that, as a solicitor, I owed responsibilities not just to the University as my employer but also to society under the rule of law.

Naturally, I couldn't expect Harriet to understand all this. She wasn't the one who had been humiliated by Mehak. I therefore said, 'If she realises the game is up, she may make a clean breast of things to Amanda. To get her side of the story in first. It would save us from having to dob her in ourselves. I can't say I would relish having to do that.'

Harriet looked a little surprised, as if she hadn't expected me to show such a conciliatory tone. But she nodded and made a brief scribble in her notebook. She'd done well while I was away. And I'd done well to entrust her with such responsibilities.

'There is something else, Alan,' she said.

My heart skipped a beat. Perhaps she was going to say she'd missed me during my week away. 'Go on,' I said.

'It's my car. When I went to the car park on Friday, I saw it had been scratched. Keyed, that is. All the way along the driver's door. Someone must have done it on purpose.' And Harriet's large brown eyes filled with tears. A moment later, a tear ran down her left cheek, leaving a gentle line in her understated make-up.

I pride myself on keeping the dividing line clear between myself and my work colleagues, but I felt this was an occasion when an exception could be made. I reached out with my right arm and laid it gently upon her left shoulder. I was expecting her to reciprocate by leaning towards me so that I could hold her tight in a gesture of professional support. Instead, she remained bolt upright, saying nothing and leaving me feeling slightly foolish. After a few seconds, I withdrew my arm and scratched my nose before letting the arm rest back on the table. It was all slightly awkward. And I felt a blaze of anger. I couldn't imagine her reacting in the same way if Hugh, or Lewis, or that shit Jeff Parker had tried to console her like I had done. What did they have that I didn't?

I pulled myself together. 'That's terrible,' I said. 'Do you have any idea who did it? There must have been other people around. And there must be CCTV too, surely?'

'No one's said anything about seeing it happen, and I've been too embarrassed to tell anyone I work with in case they thought I was accusing them. The CCTV system doesn't cover the car park, according to the security guy I spoke to. I've been racking my brain as to who might have done it. I didn't think I had any enemies. And it's not like I've got a big expensive car that someone might be envious of.'

I am deeply ashamed to admit it, but the idea that someone might dislike Harriet enough to key her car did trigger in me a feeling of *schadenfreude*. For a moment, I was again the bullied schoolboy who could take comfort in the fact that, for once, the bullies were picking on someone else.

I said, 'Some people just behave badly, I'm afraid. Might you have upset someone without realising it?'

She was silent for a few seconds. I could see her thinking. 'Well,' she said, 'there are a few people, but surely none of them would do something horrible like this. There's Lewis's wife, Ruth. She still seems to blame me for what happened with her husband even though I've explained to her, woman to woman, that I didn't know that she and Lewis were still together. There's Hugh, I suppose. He's pissed off that I've got a second date with someone tonight. But I don't know why, as he's normally cool about me seeing other people now. And there's Richard. He's been sulking about me grassing him up to you – as he put it – over that contract with the middle bit missing. Oh, and I suppose there's my landlord. I went into his shop as you suggested and mentioned what we'd worked out about the gas safety certificate. He definitely didn't look happy. But, come on, what sort of person goes out and keys another person's car just because they've had a falling out? We're all professional people, after all.'

I felt a bit uncomfortable. I can truthfully say that I've never keyed a car. But if I am totally honest, I can see how, in certain situations, some people might find it a tempting thing to do. It isn't always practical to speak one's mind to someone who has behaved badly towards you, and in extreme circumstances having their car keyed might be a lesson which they could learn from. I didn't say this to Harriet, though. It wasn't the right time for that kind of philosophical discussion.

'It's unbelievable what some people will do,' I said. 'I don't think you can rule out any of those you mention. Hugh has no

117

right to be jealous, of course. You're free to go on a date with whoever you want. Is this someone from that app you use?'

'No, it's Jeff from Doveley's.'

A torrent of disbelief and rage swept over me. Christ, that man had no shame. I looked down at my hands to prevent my expression from being visible to Harriet. 'You mean Parker?' I almost spat out his name. 'But he was away all last week, like me.'

'Yes, but he messaged me while he was away. He said how much he'd enjoyed our last drink and asked if we could meet up tonight after his first day back at work. I said yes, obviously.'

Obviously. What the hell does she see in that man who can't keep his hands off women? Doesn't she have any idea how many women he's had over the years? Doesn't she realise the effect that he has on me? Or doesn't she care as long as she gets what she wants?

I was really struggling not to show my emotions. I remembered how I'd felt when Jeff Parker was going out with Helen while we were all at Doveley's, and how I had to continue to behave professionally towards them both when all I really wanted to do was to catch Parker unawares and rip his head off. And now it looked like it was going to happen again. I imagined how I was going to feel when Harriet started coming in each morning with a smile on her face like the proverbial cat that's got the cream. I honestly didn't think I could cope with that. And, worst of all, Jeff would be praised at Doveley's for what he was doing. No one would be crass enough to congratulate him openly for shagging the client, but I could imagine the unspoken kudos he would receive, from trainees through to equity partners.

I racked my brain for a way in which I could blame Jeff for keying Harriet's car, but I quickly realised how ridiculous that would sound. I had to say something, however. Harriet was still visibly upset and waiting for a response from me.

'My guess is that either Hugh or Lewis is responsible,' I said eventually. 'They must both be feeling angry that you've moved on from them. It won't be Richard or the landlord. They may be annoyed with you, but not enough to do something vindictive like that. And it won't be Ruth. She may not want to admit it to you, but she'll know perfectly well that it was all Lewis's fault. Do you want me to say something to Hugh and Lewis?'

I wasn't quite sure what I would say. It's hardly the best look to march into your line manager's office and accuse him of keying the car of one of his team members. And my ball sack tightened just at the thought of confronting Hugh in front of his crew on the first floor. But I had to offer to do something. Harriet was seeking my help.

Fortunately, she didn't take me up on my offer.

'It's all right, Alan,' she said. 'Leave it with me. I'm hoping it's only a one-off. I'll just have to be a bit more careful about where I leave my car in future. Thank you for listening, though. You are such a nice man.'

21

For much of the rest of the morning, I couldn't stop ruminating over what Harriet had said. I'd temporarily lost interest in what Amanda, Simon Fuller and Mehak had been up to. I was more focussed on Jeff Parker and his date with Harriet that evening.

Harriet had said that I was a 'nice' man. Well, I may be nice, but she still wasn't planning to spend her evening with me. Instead, she was going out with a man whom I'd never once heard described as nice, not even by his closest buddies at Doveley's. Why, then, was Harriet so keen to go on another date with him? To my mind, there could only be one answer and it made me feel physically sick. I kept turning my head to look at Harriet in case she had something more to say on the subject, but she was engrossed in reviewing a new research contract that had landed on her desk.

In the end, I realised I had to find something to take my mind off Jeff, and fortunately I had plenty to do.

My main task was to provide advice to the Dean of the School of Engineering. One of the School's modules was designed for students who wanted to work in the cycling industry and included a guaranteed term-long secondment with a professional road racing team. However, the secondment was being discontinued, and the Dean wanted to know the extent of the School's potential liability to students who claimed that the secondment was the only reason they'd chosen the University of East Cambridgeshire. Fortunately, I hadn't been responsible for drafting the contract that applied to these particular students; it seemed to have come from either Tom or Richard, under Lewis's so-called supervision. I could therefore take some pleasure from having to advise the Dean with regret that – although I avoided this colloquialism – the School was stuffed.

Next, I spent some time, separately, with Tom and Richard, wheeling my chair around to each of their desks in turn. Neither of them said anything to show they were pleased to have me back.

'You haven't described the student project,' I said to Tom in as calm a voice as I could manage, as I reviewed a contract he was doing for the School of Performing and Creative Arts. 'You're using the right template, but you've left the words "Project Description" in square brackets. You're supposed to replace these words with your own description of what the project is.'

Tom sucked the end of his pen. I wondered what thoughts were going through his head. 'Could we say "the project at the School of Performing and Creative Arts"?' he eventually asked.

Lord, please give me strength, I thought. 'How does that differentiate this project from others at the same School?'

'Good point, Alan. Could we say "the project at the School of Performing and Creative Arts to design a new range of children's clothes"?'

It wasn't perfect, but I wouldn't labour the point. 'It'll do,' I said.

Richard had sufficient intelligence to avoid that kind of error. I was more concerned with what he might hide from me: perhaps a complaint from an internal client or a missed deadline. I also remembered what Harriet had said about him bearing her a grudge for having grassed him up to me. I wouldn't put it past him to have keyed Harriet's car even though I had my own reasons for hoping that it had been Lewis or Hugh.

'You told me to get the contract signed, Alan,' he said, after I got out of him that the School of Social Sciences had a payment dispute with a supplier.

Again, I found myself biting my tongue. 'Richard,' I said, 'I asked you first to check that the School's suggested payment schedule was OK. But you didn't, did you?'

'I thought it was OK,' he said.

Typically, he was avoiding giving a direct answer. He really was an unpleasant weasel of a man. 'But it wasn't OK,' I said. 'It isn't clear if the School has to pay before the deliverables are handed over, or afterwards. That makes a big difference.'

I paused. All I wanted was for him to make some kind of apology. We all make mistakes – Christ, I'd made enough in my career – but Richard simply would not own a mistake. It was always someone else's fault, as far as he was concerned.

'But the School said—'

'I don't give a toss what the School said,' I snapped. 'It's our job as lawyers to get these things right.' I took a deep breath. I had enough to worry about without giving him the earbashing he deserved. 'Look, Richard, tell the School that the wording isn't clear. But tell them also that the supplier will want an ongoing relationship with the University. They won't be stupid enough to jeopardise that over a few thousand pounds. Then, assuming the Dean agrees, call the supplier's MD and offer on a without prejudice basis to pay half before delivery and half after. Can you manage that?'

Richard nodded, averting his eyes. Was it really too much to hope for that he might thank me for once? Not for the first time, I rued the fact that in private practice, at a leading firm such as Doveley's, I could be guaranteed a certain level of competence in my trainees. In comparison, in-house legal practice, particularly in the public sector, could be like the Wild West.

*

'That was Hugh.'

After putting down her phone, Harriet turned in her seat towards me. She was biting her lower lip.

'What did he want?' I asked, slightly superfluously.

'To discuss another KTP. He asked if I could pop down. He said it would be quicker than him having to write me an e-mail. Obviously, he's right, but—'

'You're worried in case he's the person who keyed your car?'

She nodded. 'I can hardly ask him outright if he did it, can I? But if I don't, it's going to be a massive elephant in the room. What should I do?'

As always, I was flattered when Harriet revealed how much trust she had in me. It wasn't her fault that her good nature was taken advantage of by the likes of Lewis, Hugh and now Jeff Parker. It just made it even more important that I was there for her.

'Go and see Hugh,' I said. 'But be completely professional. Don't mention the car at all. And don't let him distract you with other non-work stuff either.'

I watched her head off across the second floor. Just before she reached the door, Amanda and Deborah came in together. The three women stopped and spent a minute or two chatting. I saw Deborah throw back her head and give a great guffaw. Amanda's face creased with amusement. It reminded me how genuinely popular Harriet was at the University. In contrast, even before the recent dressing-downs I'd had from Deborah and Amanda, they'd never shown any inclination to stop and have a casual chat with me when our paths crossed.

As Harriet disappeared through the door, I automatically glanced at her desk. I noticed that, as often happened, she'd left her personal mobile phone next to her keyboard. I turned back to my computer screen, but before I could pick up the thread of my work, something occurred to me and I looked at the phone again.

I tried to resist my line of thought but was unable to do so. Without turning my head in their direction, I glanced sideways at Richard and Tom. Both of them were, for once, concentrating on whatever was on their desks. I knew Lewis wasn't in his office, and Harriet's desk wasn't in anyone else's direct line of sight. I continued to stare at the mobile phone. Part of me wished Harriet would at that moment arrive back at our pod following her visit to Hugh. But she didn't. I counted silently to ten. I looked up at the door. Still no sign of Harriet. And no change in what Richard and Tom were doing.

I took a deep breath, yawned and stretched out my left hand towards Harriet's desk. Without actually looking at my hand, I put my fingers around her phone and dragged it quickly onto my desk. Now that I'd crossed the Rubicon, I worked quickly. I pressed the button on the side of the phone to light up the home page. Then I tapped in the four-digit code to unlock the screen. Unlike some people, Harriet had never been one to go through the charade of covering up the movement of her fingers when unlocking her phone. Without having had any specific plans, I had once watched and memorised her code. Now I found myself on the unlocked home page. I double-clicked on the WhatsApp icon. I quickly scanned down the list of people who had been messaging her and, as I feared, spotted Jeff Parker's name. Next to his name was his profile picture – there he was, grinning like a bloody idiot. I clicked again to open the message thread.

Hey H

Can't wait to see you tonight. A week's been too long.

I'll be outside the pub at 7 p.m. We'll have a drink there, then go on to where I've booked a table for dinner. Hope you've got a big appetite and a raging thirst. (Hope you're in the mood for some food and drink as well!)

Until later,
J x

Fuck, how I detested the man. Towards the end of my time at Doveley's, we'd come to an unspoken truce regarding Helen's death. He'd revealed some of his own vulnerabilities. I'd occasionally even thought that perhaps he wasn't as bad as I'd been painting him.

But now this. He'd had one drink with Harriet so far. One bloody drink. And here he was, flirting with her and indulging in obscene innuendo. He really deserved every name I'd called him in my darkest thoughts. What right had he to message her in this way? I'd helped Harriet in so many ways over the last few months, and I would never have dreamt of sending her a message like this.

My first reaction was to want to show the message to Harriet and tell her that Jeff should be reported to both Amanda and Doveley's. But it only took a second or two for me to comprehend that I mustn't do this. Harriet would never forgive me for looking at her phone. I also couldn't avoid wondering if Harriet had encouraged Jeff. I remembered her pretend disappointment that Jeff hadn't made a move on her during their first date.

In all the months I'd known her, Harriet had never said or done anything to suggest that she would like me to make a move on her. Of course, she would know that it would be impossible, professionally, for me to do so. But perhaps with Jeff, with her inhibitions relaxed under the influence of the alcohol he'd undoubtedly plied her with, she'd been different. It was obvious, anyway, what Jeff was hoping for tonight.

Harriet had read the message but hadn't yet replied. I felt sick at the thought of her taking her time to compose an equally flirty message back.

For a while, I didn't know what to do. I even considered sending a message to Jeff from Harriet's phone and in her name, telling him to fuck off and go and have a wank if he couldn't control his urges. But this was only likely to blow up in my face. He'd hardly sent her a dick pic, after all. Then I saw the door open and Harriet came in. In a panic, I pushed her phone back onto her desk and prayed that the home screen would turn dark before she arrived back at our pod. As she walked down the central aisle, my eyes flickered constantly between her and the phone. I was just about to get up from my desk to intercept her on some pretext when I saw her phone go dark. I sank back into my chair, panting with relief. My armpits were sticky and my head span. I don't know what I would have said or done if she'd caught me browsing through her phone.

'Is everything OK, Alan?' she asked as she sat down.

'Yes, fine, any reason it shouldn't be?' It wasn't the best of responses, as it made me sound bad-tempered. But I was still recovering from the shock of reading Jeff's message.

'No, not at all,' she said. 'It's just that you looked a bit stressed.' She then smiled. 'Thanks for the advice regarding Hugh. The KTP thing was clearly an excuse. He really wanted to know about my date with Jeff tonight. It's funny, because he didn't seem too bothered when I finished with him, and he wasn't that bothered either by the guys from the dating app. I guess Jeff the high-powered lawyer makes him feel inferior.' She laughed, as if to reassure me she didn't really think that Jeff was high-powered. 'Anyway,' she continued, 'I did what you said and kept it all very professional. Oh, and I also spoke to Mehak while I was down there. She looked worried when I hinted at what I knew about her dealings with agents. She asked if she could explain things to me tomorrow. She definitely didn't like it when I said that I was going to have to discuss it with you in due course.'

She picked up her phone and entered her code. I watched as she tapped the screen a few times and then grinned like a bloody Cheshire cat while she read something. I didn't need telling whose message she was reading. She'd obviously been thinking of a response to Jeff while she'd been away from her desk because she quickly tapped out a message of her own, paused as if to check it, ran her tongue once along her upper lip, and then gave one more tap which I assumed was to send the message.

How I wished I could have read her reply to Jeff even though I knew it would torture me further. I was desperately hoping that she would leave her phone unattended on her desk again, but when she went out for lunch shortly before 1 p.m. she took it with her.

*

I don't know how I found the strength to get through the rest of the day. Fortunately, I am an excellent technical lawyer and I could do most of my work on autopilot. I had to sign off on some advice that our data protection officer had produced in draft form. He knew the legislation better than me but wanted someone else to take the blame if anything went wrong.

Deborah wandered over at around 3 p.m. to chase me regarding the agreement for Simon Fuller.

'The first draft's nearly done, Deborah,' I said. 'I can then e-mail it over to Simon to get his comments.'

'About time,' she said abruptly. 'Simon's been asking about it. I'll let him know it will be on its way.'

So, like Mehak, Fuller had now been going behind my back.

Harriet must have overheard the exchange because, as soon as Deborah was out of earshot, she said, 'Just give me a few days, Alan, and I expect I'll have what I need.'

Then it was Amanda's turn. It was as if she'd been waiting for Deborah to bring me to the ground before she came over to put the boot in. 'About the Landlord Relax spin-out,' she said, 'I see Jeff Parker e-mailed over a set of documents first thing this morning. Have you looked at them yet?'

Truth be told, I hadn't even opened them. Everything Jeff said rubbed me up the wrong way, and I knew that once I started looking at anything he sent over for review, I would never stop. But I couldn't admit to that. Jeff had, like me, been away the whole of the previous week, so I assumed Lucy had done the drafting and got him to bless the documents as soon as he was back in the office.

'I'm sure they'll be fine,' I said, avoiding any deliberate lie. 'What he's drafting is all pretty straightforward and low-risk. I just need to clear some time in my schedule for a full read-through. I'll then report back to you.'

I could tell that Amanda wasn't entirely happy with my response but that she couldn't make up her mind what to say in reply. I knew it made me sound lazy, but Amanda clearly wanted the deal done quickly without me dropping a spanner in the works. I would love to have had an emergency task that I could have tossed onto Jeff's plate right at the end of the day, forcing him to cancel his date with Harriet. Unfortunately, though, Landlord Relax wasn't the type of matter that ever needed anything doing urgently.

I left the office before Harriet, just after 4.30 p.m., having e-mailed my draft assignment of intellectual property rights to Simon Fuller. I had some documents to drop off at the School of Business and was glad of the chance to slip away without having to listen to Harriet asking me to wish her good luck with Jeff.

On my way down the stairs, I passed Mehak on the landing of the first floor. I was gratified to see a look of alarm flash across her face. She must be worried, I thought, about what she's going to have to explain to Harriet and what Harriet is then going to tell me.

There was no one at the School of Business when I arrived shortly before 5 p.m. For a School that held itself out as teaching students about the world of business, they seemed remarkably reluctant to work normal commercial hours. I left the documents in the Dean's pigeonhole and headed off to the car park.

22

Almost my first action when I got home was to open a bottle of wine. I can't deny that I was feeling guilty about my nosey through Harriet's messages. Most people, I conceded, would disapprove of what I'd done. However, I'd done it with Harriet's best interests at heart. I was aware, more than most, of what Jeff Parker was like, and if Harriet took up with him it was bound to end in tears.

I sat on my sofa, mulling over the events of the day. I couldn't understand why, in my personal life, everything seemed to go wrong. Harriet had said that I was 'nice', but perhaps I was too nice for my own good: too nice to attract the right type of women. I'd gone out of my way to show kindness to both Mehak and Harriet, putting in extra hours to help them with their work, but they both seemed to prefer to make themselves available to men who were only after one thing. Not that I would have allowed Harriet to make herself available to me, as I pride myself on my professionalism. However, if she had hinted at wanting something along those lines, we could at least have had an adult conversation about it even though it would have ended in a regretful agreement not to pursue things. In Mehak's case, of course, there would have been no such professional obstacle. For the umpteenth time, I recalled how she'd said she couldn't go out with me because she already had a boyfriend and how I'd subsequently found out that she was playing around with two men simultaneously.

What was so special about all these other men compared to me?

After a while, I noticed I'd been too involved in my thoughts even to pour myself a glass of wine. The open bottle of red Californian Zinfandel seemed to taunt me. I could almost hear it asking: are you going to sit there all evening leaving me on my own? I knew that if I poured just one glass, the course of the evening would be set. I would gulp down half a bottle in about ten or twenty minutes, then find something quick and easy to cook – perhaps a frozen pizza from my stash in the freezer. I would finish the bottle with my food and spend the rest of the evening scrolling through my phone while I half-watched some rubbish on the TV. Finally, I would drag myself off to bed, only to wake up after an hour or two's sleep with my mind overflowing, like a river after heavy rain, with my thoughts.

So tonight I continued to resist the temptation of the wine. But when I next looked at my watch, it still wasn't 6.30 p.m. Jeff and Harriet wouldn't yet have met up outside their riverside pub. I assumed Jeff still lived in Cambridge, so he would now be on his way to Ely, not wanting to risk being late. If he was taking the short twenty-minute train ride from central Cambridge, he could walk from Ely station to the pub in less than ten minutes. If instead he was driving, he could easily park on a Monday evening in any number of places near to the pub – although if he wasn't familiar with the area, he would probably choose the supermarket car park next to the station. Knowing Jeff, he would have chosen whichever mode of transport best fitted in with his nefarious plans. If he came by car, he could at an opportune moment say to Harriet that he daren't risk another drink in case it put him over the limit, giving her the opportunity to offer him a couch for the night at hers. And he would take it from there. That was just how the bastard operated. I'd heard him discuss these types of ploys with his male intimates at Doveley's enough times over the years.

And what about Harriet? What was she doing? It was a ten-minute walk at most from her house to the pub, and she wouldn't want to arrive before 7 p.m. and have to hang around on her own outside. She was probably therefore still getting ready. I wondered whether, during her shower, she'd imagined what Jeff might want to do to her naked body were she to give him any encouragement and, if so, whether this prospect had excited her. I pictured her putting on her make-up in front of a mirror and mulled over whether, as she applied her lipstick, she envisaged what her lips might do later that evening.

I wished I didn't have these thoughts. I knew what they made me look like. But I couldn't drive them from my mind.

Then, I had an idea. For a few seconds, it seemed the most natural thing to do. Until I started thinking about all the possible consequences. Not just the consequences of being caught, but also the consequences of finding out the truth. These all terrified me. But already it was too late. I had to do it. If I didn't, I might never forgive myself.

*

It was a slightly odd time of year to have a date down by the riverside rather than in the centre of Ely or in the Ely Leisure Village.

In the summer, the riverside thronged with both residents and tourists, admiring the narrowboats moored along the near bank of the River Great Ouse or watching the crews of rowers practising their strokes under the barking orders of their coxes. There were plenty of places to eat and drink, browse antiques, view watercolours or just buy an ice cream, and when I'd first moved to Ely, I'd often enjoyed nursing a cold lager in the sunshine while I observed people and boats go by. On a cold, wet Monday evening at the end of October, though, there would be no tourists and few residents down by the riverside. For that reason, I assumed the choice of venue had been Harriet's. She was always raving about the place and had an artist friend who seemed to spend most of her time on one of the narrowboats.

I'd parked my Aygo in the big car park which is halfway up the hill on the road from the station to the centre of Ely. The supermarket car park next to the station would have been nearer, but I didn't want to risk being spotted by Jeff even though I'd changed my car since the last time he'd seen me driving. Before getting out of my car, I checked myself in the driver's mirror. I'd pulled the hood of my anorak over my head and tightened it around the sides of my face, so my only easily recognisable feature was my dark-framed, rectangular glasses – which I always considered struck a nice balance between seriousness and coolness.

Just after 7 p.m., I walked down the hill and, shortly before reaching the station roundabout, crossed over into a narrow residential road which led directly to the riverside. Although the night was dark, the central riverside area was fairly well illuminated by a mixture of lampposts and other lights from the various venues that were open in the evening. The river, just a few yards away, was very still, looking like a thick band of tarmac laid on the ground. Most of the moored narrowboats were dark and empty, and nothing moved on the water.

I was fairly sure that Jeff and Harriet were already enjoying the warmth of their chosen pub, but as I approached it from the front, I was ready to dart off in a different direction if either of them appeared. I went round the side and tried to peer through a window to see where they were and what they were doing, but it was surprisingly busy inside and I didn't dare spend too long at the window in case I was seen. I therefore took up position behind the massively thick trunk of a tree that stood between the pub and the river. From here, I would be able to see them when they came out, and I could keep the trunk between us regardless of the direction in which they headed.

It was almost 8 p.m. when Jeff and Harriet left the pub. They were laughing together at something. He didn't yet have an arm around her shoulders, but I was sure that this would only be a matter of time. I noticed that, despite the cold, Harriet was wearing a short skirt above the knee that showed off her shapely legs. Jeff was wearing a lawyer's typical dark, heavy overcoat. There were very few other people outside, so I stayed behind my tree as they turned and walked along the riverside. There weren't many eating places they could choose from and I wasn't at risk of losing sight of them. Nevertheless, it was a relief when soon they stopped at a restaurant and disappeared inside.

I hadn't thought this far ahead, but now I had to decide what to do next. They were likely to be in the restaurant for at least an hour and a half, and I wasn't sure what I would achieve by hanging around outside for all this time. I wasn't stupid enough to think that I could burst into the restaurant demanding that Jeff keep his hands off Harriet. In fact, there was nothing I could realistically do to stop whatever they might be planning.

So why was I outside the restaurant in the cold and the dark, finding it impossible to go home? It took me a while to work out the answer. And the answer was that, for good or for bad, I simply had to know what was going on, even if the outcome was going to be the worst possible news for me. I remembered reading how, in the days of capital punishment, it was often a relief for the condemned man to be informed by the prison governor that the home secretary had denied a last-minute reprieve and that he would definitely now be hanged at the appointed hour. For these men, it was easier to come to terms with the prospect of imminent death once all hope was gone.

And so it was for me. The thought of Jeff and Harriet in bed together brought me almost unbearable pain. But I still had to hit rock bottom before I could hope to get back up. Once I knew the awful truth, I might – perhaps – eventually even come to terms with it.

Though I might also have an opportunity to get my own back. If Harriet was determined to throw everything away on some sordid sexual adventure with Nosey Parker, I would do my damnedest to make sure that he lived to regret it.

23

Once I was certain that Jeff and Harriet were settled into their restaurant, I went for a long walk along the path which ran next to the river. I went past a narrow bridge which led to the marina on the other side of the river, then past a tea shop and an art gallery, meeting fewer and fewer people as I got further away from the main commercial area of the riverside. One of the narrowboats was brightly lit up, and as I walked alongside I could see a man and a woman, both hippy-looking types, sitting on one side of a table with bottles of beer in their hands, with two young children enjoying some kind of drink in a mug on the other side. They wouldn't have seen or heard me, and they had no inkling that I even existed.

Presently I came to a fork, from where I could either turn left into a car park or right under a railway bridge. I chose right, and as I emerged on the other side of the bridge, I appreciated for the first time just how dark the night was. Ahead of me, the river and the surrounding fields were indistinguishable from each other, looking like a black blanket laid on the ground. Above me, the sky was a little lighter, although whether from the moon or the stars or simply the lights of Ely, I couldn't have said. There was just enough illumination for me to follow the footpath without stumbling into the river. I was completely alone.

For a while, I took some comfort in a brief fantasy of filling the pockets of my anorak and trousers with stones and wading into the river until I was out of my depth and was pulled beneath the surface. I didn't know if drowning would be a painless death, or if a sense of self-preservation would take over and I would desperately try to empty my pockets of the stones and struggle to the surface, fighting for every breath. It was a not uncommon occurrence in the Fens of eastern England to read about police divers having to recover bodies from cars that had gone into a river, and I had often been curious about what it would be like to die that way.

What would people say if they learnt I had drowned? Harriet, I hoped, would be devastated, asking herself if she was to blame and what she could have done differently to save me. I pictured her, tearful at my funeral, trying to imagine her life without me as her mentor. Then another image came into my mind: of Jeff Parker alongside her at my funeral, putting a consoling arm around her and holding her tight. I clenched my fists in absolute fury. No way would I give that fucking shit the satisfaction of comforting Harriet in her time of need.

My moment of weakness had passed, and I strode on along the footpath until I reached a gate to a road which would have taken me on a circuitous route back into Ely. I stayed at the gate for a long while, full of angry thoughts about Jeff Parker and life in general. Then, looking at my watch, I realised I'd better get back to the vicinity of the restaurant in case Jeff and Harriet left sooner than I anticipated. I had no doubt that Jeff had planned every step of the evening in advance and that he knew exactly what he wanted to do after they finished their meal. I wondered how much wine he'd poured down Harriet's throat and what wheedling words he'd used on her.

*

Back near the restaurant, I found a bench – shaded from the lights of the riverside – from where I could observe the entrance without getting too close. There was a risk that, after leaving the restaurant, Jeff and Harriet might head for a walk in my direction, but I thought it unlikely. That wasn't the way to Harriet's house, and if Jeff had made enough progress to bed her, he wouldn't want to waste time. I got my phone out and scrolled through photographs in my 'Favourites' album in case anyone was watching me, but the few people out and about probably had other things on their minds.

At around 10 p.m., Jeff and Harriet came out of the restaurant. They were about forty yards away from me. Even if they'd looked in my direction, I'm sure they wouldn't have recognised me, with my anorak hood up, in the gloom. For a couple of minutes, they chatted in the doorway before, to my amazement, I saw Harriet give him, in quick succession, a hug, a kiss on the cheek and a wave. Then she headed away from me, along the path next to the river, in the opposite direction from where I'd taken my walk. To my slight surprise, Jeff made no effort to detain her. If he had, and particularly if he'd got hold of her, I would have had no hesitation in striding over and interceding on Harriet's behalf. Earlier in the year, I'd had to use force to detain Helen's murderer after a desperate fight for my life in the centre of Cambridge, and although no one else had particularly praised me for this it had given me considerable confidence in my abilities in a rough and tumble. I don't mind admitting that it would have given me great pleasure to defend Harriet's honour by punching Jeff in his podgy face, followed by a couple of well-placed kicks to the groin as he went down to the ground.

Instead, Jeff turned and made his way towards the cut-through that I'd used earlier that evening. Within a few seconds, he was out of sight.

What on earth was Harriet doing? Even though she appeared to be going home without Jeff, the quickest route for her was via the same cut-through that he'd just taken. And it was hardly as if they were parting on bad terms. Whatever proposition he might have made to her, and whatever her response had been, she hadn't been storming off in a different direction from him. I couldn't make it out. However, I had to make a decision quickly; already, she was moving out of the lights of the main riverside area into the blackness which lay beyond.

On a warm summer's day, this wouldn't have been a bad choice of route for Harriet, especially if she wanted a few extra minutes to mull over the events of the evening before discussing them with Kat, her housemate. In less than half a mile, there was an exit from the riverside footpath to the main road from Soham to Ely, from where it was an easy walk back to her house.

Tonight, though, it was dark and cold, and although Ely was as safe a place as any, it was difficult to imagine any sensible woman wanting to walk home this way on her own. Then I remembered Harriet's friend. The friend's narrowboat was apparently moored along this stretch of the river. Harriet must be planning to call on her, to tell her all about her date. That was what women often did. It all made sense now.

Oh, how I wished I knew what had gone on between Jeff and Harriet. Had they discussed having sex and had Harriet perhaps made some practical woman's excuse why another night would be better? Or maybe they'd both realised that if they spent the entire night having sex, neither of them would be any good for work the next morning? I had to know more; I couldn't go home and wait to see what I could get out of Harriet the next morning. For a moment, I thought about rushing after Harriet to catch her up, saying that I'd spotted her while I was out enjoying an evening stroll by the river. But I doubted I could carry this off. Harriet might suspect that I had been spying on her, and I didn't want to have to explain that I was only looking after her interests.

Consequently, without quite knowing what I was trying to achieve, I followed Harriet along the footpath, keeping my distance.

It was as dark this way as it had been on my earlier walk in the opposite direction. But there was just enough light from one source or another for me to keep her in sight even though she was often not much more than a movement ahead in the blackness. I daren't fall too far behind, but it had started to rain and the sound of the raindrops falling on the ground and the river would help camouflage any noise from my footsteps. A few times, I had to pause to wipe my glasses in order to have any hope of seeing anything.

One after the other, maybe twenty seconds apart, we passed a boatyard on the right, then shortly afterwards went under the bridge which carries the railway line into Ely station. As I went under, there was a thundering roar as a train went overhead, and I worried for a moment that Harriet might turn around to watch the train and see me. After the bridge, there was a series of moored narrowboats on my left, all but one lying quiet and dark against the riverbank. Harriet veered off the path towards the only narrowboat that was showing an interior light. I hung back, making sure that I stayed out of the reach of the light. With what looked like practised ease, Harriet stepped onto a short plank between the riverbank and the narrowboat and from there onto the platform at the rear of the boat, and disappeared below.

I got closer to the narrowboat, stopping about ten yards away in the deep shadows of a tree on the other side of the path. Through a window, I could see Harriet and another woman in what looked like the main living area. They had just finished giving each other a hug and were now talking animatedly, with lots of smiles and arm movements. I was debating with myself whether I could risk getting even closer, perhaps even somewhere on the boat from where I could listen to their conversation, when I heard a slight sound behind me.

I turned my head and saw a movement about twenty yards further back on the path. As I forced myself to look harder into the darkness, I twigged that someone else was there. The veins in my head pumped with blood as if a switch in my brain had been flicked on, and I felt physically sick. Someone was watching me watch Harriet.

Christ, was it Jeff?

Had I got it all wrong? Had he only gone off, say, to collect something from his car, intending to join Harriet a few minutes later on the narrowboat with her friend? Was Harriet going to introduce him to her friend as her new boyfriend? How on earth was I going to explain what I'd been doing? I could just see the smirk on Jeff's face, and the disbelief on Harriet's, if I said that I'd merely been enjoying a solitary evening stroll. They, and everyone they told, would think I was some kind of stalker. No one would listen to my side of things.

Not stopping to think further, I broke into as hurried a walk as I could manage without actually running, away from the secret watcher and in the direction that Harriet and I had previously been heading. I put my hands over my anorak hood to make sure it was as tight around my head as possible, and I averted my face from the narrowboat until I was well clear. I was dreading to hear a cry of 'Stop, Alan' from behind me, but to my relief all I could hear was my panting. I didn't dare turn around to see if I was being followed.

Within a couple of minutes, I'd reached the bridge which carried the road from Soham to Ely over the river. I went up the slight incline to the side of the bridge, and as soon as I reached the top and turned right onto the pavement I broke into a run. Even if I was being followed, I had enough of a head start to keep ahead of my pursuer. Jeff still played rugby, but the rugby at his level was more of a preliminary to a boys' piss-up in the bar afterwards, so fitness-wise he had nothing on me.

I crossed the road to go under the low railway bridge just before the supermarket – the bridge which, rightly or wrongly, has the reputation for being the one in England which is most often hit by high vehicles. I ran past the supermarket car park and across the roundabout and only slowed down when I started the climb up the hill towards my car park. Finally, I gave into the temptation to look behind me and, as far as I could tell, I wasn't being followed. However, I still maintained a brisk walk all the way to the car park. I had another look round when I reached my car, as anyone who recognised it as mine would figure out that no one other than me would be climbing into it. I could still see no one obviously following me, so I assumed that Jeff – if it had been him – had joined Harriet on the narrowboat instead of chasing me.

As soon as I got home, I went to the toilet through sheer nerves and then automatically checked myself out in the bathroom mirror. Although I was still in shock, I didn't think

I looked any different from how I'd been earlier that evening. I started to think I might have got away with it. There was no way that Jeff, if it was him spying on me, could have known for sure that it was me. And Harriet, I was positive, hadn't spotted me. So even if Jeff did say something to her about thinking that he'd seen me, I could say that I'd spent the whole evening in my house. Nobody could prove otherwise.

*

The opened bottle of Zinfandel was still waiting for me in the kitchen area of my house. It seemed to wink at me, as if to ask if I thought I might have been better off staying at home. I wished now that I'd done so. I'd been a fool. I'd allowed my heart to rule my head and I'd risked putting myself in an embarrassing situation professionally and personally. I doubted I could ever show my face in Senate House again if the truth came out. I could picture the sneers on the faces of experienced players such as Hugh and Lewis, and the looks of disgust on the faces of women such as Deborah, Amanda and Mehak. I would even struggle to maintain any authority over the likes of Richard and Tom.

Normally, I liked to savour the taste and smell of my fine red wines, but I finished the bottle as quickly as I've ever done. I must have been two-thirds of the way through before the effect of the alcohol hit me. The rest of the bottle went down my throat almost as an afterthought.

On most occasions, that amount of wine would quickly send me off to bed and sleep. But tonight, I stayed annoyingly sober. I toyed with opening a second bottle but knew I would then sleep badly. And I might need my wits about me tomorrow.

I wanted something to take my mind off that evening's events. I picked up my phone and started browsing one of my favourite websites covering the history of capital punishment in the United Kingdom. I found some material, new to me, about a case I had long been interested in: that of a young man hanged in the early 1960s for the murder of an elderly widow who lived almost opposite the house which he occupied with his own family. It had been the last ever hanging at that provincial prison, and the night before the execution the other prisoners had staged a noisy protest in his support. I found some archive news footage on the Internet, again from the day before the execution, of the doomed man's father, understandably looking very haggard, arriving at the prison gate to say his final goodbyes to his son. I tried to visualise what their last conversation might have been like.

Not for the first time, I wondered how I would handle my last days in a condemned cell, knowing to the second when I was going to die. I wondered also who would visit me before I died. I expected my parents would make the long journey south, through duty if nothing else, but I couldn't immediately think of anyone else. Usually, I took a strange comfort in reading about murderers awaiting their last walk to the gallows, recognising that whatever mood I was in my plight could hardly compare to theirs. Tonight, however, I got no pleasure from my reading. I couldn't stop thinking about Jeff and Harriet.

Eventually, I went to bed, recognising that I needed a good night's sleep before tomorrow. I had resolved to tackle Harriet directly in the morning. I would ask her exactly what was going on between her and Jeff. I had a need to know.

24

'Alan, can you step into my office, please?'

This was Lewis. He was standing in the doorway of his office. It was 2 p.m. on the following afternoon.

Until then, I couldn't have told you if Lewis was even in his office. I'd been on edge ever since I got in that morning, waiting for Harriet to arrive so I could find out what had happened on and after her date with Jeff. However, I'd been more irritated than worried when she hadn't put in an appearance by the early afternoon. I'd noticed in our shared team diary that she had a few meetings scheduled in the course of the morning. It therefore seemed likely that she'd gone to the first of these straight from home, and had then gone from one to the next for the rest of the morning without feeling the need to show her face in Senate House. She had nothing scheduled at lunchtime, but given how many people she was friendly with around the University it was perfectly possible that she'd had an impromptu lunch with someone she bumped into. She hadn't told me in advance that she was going to do this, though, and while I didn't like to micromanage her, I did prefer to know where she was throughout her working day. Harriet's desk phone had rung during the morning and bounced to Tom. I heard him say, 'No, sorry, she's not in yet,' and then after he put the phone down I heard his muttered aside to Richard, 'That was a solicitor from the firm that's just been appointed.' It was typical of the man's lack of imagination that it didn't occur to him to speculate why the solicitor, whom I presumed was Jeff Parker, wanted to speak to Harriet rather than to me or Lewis.

'Take a seat, please, Alan.'

I noticed Lewis had now said 'please' twice. On the occasion of my previous summons, when he'd had a go at me over Mehak, he'd merely gestured at me with his finger to sit down. I took the chair facing him across his desk and waited to hear what unpalatable favour I presumed he was going to ask of me.

'I have some bad news, I'm afraid,' he said after a few seconds of silence. 'There's no easy way for me to tell you. I had a phone call a short time ago to say that ... that Harriet's body has been recovered from the river. She appears to have had an accident last night on her way home. I'm very sorry to have to tell you this. I know how much you valued her ...'

Lewis had clasped his hands together on his desk and he looked down at them as he spoke, like I can imagine an oncologist does when telling a patient that their condition is terminal. His words sounded rehearsed, as if he'd given some thought as to exactly what he was going to say.

It probably seems strange that I was able to analyse Lewis's manner and tone so objectively. Looking back at those moments afterwards, as I did many times in the days to come, I think there must have been some kind of disconnection between what I was hearing and what I was feeling. Although I heard and understood every word, I couldn't accept that they were true. Harriet – the woman who sat next to me every day of the working week and whose look, voice and scent I knew so well – simply couldn't be dead. I'd seen her alive only yesterday. It wasn't possible that I would never see her again.

I began to feel dizzy. I remember experiencing some detached curiosity about whether the dizziness was because blood was rushing to, or from, my head. My heart was also pounding, but rather than quickening as I would have expected, its beat seemed to be slower than normal, like the beat of a drum on a military funeral march. My breathing had become very rapid, yet I couldn't get oxygen into my lungs.

'Here, Alan, have a drink of this.' I hadn't noticed Lewis

143

getting up and coming around his desk, but now he was holding a water bottle to my lips. 'Good. Now put your head down between your legs and take some slow, deep breaths.'

I felt his hand on the back of my head, pushing it down gently but firmly. Except for the rasping, almost animal-like sounds coming from my mouth, there was complete silence in the office.

Slowly, probably over a couple of minutes, the dizziness passed. I noticed too that my breathing had slowed.

Lewis's hand was still resting on the back of my head, and I couldn't stop myself from thinking about how often he had rested that same hand on the back of Harriet's head. Even now – and despite my loathing for Jeff Parker – I found it impossible to forget what Lewis had also done with Harriet.

'I can't believe it,' I said. 'I was with her only yesterday.' These words came out spontaneously, as if sub-consciously I thought I could rationally argue away the fact of Harriet's death. In reality, I wasn't stupid enough to suppose that Lewis was joking or mistaken. But that still didn't mean I could accept that she was dead.

I can't now be sure, but I suspect I was also remembering that morning at Doveley's, earlier in the year, when Sam Snape had announced Helen's death in an all-staff e-mail. Sam had known how much Helen meant to me, but he hadn't had the courtesy to break the news to me in person. Whether he'd done this on purpose – to hurt me further – or just unthinkingly, I still had no idea. If I was indeed remembering that morning, then I suppose I must also have recognised that at least Lewis was having the decency to tell me about Harriet's death in private, although I was hardly going to forgive him anything for that.

'I can't believe it either,' Lewis said. 'She will be greatly missed. Especially by me. I'd got to know her quite well.'

Quite well indeed, you bastard. You'd been bloody shagging the girl behind your wife's back. But I had no idea if Lewis knew that I knew, so I wasn't going to mention that.

I had to steer the conversation away from anything likely to make me lash out at him. 'What happened?' I asked.

'I had a phone call at lunchtime from Harriet's sister. She'd received a phone call during the morning from Harriet's housemate. Someone on a narrowboat spotted Harriet's body in the river at dawn this morning. I don't know if they tried to get her out themselves, or called the police, but there was nothing anyone could do. She'd been dead a while, apparently. It happened somewhere between the main business area of the riverside and the bridge near the supermarket. I don't have a clue what she was doing down there, but it sounds like she slipped on the footpath and fell in. When did you last see her, Alan?'

I had to think quickly. I certainly wasn't going to say that I'd been just a few yards away from her yesterday evening. He might ask what I'd been up to. But I also couldn't risk saying anything which, if I was unlucky, could later be shown to be untrue.

'We last spoke when I left here yesterday,' I said. 'About four-thirty.' I realised this might sound like I'd been wagging off work early. 'I had to drop something off at the School of Business before I went home,' I explained.

Lewis paid no attention to my explanation. 'Any idea what she was going to do last night?'

'She didn't tell me.' Again, I was careful not to tell a lie.

'Reading between the lines,' he went on, 'it looks like she'd been drinking. Her housemate said she was meeting someone for a drink and a meal after work – she didn't say who – and was then going to see a friend who lives on a narrowboat. It would have been dark down there. There are hardly any lights once you get away from the main riverside. And it had been raining, so it would also have been slippery. It's easy to see how a terrible accident could have happened. It goes to show that water and alcohol don't mix.'

Lewis nodded to himself slightly, as if acknowledging the wisdom of his own truism. I half-expected him to give his moustache a stroke, as the equivalent of patting himself on the back.

'What can I do?' I asked. It sounded like a stupid question, but

I had to say something.

'Actually, you can help me out here, Alan. I have to break the news to the senior management team. Harriet was very well respected by all of them. So if you could tell Richard and Tom, I would be grateful. Feel free to send them home for the rest of the day if you think it appropriate.'

'Yes, of course.'

Lewis was now looking and sounding like the consummate manager. His tone was no different to how it might have been if he'd been asking for help in announcing the roll-out of a new expenses policy. OK, he'd had longer than me to come to terms with the fact of Harriet's death, but even so ...

Then I understood why he appeared to be taking Harriet's death in his stride. Deep down, it solved a problem for him. Harriet had been the cause of the blazing row the other week between him and his wife. As long as Harriet was at the University, working in his team, she was a potential source of marital discord for him. But Harriet would never now come to work at the University again. I had no doubt that, in his own way, Lewis had been fond of her. But he hadn't been fond enough of her to leave Ruth. Moreover, it couldn't have been much fun for him to watch her subsequently drop her knickers for a second-rate BDM such as Hugh. If he was anything like me, he would have been agonising over whether Hugh's sexual performance was better than his own.

'One other thing, Alan.' Lewis was speaking again. 'I also had a phone call from the police officer who's dealing with Harriet's death. She's coming to Senate House tomorrow morning to confirm a few facts. I said you'd be the best person to do that. I can't see it taking very long.'

*

'It's awful, Alan. Just think, she was here yesterday, doing normal stuff, and she had no inkling that it was her last day alive. The same thing could happen to any of us, I suppose.'

146

Tom's platitudinous response to the news of Harriet's death was the sort of thing I had expected: the words of a kindly young man who was out of his depth. I wondered if he'd ever before had to deal with the unexpected death of a young person whom he knew well. His expression suggested that he hadn't previously comprehended how cruel the world could be.

'Very true,' I said. I was still too shaken to indulge in any kind of philosophical discussion about the frailty of life.

'Is there anything I can do?' Almost the same clichéd words that I'd used with Lewis.

'Work-wise, I can deal with everything today,' I said. 'Outside work, her sister's on the case. So I suggest you continue as normal for now, but be prepared to pick up some of Harriet's work when I reallocate it. But don't worry, Tom, I'll make sure you have time to mourn and remember her in due course.'

In different circumstances, I would have taken pride in my words. They struck the right balance, I thought, between respect for the dead and a practical acknowledgement that life must go on.

Meanwhile, Richard had been silent. He now said, 'I'll pick up what I can of Harriet's work, but I do have a pretty full load at present.'

He really was a little turd. I bet his first thoughts had been about how Harriet's death might impact negatively on him. No doubt his second thoughts would be about whether he might benefit from her death. Well, if he thought he was going to be having cosy one-on-one chats with me, he had a shock coming.

'You're not the only one to have a full load already, Richard,' I said. 'But we'll all have to take more on. That includes you, I'm afraid.'

I didn't say that he would also have time to mourn and remember Harriet in due course. The words would have stuck in my throat. I hadn't forgotten the keying of Harriet's car and the possibility that Richard was the culprit.

I'd been half-minded to send Tom and Richard home for the rest of the day, as Lewis had suggested. But I could hardly send one home and not the other. And I was buggered if I was going to give Richard the rest of the day off. Moreover, I was irked with them both for another reason. I tried to be scrupulously fair in how I treated my team, but Harriet had undeniably been the most talented and committed of the three and it had therefore only been natural that I should develop a special working relationship with her. Yet neither Tom nor Richard had expressed a word of sympathy for how they must have known I was feeling. Did they really have that little emotional intelligence?

*

I left work as soon as I decently could, soon after Richard and Tom. They'd said their goodnights to me as if nothing out of the ordinary had happened.

Word about Harriet's death had spread around the second floor during the afternoon, presumably filtering down from senior management. From time to time, someone from another team would come over for a whispered conversation with Richard or Tom, and then go back and have another whispered conversation with their own team. I was numb, and in no mood to speak to anyone, but I was still irritated that they went to Richard and Tom for information rather than me. I couldn't help but notice too that not a single person said anything to me about being sorry for my loss.

I had no idea if Hugh and Mehak had yet heard about Harriet's death. If not, I certainly wasn't going to tell them. I couldn't imagine they would express much sympathy for me either.

Back at my house, shortly after 5.30 p.m., I threw myself onto the sofa in my downstairs living area. My house was always quiet, but tonight it felt eerily so – almost lifeless. I desperately wished that there was someone I could talk to. If I'd known my neighbours better, I could have knocked on their doors and explained about Harriet's death, perhaps apologising in advance if I wouldn't be my normal self for a while. But the neighbour with whom I'd exchanged most words was the oaf who had objected to my complaints about him parking in my allocated spot. The other houses were mostly occupied by elderly couples, and I'd never done more than swap banal comments with them about the weather on my way to and from my car.

I felt I should be crying. I'd seen how easily other people, particularly women, could shed tears in appropriate circumstances. And nothing could be more appropriate than the loss of a talented young woman of whom, I don't mind admitting, I'd been very fond. But the tears wouldn't come. My cat took up position on the arm of the sofa, and as I mechanically stroked the top of her head and tickled her ears, I pondered whether she could sense what I was going through.

As I continued to mull over the day's events, some of the numbness I was feeling turned into anger. At first, it was a general anger: anger at the fact of Harriet's death and how unfair it was. But after a while – and I'm not proud to admit this – some of this anger was directed at Harriet. Why the hell had she gone out on a date with Jeff Parker and got so drunk? If she hadn't done so, she wouldn't have had her accident and wouldn't now be dead. And it hadn't just been Jeff, either. Before him, there'd been Lewis and Hugh, both people with whom she had a professional relationship. And yet, in all the months I'd worked alongside her, she'd never once hinted at wanting to step outside our professional boundaries. Of course, if she had done so, my duty would have required me to rebut her advances, gently but firmly. Nevertheless ... nevertheless ... it would have been nice to have been asked.

There, I'd finally admitted it to myself.

Yes, I would have liked her to want to go to bed with me. And yes, I'd been jealous of what she'd done and had planned to do with other men even though I'd tried to pretend otherwise even to myself. And I knew now – and this was what was making me most angry – that I'd never have the chance to know her in the way that Lewis and Hugh had done, and that no doubt Jeff would soon have done.

But what if I'd been the one to suggest that we should cross the line?

I wanted to imagine that she would have fallen into my arms, perhaps after an earnest discussion of whether or not this was a good idea. However, try as I might, I couldn't make this work. I didn't think that she would have laughed at me, or lied that she already had a boyfriend like Mehak had done; she was too kind to do that. But I could picture the look on her face as she asked herself how she could tactfully extract herself from this embarrassing situation. I remembered other occasions, at school and university parties, when women whom I'd found the courage to proposition had suggested that things were 'too complicated' or that we shouldn't 'risk spoiling a nice friendship' – only for me to see them an hour or so later sticking their tongue down the throat of some brainless buck whom they hardly knew.

For far from the first time, I tried to envisage what it must be like to be a Jeff Parker: to be able to make a move on a woman knowing that the odds were in your favour, but that even if you were unsuccessful, there would be no hard feelings or awkward aftermath because it was simply part of the overall game of life.

I didn't think I would ever get over my loathing for Jeff. He'd taken Helen from me at Doveley's and had clearly planned to take Harriet from me here at the University. The only meagre consolation I had was that he hadn't, as far as I was aware, got what he wanted from Harriet before she died. Thank God for that.

And then, out of the blue, another thought occurred to me.

Was there a chance that Jeff was responsible for Harriet's death? In one sense, undoubtedly, he was responsible. He'd poured alcohol down her throat, and that had probably been a factor in her accident. But had there been more to it? Had he been the person watching me follow Harriet and, if so, had he got her even more drunk later that night in the hope of being invited back to her house, and had that further drunkenness made all the difference? Or had he said something to upset her, so she lost concentration and fell into the river? From nowhere, I recalled the tragic death of a student during my time at university; she'd run across the road and been hit by a car after a drunken late-night row with her boyfriend.

When I finally went to bed at around 10 p.m., I was still devastated by the news of Harriet's death. I was dreading the next few days in particular. But at the same time, if there was some unpalatable truth to be uncovered regarding why and how she died, I knew it would be my duty to do so. For Harriet's sake.

25

'Alan, there's a police officer here to see you.'

For a moment, I felt like I was a character in a second-rate comedy thriller. The receptionist's words down the phone were almost exactly the same that my secretary at Doveley's had used earlier that year, on that fateful morning when the police had called to talk to me about the circumstances of Helen's death.

'I'll come straight down,' I said.

Richard and Tom were at their desks, and although this was going to be an informal meeting, I had no wish to advertise whom I was seeing. Neither of the 'boys' had bothered to ask me what sort of night I'd had when they got in that morning, and they'd even spent the first few minutes of the day discussing a televised football match from the night before. It was as if Harriet's death was water under the bridge. When they finally deigned to turn their attention to work, I had to bite my tongue when Tom showed me the mess he'd made of a simple disclaimer.

In some ways, therefore, it was a relief to head down the stairs to the reception area of Senate House. The only uniformed people normally to be seen in the building were from security, so I spotted the police officer as soon as I turned onto the last flight of stairs that led to the reception desk. The officer was standing with her back to me, and until she turned on hearing my approach, I had no inkling of who she was.

'Hello, Alan,' P.C. Dawn Smith said.

You could, as they say, have knocked me down with a feather. I hadn't spoken to Dawn Smith since that late Sunday night in

March when she had telephoned me at home to tell me whom the police had charged with Helen's murder. I was still expecting to give evidence at the trial, but it had all gone quiet and I certainly had no incentive to make enquiries about what was going on.

'Er, hello, Dawn,' I replied. 'I hadn't expected to see you here.'

I was itching to ask why she'd been chosen to see me, but she must have been reading my mind. 'I've moved to the area since getting married in the summer,' she said, 'so I'm working locally now rather than in Cambridge.'

I remembered now the engagement ring she'd been wearing when I first met her at Doveley's. It was on the tip of my tongue to ask what her husband did, but I'd already worked long enough in the public sector to know that this type of hasty assumption regarding a person's sexual preferences was frowned upon.

So I said, 'Does your, er, other half work locally too?'

'He's a student here, actually.'

My God, she's a cradle-snatcher, I thought. I bit back a witticism. I'd learnt from my experiences earlier in the year that it was a good idea to keep the police onside.

Again, it was as if Dawn could read my thoughts. 'He's doing an MBA,' she said. 'Sponsored by his employer.'

I would like to have asked why he was doing an MBA at the University of East Cambridgeshire rather than at any of the better universities in Cambridgeshire. But that was likely to piss off both her and the listening receptionist, so I resisted the temptation.

'I'm sorry we're meeting again under such sad circumstances,' Dawn went on. 'I didn't know the lady who died, but I understand she was highly regarded by everyone. Please accept my condolences.'

Perhaps I was being too sensitive, but there seemed to be an implication that Harriet had been more highly regarded than me. I wondered who she had already been talking to.

Greetings over, we went to the meeting room on the ground floor which had been allocated to us: the one where we'd held the last Enterprise Board meeting. As it was the largest of the meeting rooms, it occurred to me that the receptionist might have been trying to impress the police with the lavishness of the University's facilities.

Dawn was evidently still in the habit of underplaying her femininity when dressing for work. She had a pleasant enough face, but she wore no make-up and her nails were unvarnished and cut – or possibly even chewed – very short. Her blonde hair was fastened up at the back above her collar, so it was impossible to tell how long it would be when allowed to fall loose. I made a mental note to look her husband up when I got the chance. It would be interesting to see the type of man that P.C. Dawn Smith went for.

'This time it really is a routine enquiry, Alan,' she said as we sat down opposite each other. 'We have to collect all relevant information for the coroner. Normally, we'd get this from the family. But as none of Harriet's family live locally or see her regularly, we're speaking to her housemate and to people who knew her best at work.'

'I understand,' I said. 'I am a lawyer. What do you want to know?'

'Well, first of all, what was her state of mind before she died? Was anything worrying her? Anything that might have meant she was likely to pay less attention to what she was doing?'

'She was a lawyer, too. Our job involves working to deadlines under pressure. The consequences of getting things wrong can be enormous. So, yes, unless you're a completely unimaginative person, which Harriet wasn't, you're always going to be worrying about things at work. But Harriet had me. I made sure she wasn't overburdened or unsupported.'

'What about her personal life?'

'She'd recently ended a relationship with one of the BDMs. Business development managers, that is. But it hadn't been very serious. I gather she'd dated a few other men. I didn't like to pry, though.' I decided not to mention Lewis. That might rebound on me.

'How did you feel about that?' Dawn's tone remained casual, but she looked me straight in the eyes.

'What do you mean?'

'How did you feel about her dating other men?'

For God's sake. Talk about being judged. I hadn't behaved perfectly in the aftermath of my break-up with Helen, but it sounded like Dawn had formed an impression of me which I didn't like the sound of.

'It was entirely up to her,' I said. 'Occasionally she sought my advice, and I was happy to help in any way I could. Other than that, my only concern was that her work wasn't adversely affected by anything in her private life.'

'How did you feel about her seeing Jeff Parker?'

I assumed she'd heard about Jeff from Harriet's housemate. I was increasingly ill at ease and tried to keep my voice neutral. 'I don't mind admitting that I was a bit surprised. Jeff Parker is one of the University's external lawyers, so it's important for us in Legal not to blur the lines between our work and personal lives. But apart from that consideration, it was a matter for Harriet with whom she spent her time.'

I stopped there. It would only reflect badly on me if I went off into a rant about the sort of person Jeff Parker was. Dawn had met Jeff earlier in the year during the inquiries into Helen's death, and she'd clearly fallen for his superficial charm.

'Who do you think keyed Harriet's car?'

The change of direction completely threw me. Dawn waited patiently, but I fancied I saw a flicker of a smile on her face. She'd seen some of my imperfections before, and I supposed it was only natural that she should find some enjoyment in my discomfiture.

I stalled for time. 'How did you hear about that?'

'Her housemate told me. Harriet had been very upset. Understandably so. It must be horrible to have someone deliberately damage something precious to you. Given how well you knew Harriet, surely you must have some idea of who could have done it?'

155

The natural response would have been for me to name Hugh, or Lewis, or Richard. Or even Ruth. All of them had a motive. But I couldn't. The last thing I wanted was some kind of official investigation into Harriet's life in the days leading up to her death. CCTV was everywhere nowadays, and I didn't want the police to find footage of me watching Harriet and Jeff down by the riverside on the evening of her death. My mouth felt dry just at the thought of me having to explain my movements away.

'I'm sorry, I don't have a clue,' I said. 'I assumed it was some passing toe-rag who saw the car and, er, just keyed it.'

'You didn't key it yourself, Alan?'

For fuck's sake. Is this really what the police thought of me? OK, I knew I'd gone a bit too far in how I kept tabs on Helen after our break-up, but we'd been in a serious relationship so I thought people would understand. Harriet and I, on the other hand, had never even kissed. Why on earth did this woman think I might have been tempted to key Harriet's car?

'No, I bloody well didn't,' I said.

'I had to ask. I'm sorry. One final question for now. When did you last see Harriet?'

I decided to adopt the same strategy as I had done with Lewis. 'We last spoke at about four-thirty on the night she died,' I said. 'I left work a bit early to drop something off at the School of Business.'

'And you didn't see her later that evening?'

She was definitely more on the ball than that randy goat Lewis. I knew I had to make a decision and stick to it. If I lied, there was the risk of being caught out. But I couldn't tell the truth. No one would understand why I'd felt it necessary to keep an eye on her and Jeff that evening.

'No, my last sight of her was at her desk upstairs on the second floor. If only I'd known that I wouldn't see her again, I would have …' I let my voice trail off, then bowed my head to avoid Dawn's gaze. I knew I should tell her about the person who'd watched me following Harriet along the riverside, but there was no way of doing so without making myself look like a jealous obsessive.

'I'm sorry to upset you, Alan. I had to double-check.'

'May I ask what actually happened? I heard that Harriet probably slipped and fell into the river after she'd been drinking on a narrowboat with a friend. Is that right?'

'You know I can't disclose too much information. But yes, that's what seems to have happened. A tragic accident, in other words. There are no suspicious circumstances. From what you and her housemate say, it looks like she had a few things on her mind that night. These might have encouraged her to drink more alcohol than usual and caused her to pay less attention to what she was doing when she left her friend's boat.'

'But how did she die?'

Dawn shook her head. 'That will be for the coroner to decide. All I can say is that she was found dead in the water at dawn on Tuesday.'

And that was that. Once Dawn had the information she wanted from me, she showed no wish to continue our conversation. We weren't best buddies, but I had earlier that year been instrumental in catching a murderer and had nearly lost my own life in the process. I'd expected Dawn at least to acknowledge this, perhaps by sharing some of her thoughts about Harriet's death as a way of showing that we were on the same side.

Instead, she was quickly on her feet. 'Goodbye, Alan. I'm sorry again for the loss.'

I couldn't help but notice how she referred to 'the loss' rather than 'your loss'. She was another one who didn't seem to understand what effect Harriet's death was having on me.

I followed her out of the door and almost the first person I saw was Mehak, who was ascending the stairs to the first floor in the company of a couple of her colleagues from International. She must have been twenty yards away, but I saw her mouth open in shock at the sight of me in the company of a uniformed police officer. She continued to walk up the stairs, with her head half-turned so she could keep me and Dawn in her sight. For a second,

I wondered if she was going to stumble on the stairs, but then she turned her head away from me and continued upwards.

I turned around, but Dawn was already walking out of the main door of Senate House. I headed back upstairs, lost in my thoughts.

26

I hunkered down at my desk for the rest of the day. My work was the only thing capable of taking my mind off the aftermath of Harriet's death.

The University was planning to register its name, logo and crest as a trade mark in a number of countries around the world, and I had to determine the categories of goods and services in respect of which the trade mark was to be protected. Personally, I thought it was a complete waste of time and money, as I couldn't imagine anyone wanting to pass themselves off as being associated with a Mickey Mouse university such as ours. But Amanda had recently come back from a conference of university big cheeses who had been boasting about their international trade mark portfolios, and she had decided that this was something we also had to do if we wanted a chance of eating at the top table. I had to choose my battles carefully at the University, and this wasn't one to fight.

All around me, the second floor seemed, at least on the surface, to be back to normal. Amanda and Deborah were endlessly in and out of their offices, making themselves look important without actually doing very much. Lewis was mostly motionless at his desk, doing whatever he normally found to do when he was there: bugger all of any value, if you asked me.

After a while, I sent an e-mail, copying in Lewis, to the IT helpdesk:

Hi

You've probably heard the sad news about Harriet Wells. I was

her line manager. To help me pick up her work and re-allocate it
amongst the rest of the team, please can you give me access to her e-
mail account and to any documents she created that aren't on the
team shared portal. I'm sure Lewis (cc'd) will give you any necessary
authorisation.

Thanks,
Alan

Lewis would be uneasy about me gaining access, but my request was a reasonable one and he would have to OK it. I was curious to see if there was any evidence about how his affair with Harriet had started. If there were any work e-mails in which they had flirted with each other before they hooked up, I wanted to see them.

I left the office as soon as I decently could at the end of the afternoon, feeling slightly guilty as I joined the clock-watchers flooding down the stairs and out of the main door of Senate House. However, there was somewhere I had to be.

*

I parked as close as I could to Harriet's house. I didn't know what hours Kat worked, but 6 p.m. seemed as good a time as any to catch her at home. I heard footsteps from inside almost as soon as I rang the doorbell. The door opened a few inches and a woman in her mid-thirties peered around the door. She looked tired, and also older than I expected based on Harriet's descriptions of her, but I was too much of a gentleman to pass comment on that.

'Hello, Kat?' I asked tentatively.

'I'm not Kat. She's having a shower. Can I help you?'

I thought she was being unnecessarily brusque, whoever she was. But I wasn't there to pass judgment. 'I'm Alan Gadd. From the University. I was hoping for a word with Kat. Do you know if she'll be long in the shower?'

The woman looked at me as if she thought I was an idiot or a pervert. 'It's not a great time to call, to be honest,' she replied, not answering my question. 'Is it important?'

'I'm sure Kat will think it is,' I said, feeling slightly irritated. 'Are you, er, a friend of hers?'

'I'm Zoe. Harriet's sister. Harriet lives … lived here.' There was a catch in her voice, and I realised that her passive aggressiveness was probably being used to conceal some deeper emotions.

'I'm sorry,' I said. 'I understand how you must be feeling. Your sister's death has upset me very much too. I was her line manager.' I wanted to say that Harriet had spoken of her sister many times, but in truth her name had barely ever come up in conversation.

Zoe said, 'I don't remember Harriet mentioning you, I'm afraid. You must be new at the University because I always thought that Harriet's line manager was Lewis Morgan. A lovely man, from what I heard. It's very kind of you to call, though.'

I tried not to show my annoyance. I liked to think that I'd been Harriet's mentor as well as her line manager; and, indeed, her friend. I found it difficult to believe that Harriet either hadn't mentioned me at all to her sister or had done so in such a passing way that my name hadn't stayed in her mind. But perhaps it was just an indication that Harriet and Zoe weren't very close.

'Harriet and I have been working closely together since I joined the University in July,' I said. 'Lewis hasn't been her line manager since then. In fact, I don't think she and Lewis have had much to do with each other recently.' I thought it best not to say more about Lewis at this point. 'I'm very glad,' I went on, 'to have had the chance to convey my sympathies personally. However, I had called to speak to Kat, if you think she'll have finished her shower soon—'

'Hello?'

The door was suddenly pulled further open and another face appeared next to Zoe's. The new arrival looked younger than Zoe, and her face had the kind of jolly features that make you think she must spend most of her time in a good mood. She was wearing a bathrobe, and instinctively I noticed that it was falling slightly open at the front, revealing the upper slopes of one of her breasts from which I carefully averted my eyes. Although I hadn't met her before either, I knew who this would be.

'You must be Kat?' I asked all the same. There was a polite smile and a nod. 'I'm Alan Gadd, Harriet's line manager. I'm calling to say how sorry I was to hear about Harriet's death and to see if there is anything I can do to help.' That wasn't, strictly, why I'd called, but I pride myself on being able to say the right thing at the right time.

'So you're Alan, then,' she replied, with a hint of what, in a different situation, I would have interpreted as a slightly mischievous smile. 'Harriet mentioned you a lot. In fact, she was only talking about you on Monday before she went off for a meal with the lawyer she'd met.'

I didn't like the sound of that. Call me paranoid, but I couldn't imagine that Harriet was discussing my technical abilities as a lawyer while getting ready for a hot date with Jeff Parker. I wondered if she'd picked up on any of my reservations about Jeff and passed them on to Kat.

'I was devastated when I heard the news,' I said. 'Harriet had such a bright future ahead of her. You must have been one of the first to hear?'

Kat sighed. 'Yes, there was a ring at the door just before I left for work. Two police officers. Both very pleasant. You could tell they'd done this sort of thing before. They said that Harriet had been found in the river on that stretch between the commercial area and the bridge near the station. They didn't tell me a huge amount, as you'd expect, but I had a phone call later on from Harriet's friend. The friend who found her. She lives on one of the narrowboats, and I've been down there with Harriet a few times. Apparently, Harriet and the lawyer – a very decent chap, I gather, called Jeff Parker – had their date down by the riverside. After saying goodnight to him, Harriet called to see her friend.'

I'd winced at the description of Jeff as very decent but decided not to interrupt.

'Anyway,' Kat continued, 'Harriet and her friend had quite a lot to drink. In Harriet's case, this was on top of what she'd already drunk with Jeff. Both girls were therefore pretty wasted by the time Harriet left, just before midnight, although Harriet was in a worse state. Harriet's friend said she gave Harriet a hug and a kiss below deck, but left Harriet to jump ashore on her own from the stern of the boat. She's feeling very guilty now that she didn't walk with Harriet to the bridge, although to be fair to her it's only a couple of minutes away even in the dark. Shortly after Harriet had gone upstairs to the stern, the friend heard a big splash. She assumed, and again remember she was pretty drunk, that it was something to do with one of the other boats that are moored along that part of the riverside. People come and go at all times, even during the night, and there's a lot of drunkenness. Anyway, she went to sleep. She got up at daybreak and went up onto the stern of the boat for a cigarette. She saw something floating in the water just behind the boat, caught in a loose mooring rope. She saw a tangle of hair, and then a colour which was the same as Harriet had been wearing the night before. And when she looked closer, she ... she realised it was Harriet. She couldn't get her out of the water herself, so she dialled 999.'

All three of us were silent for a few seconds as we pictured what the friend must have experienced.

'So do the police think she fell in because she was drunk?' I asked, after what I thought was a sufficiently respectful pause.

'Yes, that's the impression I got, although they will need to wait for the post-mortem to be sure. Harriet's friend was there when ... when they pulled her out of the water. From what the police were saying to each other, it looks like she may also have banged her head on the side of the boat as she fell. If so, well, it's hardly a consolation, but it means she may not have suffered if she was knocked unconscious. I'd hate to think that she died, fully conscious, trying to reach the riverbank. She'd never learnt to swim, sadly. It was one of those things that she was oddly slightly proud of.'

I could tell from the two women's body language that they

wouldn't welcome a discussion of the mechanics of drowning. 'And, Zoe, you then heard from Kat?' I ventured.

'Yes. Kat didn't want me to have to wait until the police sent someone round. She phoned me as soon as they'd gone. I drove straight down from Peterborough. There was nothing I could do, but I wanted to be close to where ... to where it happened. I'm staying in Harriet's room for a few nights. At the moment, I'm going through her things and letting family and friends know. Mum and Dad are devastated, as you'd expect.'

I was also devastated. However, there was no point in getting involved in a hierarchy of grief. I scratched around for a way to break a silence that was becoming uncomfortable. 'Funnily enough,' I said, 'I was last here only a short while ago. Harriet had been concerned about the safety of the gas appliances and asked me to advise her. Fortunately, I could identify the problem and provide a solution. Did she mention this to you, Kat?'

Kat gave me a look as if I'd released a sulphurous burp in her face. 'Harriet did say something, Alan. But it hardly matters now, does it?'

'Very true,' I said, trying to sound philosophical.

Again, there was a silence. Neither of the two women had invited me into the house, and it occurred to me they might be wanting to bring our conversation to an end.

'Well, I suppose I'd better be off,' I said. 'It was nice to meet you both. I only wish it had been under happier circumstances.'

Neither woman said anything, but Kat gave me what looked like a sympathetic half-smile. I remembered again her comment about having talked about me with Harriet. I wished I knew what they'd said. I hadn't expected Kat and Zoe to stand at the door waving until I drove out of sight, but I was a little put out that Zoe shut the door within a second or two of me turning to walk down the footpath to the road.

*

Rather than go straight home, I drove the short distance to the supermarket car park next to the station. From there, it was only a five-minute walk to the bridge over the river. The bridge was well-lit, and as I stood looking down over the parapet into the gloom, I couldn't at first even distinguish the river from the riverbank. As my eyes grew accustomed to the dark, I gradually became able to make out the footpath and the shape of narrowboats moored sporadically alongside.

I walked down the incline at the side of the bridge and made my way gingerly along the footpath towards Harriet's friend's narrowboat. There were no lights showing inside. After what had happened, I couldn't imagine Harriet's friend enjoying a jolly night at home on the river. The only sounds in the darkness came from cars crossing the bridge behind me. I took out my phone and switched on the torch for a few seconds. There was a short plank, shiny with slippery-looking mud, between the stern of the boat and the bank. Beneath the plank, the water was like black treacle: thick and sticky.

How easy it would be, in the dark and after a skinful of alcohol, to lose one's footing on the plank and tumble headlong into the water. The bank was a couple of feet above the river, and even a decent swimmer, sober, would have to make a big effort to pull themselves out of the water. As for a non-swimmer: drunk, weighed down with wet clothes, perhaps not even knowing in which direction the bank was … well, I wouldn't bet any money on them being able to get themselves out onto dry land. And if they'd banged their head on their way in, then even if they weren't rendered unconscious it would be almost impossible for them to save themselves.

Poor Harriet. What an awful way to go. And so needless too. If she'd chosen to spend the evening with me rather than with Jeff, she would still have been alive.

Then, as I switched off my light and was again surrounded by darkness, I thought about the person who – I had assumed – had been following me. Why hadn't they continued to follow me away from the riverside and up the hill towards the car park? That they hadn't done so, I was sure. But if they hadn't been following me, what were they doing? They must have been following someone else. And that someone else could only have been Harriet. If so, surely they would have hung around until she came off the boat. That's certainly what I would have done if I hadn't been frightened away. And if they had hung around, they would have seen her slip and fall into the water, and then they would have tried to help her themselves or at least summoned help.

Unless ... and I kicked myself for not having thought of this before. Unless the person following Harriet had wanted to do more than just follow her. Had they wanted to have something out with her? Had they had an argument by the riverside which had resulted in Harriet losing her balance? Or, and this sent a chill down my spine, had they pushed Harriet into the water, or even – God forbid – hit her over the head with something and caused her to fall into the water?

It scared me even to think about it. But on Monday night, had there been a killer only a few yards away from me in the dark?

I was shivering now, and this wasn't because of the coolness of the night air. I was shivering with the realisation that I may have been close to the scene of a crime. A crime that no one else even suspected. I was the only person who knew there had been a secret watcher down by the riverside that night, and unless I did or said something, no one else would ever know. And no one else would ever believe that Harriet's death had been anything other than a tragic accident.

27

I found it impossible to settle when I got back to my house. Every time I sat down on my sofa, I felt the urge within a few seconds to jump back up to my feet and pace up and down.

I was shaken by my realisation that Harriet's death may not have been an accident. I was also – I don't mind admitting – frightened by the thought that I might have been within a few yards of a killer.

But most of all, I was getting angry. Initially, my anger was aimed solely at whoever might have been responsible for Harriet's death. However, as I went over the events of the last few days again and again, I became increasingly angry also about the way people had behaved towards me.

I could understand that Kat and Zoe had more important things on their minds than me, but it would have been nice if they'd shown some appreciation of my role in Harriet's life. The way they'd shut down my mention of the gas safety issue bordered on rudeness. Similarly, not one person at work had expressed any genuine sympathy for what I was going through.

My main ire, though, was directed towards P.C. Dawn Smith and the police. I'd met Dawn voluntarily, eager to do my bit as a responsible citizen, and she'd repaid me by asking if I'd keyed Harriet's car. For fuck's sake, I was a solicitor. I don't think I'd ever knowingly broken the law, other than in relation to things like unreasonably slow driving limits. The fact that Dawn remembered me from the investigation into Helen's death earlier that year made it worse. What sort of person did she think I was? Although she would be reluctant to admit it, she knew I had been instrumental in the arrest of Helen's killer. I've always suffered from *l'esprit de l'escalier*, and I wished now that I'd asked Dawn what response she got from the Vice-Chancellor, from the Secretary and Registrar, and from all the University's unnecessarily large gang of pro-vice-chancellors when she asked each of them if they had keyed Harriet's car. Unless – surprise, surprise – she hadn't asked them this question, in which case what was so special about me?

The police, I concluded, needed to be put in their place. They also needed to be encouraged to do their job properly. If they hadn't even considered the possibility of foul play, they were clearly lacking in investigative skills. I bet they hadn't dragged Jeff Parker off the streets for questioning, as they should have done. If that sod hadn't poured alcohol down Harriet's throat on Monday night in an attempt to get into her knickers, she would still be alive. He should be made to pay for that if nothing else.

After a while, I opened my laptop. I switched on my VPN, went into incognito mode and logged into the anonymous e-mail account I had set up in order to e-mail Ruth about Lewis's affair with Harriet. I searched for the contact e-mail address for reporting crimes to Cambridgeshire police. Then I wrote:

Dear Cambs Police

You should be investigating the death of Harriet Wells properly. You think it was an accident, don't you? Well, have you found out who was following her that night down by the riverside? Have you also found out who keyed her car a few days earlier? Has it occurred to you that the two may be connected? Who might she have pissed off at work? Who had she been in a relationship with recently? What might her landlord have been up to (hint, gas safety)? Lots of questions for you. You need to find out some answers.

Do your job, rozzers!

From a concerned citizen of Ely

At first, I was pleased with my proposed e-mail. I was

trying not to sound like a lawyer. I had in mind some of the complaining letters I saw from time to time in the local rag from semi-educated locals, although I thought it would be over the top to scatter random capitals throughout like they often did. It was a nice touch, I felt, how I pointed the finger at those who might have borne Harriet a grudge. I fell into none of these categories of people, so I wasn't putting myself at risk.

But then, as I sat on my sofa reading the e-mail over again, I realised that it probably wasn't the wisest thing to send.

For a start, if the police ever compared notes with Ruth, they would spot straightaway that the two e-mails had come from the same anonymous account, and my knowledge of Harriet's affair with Lewis would narrow the field of possible writers somewhat. But even if I set up another anonymous e-mail account, were there ways in which the police could track where an e-mail had been sent from? Technology was advancing all the time and the most recent developments would probably not yet have been reported. What if the police went to the VPN provider and said they needed their cooperation in identifying a suspected murderer?

My other concern was the possible consequences for me if the police tried to identify who was following me – or Harriet – that night. Although I was pretty sure there were no CCTV cameras overlooking the spot where Harriet had died, I was less sure regarding the commercial area where Harriet and Jeff had gone for a drink and a meal. What if the police did a full review of CCTV footage for that night of everywhere that Harriet and Jeff had been? I could easily be picked up somewhere. I felt sick as I imagined the look on P.C. Smith's face when she asked me why I'd been spying (as I was sure she would call it) on Harriet and Jeff, and whether I was quite sure that I wasn't the person who had keyed Harriet's car. There was no guarantee that CCTV footage would reveal the person whom I'd seen following me, and I could end up putting myself in the frame.

How much easier life must have been in the olden days. No CCTV, no tracing of digital footprints. I occasionally wondered how any villains ever actually got caught – although, reading between the lines of the books in my true crime collection, it did sometimes sound like either the truth was beaten out of suspects or they were simply 'verballed' in the old-fashioned way. I'd lost count of the number of murderers I'd read about who had gone to the gallows on the sole basis of their 'confessions' – confessions which they tried unsuccessfully to retract later on when on trial for their lives.

After some further thought, I deleted my draft e-mail. Sending it would be too risky. Much as I would like to settle a few scores and uncover the truth about Harriet's death in order to do her justice, I had to find another way.

Who, then, could have borne Harriet a sufficient grudge to want to follow her that night, and possibly to harm her? The one didn't necessarily lead to the other, of course. Someone might have had a reason to follow her without intending her any harm at all. But then, if they'd had a row with her by the river, or if something else had triggered their anger, it would have been so easy to give her a push in the heat of the moment.

I made inroads into a bottle of red wine while I mulled over the possible suspects. It was one of my favourites: a Brazin Old Vine Zinfandel which I bought by the case whenever it was on offer. It had the usual Zinfandel aroma and flavour but wasn't so heavy that it couldn't be enjoyed on its own.

I decided that 'cherchez la femme', or in this case 'look for the man', was a natural starting point. Lewis, Hugh and Jeff Parker would all need to be scrutinised, as men who'd had a romantic or sexual interest in Harriet. Of the three, I would most like Jeff to be the guilty man. But, deep down, I doubted he was the type to want to cause physical harm to a woman whatever the provocation; he'd shown no signs of jealousy or possessiveness in all the years I'd known him. I also guessed the police would already have checked his movements after he and Harriet parted and were satisfied that he couldn't have been on the riverbank when she died.

Looking elsewhere, Ruth would have to be on my list, even

though I had no particular axe to grind regarding her.

Simon Fuller and Amanda Middleton were also two senior people at the University to investigate. I couldn't really envisage Amanda as the person prowling around in the shadows by the riverside, but it would be negligent of me not to look into what she'd been up to. Even if she was innocent of any involvement in Harriet's death, it would only be proper for me to bring to light any professional misconduct she might have been involved in regarding the Landlord Relax spin-out or the appointment of Doveley's as the University's solicitors.

I had no intention of forgetting Richard and Mehak, however. Richard was spiteful enough, and Mehak probably desperate enough, to do anything.

I would also try to find out if Harriet's landlord could have been involved. He unquestionably had a motive. If it came to light that he'd forged a gas safety certificate, he could not only be prosecuted but also be banned from being a landlord.

When I finally went to bed, after finishing my bottle of wine and downing a pizza, I felt I knew what I was doing. I still had no plan of how I would pursue some of my leads, but these were practical issues to which there must be a solution. Before going to sleep, I wound down by reading chapters from an old favourite from my true crime collection: the memoirs of one of the most famous Home Office pathologists, who'd been involved in many of this country's most notorious murders from the Second World War through to the days after the abolition of capital punishment. As always happened, I felt a pleasurable shiver run down my spine when an account of a particular murder ended with the matter-of-fact statement, almost made in passing, that the guilty party was subsequently hanged. I didn't think I would ever tire of books like this.

28

Extracts from Harriet's e-mail account:

January

[Lewis] May I leave this new matter in your very capable hands, Harriet?
[Harriet] Flattery will get you everywhere, Lewis!
[Lewis] It's not often I hear that nowadays.
[Harriet] You only have to ask!
[Lewis] Don't tempt me ... too often.
[Harriet] Why, what might you do?
[Lewis] Come into my office ... and I might show you.

*

April

[Hugh] When will I see you in my lair again?
[Harriet] When would you like to see me in your lair again?
[Hugh] That's a leading question.
[Harriet] I'm a lady who is easily led.
[Hugh] Led anywhere in particular?
[Harriet] Just astray.
[Hugh] I'm told I do that very well.
[Harriet] I'll be the judge of that!!!

*

June

[Amanda] This Alan Gadd looks like the best candidate on paper.

Loads of relevant experience. But he was on more money at Doveley's than we're offering. What's the story?

[Lewis] Reading between the lines, he seems to have left Doveley's under a bit of a cloud.

[Deborah] Any idea why?

[Lewis] Officially, no. Unofficially, he had a falling out with the partner in charge of his team. No idea what about. They clammed up completely. Completely off the record, I was told he's a loner, not very good with people. However, he's got a reference, and I've been reassured that technically he's a very good lawyer.

[Deborah] What are the alternatives?

[Lewis] None that impress. There's a litigator who has no experience in drafting contracts. There's a City lawyer who knows nothing about the HE sector. And there's an NQ who's still wet behind the ears. We need someone who can hit the ground running and supervise Harriet and the other two contracts executives.

[Amanda] OK, let's get Gadd in for an interview. Panel of four – us three plus HR. If we take him on, just make sure he's on a long probationary period.

*

June

[Lewis] Whoops, I forwarded the wrong e-mail chain. Ignore my one with Deborah and Amanda about this Alan Gadd character!

[Harriet] Already ignored!!!

*

July

[Hugh] Have you finally met your new boss, this Alan Gadd?

[Harriet] I have!

[Hugh] And …?

[Harriet] Well, he certainly knows his law.

[Hugh] That sounds like there's a 'but' coming?

[Harriet] Ha ha, I'll tell you later.

August

[Tom] *Thanks for helping with that contract, Harriet. I wish we had you as our line manager. I really try my hardest to get things right, but Alan seems to find fault in everything I do.*
[Harriet] *I know, Tom. He does mean well, though, in his own way. He's just a perfectionist. Let me know if I can help any more.*

*

October

[Mehak] *Alan still isn't replying to my e-mails.*
[Harriet] *Um, sorry. Any idea why?*
[Mehak] *Well, he did ask me out. I said no, obviously, and I had to think of a reason. So I invented a jealous boyfriend …*
[Harriet] *I like the 'obviously'!*
[Mehak] *Ha ha. Yes, indeed. But, seriously, can you do something? I need my contracts sorted.*
[Harriet] *I'll see what I can do.*

*

Be careful what you wish for.

I'd wished for access to Harriet's e-mail account, but by lunchtime I was half-wishing I hadn't. I was remembering a time in my teens, after yet another row with my parents, when I'd crept down the stairs at home in order to listen to what they were saying about me. I could only hear fragments of their conversation behind the closed kitchen door, but there was no doubt about their anger, frustration and despair. They must have heard me make a sound because suddenly the door was thrown open and my mother snapped at me, 'Eavesdroppers hear no good of themselves.'

Today, I'd been excited when IT e-mailed me a temporary password which allowed me into Harriet's e-mails and her personal work documents. Lewis must have authorised this, but typically he didn't have the courtesy to tell me himself. I needed access to catch up on Harriet's unfinished work matters and to enable me either to complete them myself or to pass them on to Richard or Tom. However, I wouldn't be human if I hadn't first had a general nosey around. I noticed Harriet had created some file notes and e-mail folders relating specifically to the matters I'd asked her to investigate. But before looking at these, I couldn't resist searching her e-mails for references to myself, and for conversations between her and Lewis, and her and Hugh, round about the time when I believed her affairs with these two shits had started, paying particular attention to anything headed 'personal' or 'private'.

I couldn't tell you which I found the more upsetting: Harriet's innuendo-laden banter with Lewis and Hugh, or the derogatory comments made about me by people I'd ended up working with. Given that most people were nowadays wary of what they wrote in e-mails sent from their work accounts, I cringed at the thought of what they must have been saying about me face-to-face. With Lewis and Hugh, there came a point where their conversations with Harriet had abruptly become entirely professional. I assumed that this was when their affairs with her had started and that they'd subsequently used their mobile phones to exchange messages with her in complete privacy.

I was curious about what had happened to Harriet's phone and whether – assuming it had survived the hours in the water – there was some way I could gain access to it. Like a child with a scab, I knew that if I had the opportunity, I wouldn't be able to resist reading all of Harriet's personal phone messages, regardless of the hurt that they might cause me.

The childish side of me wanted to go up to each of the people who'd been saying unpleasant things about me and bang their heads on their desks until they begged for forgiveness. I couldn't actually do that, but I spent the lunch hour alone at my pod as usual, mulling over ways in which I could get my own back. It wasn't right that people could be so horrible and not have to face any consequences.

29

By the next day, Friday, I'd concluded there was no mileage in being mean back to the people who'd been mean to me. First, it was all a bit schoolboyish, and I felt I should rise above that sort of thing. Second, I had an uneasy feeling that it would just confirm the prejudices that these people had about me.

A better course of action was to find out myself if any of them had either keyed Harriet's car or been the mysterious watcher down by the riverside. I couldn't risk going to the police with my knowledge at this stage, but if I could first put someone else in the frame, the police would then have no reason to investigate me. And if the police thought someone else at the University had been responsible for the things that had happened, I would get some pleasure from watching them dragging people in for questioning and generally turning the place upside down.

In the meantime, I had to take care not to neglect my legal work. I didn't want to give anyone a chance to jump down my throat.

Accordingly, I began by reviewing the set of completion documents that Jeff had e-mailed over for the Landlord Relax spin-out. If anyone had been naïve enough to think that Doveley's had drafted them from scratch, they would have been impressed by the sheer amount of paperwork. But I recognised the format and most of the wording from umpteen similar transactions for which I'd provided commercial law support when at the firm. All the documents were based on precedents: either the firm's own, or those produced by one of the commercial subscription services staffed by burnt-out lawyers who could no longer hack it in private practice.

After spending most of the morning going through the documents, I sent a reply to Jeff, copying in Amanda, saying that they looked fine from a legal perspective and noting that, fortunately, he didn't seem to have had to make many changes to his precedents. I knew that would piss him off, as it would mean that he would be limited as to what he could charge. But for me, pissing off Jeff was always the icing on any cake. I apologised for the slight delay in my response but said that the death of Harriet – which, I added, he may have heard of – had been a shock to my team and was causing the reallocation of work. I made no mention of the fact that I knew he'd spent the evening of Harriet's death with her. Jeff replied quickly, saying that he'd heard the sad news about Harriet and offering his deepest sympathies to everyone at the University who had known her.

You tosser, I thought.

Now that I'd bought myself some breathing space, I decided to try to find out if Richard had had any involvement in what happened to Harriet. He and Tom had been mostly avoiding my eye all day, getting on with, or at least pretending to get on with, their work. But Richard had now e-mailed me a document he'd been drafting from Harriet's reallocated workload: a fairly standard contract under which the University was hiring out some valuable computer equipment for use by a local charity. After reviewing the contract, I asked him to come round the pod to go through it with me. I winced as he sat down in Harriet's chair and wheeled it closer to mine, as it brought back memories of all the mornings she'd done that to me. He stank slightly of cigarette smoke, and an image came to my mind of a weasel in the wild with a cigarette in its mouth as it watched the world go by.

'It's pretty good,' I said. The unspoken words 'for once' hung in the air between us. 'The only thing you need to check is the insurance position. Does the University's insurance cover us for everything that could go wrong, including damage to the equipment or damage of any kind caused by the equipment? If not, or if there are any gaps, you'll need to include a provision setting out what extra insurance of their own the charity will need to take out to cover us. Once you've done this, and made any necessary amendments to the contract, we should be good to go.'

Richard nodded. I wasn't asking him to kiss my arse, but he might have shown some gratitude for the help I was giving. 'Do you want to see my amendments before I send the contract out?' he asked. As usual, he was looking to cover his own backside.

'Yes, run them past me, please.' If I'd said it wasn't necessary to do so, I knew he would have made a file note to that effect just in case something later went wrong and he needed to find someone to blame. 'By the way, Richard,' I went on. 'Thanks again for taking on some of Harriet's work. I know you're busy, so it's very much appreciated.'

He had taken it on reluctantly, of course, but there was a method in my madness.

He shrugged. 'I'd known her a while. She'd been good to me.'

The implication, not lost on me, was that I hadn't been good to him. Why was I always surrounded by pricks? First at Doveley's and now here at the University. People just didn't appreciate what I was trying to do for them.

'I'm still in shock,' I said, gearing myself up for what I was really wanting to ask. 'I can't believe what she must have been going through that Monday night when I was warm and dry in my house. You must feel the same, whatever you were doing?'

'I was playing online chess until the small hours,' he said. 'Like I do most evenings since my wife left me. It helps take my mind off things.'

No one had bothered to tell me he'd split up with his wife, but he was such a misery that I can't say I was surprised. However, if he was telling the truth, and a police search of his online chess account could prove it either way, he couldn't have been the person following me and Harriet on Monday.

'It's so sad that it happened just after her car was keyed,' I replied. 'Did you hear about that?'

His eyes widened. 'No, I knew nothing. Did they catch whoever did it? I always thought the car park here was safe.'

'No CCTV, apparently,' I said. 'And no, she had no idea who was responsible, but it's a pretty crappy thing to do under any circumstances. It must still have been weighing heavily on her mind the night she died. I can't believe …' I tailed off as I noticed I was about to repeat myself.

'Is there anything else I can do?'

'No, that's fine for now, thanks.'

*

'Have you finalised Professor Fuller's agreement yet, Alan?'

This was Deborah, puffing as if she'd galloped a mile across Newmarket Heath rather than walked the few steps from her office to my pod. I wondered if she'd ever asked her hairdresser to do her a style which would make her look less equine.

'My draft is with him for review,' I said. 'He needs to check my description of the technology even though the legal wording is down to me.'

I could tell she'd psyched herself up to have a go at me. Now she had to find a graceful way of backing down. 'I'm pleased to hear it,' she said. 'Let me know if you need any help in getting it over the line.'

My plan for the weekend included looking into what Harriet had found out about the relationship between Simon Fuller and Ian Davey. And I'd now bought myself enough time to do that.

*

'I don't know if you had to OK me getting access to Harriet's e-mails,' I said. 'But if you did, then thank you.'

I'd knocked on Lewis's open door and waited for him to lift his head from his computer before saying anything. He would have seen me approaching through the glass wall of his office, but I had to go through this ridiculous rigmarole as if to underline that he was the boss and I was the underling. He ran his wet tongue around his lips before speaking. I realised I disliked him almost as much as I did Jeff Parker.

'No need to thank me, Alan. It was necessary. You were her line manager, after all.'

I adopted the same approach as I had with Richard. 'I still can't believe what happened,' I said. 'The hardest bit is knowing that I was safe, warm and dry at home at the very time she was drowning. I don't know what you were doing, Lewis, but I guess you probably feel the same?'

'Ruth and I had an early night,' he replied dismissively, as if he believed I was showing an excessive interest in his private life.

As with Richard, if this was true, then Lewis could also be ruled out as the secret watcher.

*

After lunch at my desk, I left Senate House and headed into the centre of campus and the Student Centre. I went through the entrance for back-office staff, showed my pass, and once I was in the main, brightly lit office area I walked over to the same desk from where I'd previously collected my copy of the UCAS Adviser Guide.

'Hello again, Ruth,' I said. 'I was just passing, so I thought I might as well pop in rather than send you an e-mail. I've been studying the copy of the Guide which I picked up from you a couple of weeks ago. Do you know if UCAS are going to make any changes next year in their offer letters to students?'

'I don't have a clue, I'm afraid,' she said. 'Why do you ask?'

I had my answer ready from my last visit. 'I'm reviewing the University's terms and conditions for students. I want to be sure that anything we put in our terms and conditions is consistent with what UCAS tell students.'

I saw a flash of understanding and recognition in her eyes. 'You must be the Alan Gadd who works with Lewis? I didn't make the connection before. I do apologise.'

Although she wasn't particularly attractive, Ruth seemed to

have a pleasant enough personality. I couldn't remember the last time I'd heard Lewis utter a genuine apology for anything.

'No need to apologise,' I said. 'If anything, I owe you an apology for not introducing myself the last time I was here. With hindsight, it was rather rude of me.'

I didn't really think I'd been rude. But I had sympathy for anyone on whom Lewis had done the dirty. How could she bear to let that slimy toad touch her after she had found out what he'd been up to with Harriet?

'No need for an apology from you either,' she said with a smile. 'You must have worked closely with Harriet, the girl who died? It was all very sad.'

The woman was either a liar or a saint. After I'd sent her my anonymous e-mail, I'd seen her hiss the word 'bitch' at Harriet when she came up to the second floor to have it out with Lewis. She wouldn't be human if she hadn't derived some inner pleasure from what had subsequently happened to Harriet. She would have seen me then too, of course, but I wasn't surprised that she hadn't recognised me today until I'd prompted her. But now that she knew who I was, she would guess that I must have at least an inkling of what had gone on between Harriet and Lewis.

'It was a blow to us all,' I said. 'I hadn't known Harriet long, but I like to think I'd got to know her well.' I paused and there was the customary polite silence for a few seconds while we both made a show of remembering the dead. 'What's made it worse,' I went on, 'is that I was at home, safe and warm and comfortable, at the time she died. It makes me feel so useless. I guess Lewis must feel the same?'

For the first time, there was a flicker of bitterness on her face. She said, 'I don't really know how Lewis feels, to be honest.'

'But I assume he was with you when it happened?'

'Well, he certainly wasn't with Harriet,' she replied dryly.

That sounded definite enough, and I wasn't going to pry into their bedroom arrangements. I said, 'It was such a shame for Harriet, too, about her car being keyed before she died. She was very upset. She couldn't understand who would want to do something like that.'

I had Ruth down as a typical good-natured, plump woman: the type who is not unamenable to attention from men for the simple reason that she rarely gets it. I was startled, therefore, by her reaction.

'Just what are you getting at, Alan?' she snapped.

'Sorry?'

'About Harriet's car being keyed. About her not understanding who did it. I'm not stupid. I know exactly where you're going with this. How bloody dare you suggest I would do something like that. Even to a bitch like her.'

'No, I didn't mean to suggest that,' I protested. 'All I was saying was—'

'Alan, please, just go. And don't come back.'

Ruth's voice was raised and she seemed not to care who heard her. Fortunately, she was alone at her pod, but I could see faces looking at us from other pods. I turned on my heels and left.

*

'Alan, what the hell were you thinking of?'

This was Lewis. Ruth must have got on the phone to him as soon as I'd left the Student Centre. For once, he hadn't summoned me to his office. Instead, as soon as I sat down at my pod, with Richard and Tom opposite, he shot out of his office and bent his face to mine. His voice was low, but I could almost physically feel the anger in it. His breath stank of coffee.

I swallowed. 'I'm sorry, Lewis,' I said, 'but Ruth must have misunderstood. I only mentioned in passing that Harriet's car was keyed shortly before she died. Ruth thought I was accusing her. I wasn't, I promise.'

I knew this was pathetic even as I said it. If I'd had more courage, I might have asked Lewis why he'd thought it appropriate to conduct an affair with a work subordinate when he was married; or even if he'd reported his own wife to

HR for publicly calling the work subordinate a 'bitch'. But my insides tied themselves in a knot even at the thought of saying something like this. I always shied away from this type of confrontation; I relied on getting even in other ways.

I could tell that Lewis was loath to let it go, but he knew we were in a very public environment. I could see him almost physically force self-restraint upon himself. 'We'll talk about it another time, Alan,' he said in a vicious undertone. Then he went back into his office.

I looked cautiously over at Richard and Tom. They both had their heads down, avoiding meeting my eyes. They must have heard the row, though, even if they couldn't make out every word. I fancied I saw a smirk on Richard's face. I felt like I wanted to cry.

For the next couple of hours, I buried myself in work that I had to do before going home for the weekend. I drafted a term sheet for a discussion which the School of Engineering (for once not Simon Fuller) was having with another university regarding a collaborative project overseas. I gave some intellectual property advice to the School of Performing and Creative Arts about the ownership of copyright in designs created by students as part of a commercially sponsored project. And I checked some releases which Tom had cobbled together for the same School, to allow the inclusion of various photographs in an illustrated book they were publishing about the portrayal of teenage clothing in the movies.

I deliberately didn't make eye contact with anyone near me when they left at the end of the day. Richard and Tom got up together and left quietly at 5 p.m. without even a 'Goodnight'. Lewis left a few minutes later. One by one, like aircraft taking off in turn, all the pro-vice-chancellors also left over the next twenty minutes, all ostentatiously carrying some kind of official-looking bag to give the impression that they were only pausing their work for an hour or so until they got back to their home offices, rather than knocking off for the entire weekend. All the other teams – finance, procurement, insurance and so on – had left on time, as they usually did, none of them even pretending to be taking work home; and by 5.30 p.m. I was the only person left on the second floor. I left for home at about 6.30 p.m., saying my usual goodbye to the security officer at the front desk without our eyes meeting.

I had a lot to do over the weekend, and I wanted to be fresh for the task.

30

On Saturday mornings, if the weather was pleasant, I liked to go into Ely. The town centre would usually be fairly busy, but in a relaxed, unhurried way. I would see people greeting familiar faces, and children waving at other children they recognised from school or an after-school club. It was at times like this that I ached to be part of a similar family unit: with a wife to manage the relationship with other families, and children to be the main reason for meeting up, with me dipping in and out whenever I wanted.

Today, just after 9.30 a.m., I parked as usual on the far side of the main car park in the centre of town, where there were still a few spaces which hadn't been nabbed by early morning shoppers. My normal practice was then to wander down the pedestrian walkway, sometimes stopping at the library on the way, and to emerge onto the market square where I could browse the stalls and sometimes grab a coffee to enjoy in the open air. Although there was the inevitable surfeit of charity shops and estate agents, the town centre of Ely was better than most. I say 'town', but Ely is actually a city, one of the smallest in England, by virtue of its beautiful medieval cathedral which dominates the centre – a landmark which I enjoyed looking out for when driving back to Ely from my tennis club.

Most Saturdays, I ended up in the town's large independent bookshop, where the staff knew me as a regular customer. Although I bought a lot of my books on my Kindle, I still enjoyed the feel and smell of a hard copy book, and there was nothing quite like a new book on true crime, ideally with lots of revealing photographs, to excite my interest. There was a café near the bookshop, where sometimes I would first enjoy a late breakfast fry-up, being careful to wash my hands properly before crossing the road to handle the books.

Today, though, I had a particular purpose in mind. The upmarket shop I was heading towards was within easy walking distance of the market square. I knew it by sight even though I'd never had a reason to go inside. As I rehearsed what I was going to say, I could feel the pounding of my heart. My mind flashed back to a time, while I was a wet-behind-the-ears trainee solicitor in the North, when I'd been sent to do a so-called trap purchase at a shop which was suspected of selling counterfeit goods bearing the trade mark of one of the firm's major clients. The partner in charge of the matter had told me to remove all identifying material from my pockets in case I was caught and interrogated. I had nervously complied and had sweated buckets during the purchase. It was only later, after hearing smothered laughter in one of the firm's kitchens, that I realised he'd been teasing me to see how gullible I was.

I breathed a sigh of relief when I went into the shop and saw the man on his own behind the counter. I recognised him straightaway from the photograph on his LinkedIn profile. He was probably in his early fifties and had a Fens-boy-made-good look about him. He smiled a shopkeeper's standard welcome to a potential new customer.

'Good morning,' I said. 'You must be Trevor, Harriet Wells's landlord?'

I was never quite sure what books mean when they refer to someone having a guilty look, but there was nothing on Trevor's face to suggest he was worried about anything.

'Correct,' he said. 'It's all very sad. And you are?'

'I'm Alan Gadd. I was Harriet's colleague and friend. I'm helping her friends and family to, er, deal with things.'

'That's kind of you. And what can I do?'

The tone of his question was matter-of-fact. His mind was probably already working out how best to replace Harriet.

Would he try to find another housemate for Kat himself, or would he ask her to choose someone suitable – perhaps her boyfriend?

'I'm sure it's got nothing to do with what happened,' I said. 'However, as part of tidying things up, I noticed that the previous gas safety certificate for the property seemed to have been retrospectively altered. It said the gas hob in the kitchen had been checked and was safe for use, whereas I don't actually think it had been checked. Harriet had been having headaches which she thought might have been caused by a gas leak. I believe she mentioned this to you.'

Trevor gave me a wary look. 'I'm not a gas man,' he said. 'I leave that sort of thing to my tradies. Anyway, everything is safe. Harriet and Kat had a gas safety certificate to say so.'

'My point,' I said, 'is to do with the previous check and the previous gas safety certificate. I'm not a doctor, of course, but it's not impossible that if Harriet's senses were affected by a gas leak, she might have lost her balance and fallen into the water, with the tragic consequences that followed.'

I was pleased with this last suggestion, which I had carefully prepared. I could see Trevor trying to work out what my angle was. He looked the sort of man who wouldn't put himself out for anyone else unless there was something in it for him. I wondered if he was expecting me to ask him for a bribe in return for my silence, or if he was thinking he should offer me one himself.

'I don't know what you're getting at,' he said eventually. 'I understand from Kat that Harriet had a lot to drink that night. That must be why she fell into the river. As I told you, my engineer tested everything a fair time before Harriet died. So even if there had been a fault – which I don't believe there was – there couldn't be a connection with her death.'

'I assume you didn't see her then on the night she died?' This was my rehearsed rapier thrust.

Trevor, however, looked startled rather than guilty. 'I didn't see her again after the last time she came in here,' he said. 'That must have been a week or so before she died. I don't live in Ely any more. The shop's here, and my properties are here, but we live in Downham Market now. Unless I have business in Ely, I never come over. And it happened last Monday, I believe?'

'That's right, sometime during the night.'

'Well, last Monday I was home all night with the wife and the girls.'

On the face of it, that seemed conclusive. Unless he was lying – and only the police could check that – Trevor wasn't the person who'd been following me and Harriet. I could, in the right circumstances, imagine Trevor pushing someone into the water if he felt it was necessary to protect his own livelihood. But he looked a no-nonsense type: certainly not the kind of person to creep around spying on Harriet and keying her car, even if he knew where to find it on the University campus.

However, I didn't feel he should walk away unscathed. I said, 'You may be right in saying there's no connection between the gas safety issue and Harriet's accident. But I'll still have to tell the relevant authorities. I'm a solicitor, used to checking documents, and it seemed pretty clear to me that Harriet and Kat's previous gas safety certificate had been altered. And even if that had no bearing on what subsequently happened, it's still a serious matter.'

Trevor looked at me as if he was weighing up the pros and cons of how he would most like to respond. It occurred to me he was the sort of semi-educated man who might prefer to argue with his fists rather than with his tongue. I took a precautionary step backwards.

'Were you shagging Harriet, then?' he asked. 'Or were you just wishing you could shag her?'

I clenched my fists by my side. I wasn't going to waste my time explaining to this oaf the nature of my relationship with Harriet. No doubt, if he ever had a Saturday girl to help him in his shop, he would spend the whole time leering at her cleavage and making innuendo-laden remarks. He was judging me by his own pathetic standards.

'I'm only doing my duty,' I said. 'Making sure the powers that be have all the facts.'

For a couple of seconds, we glared at each other, although I kept half an eye on both of his hands in case they suddenly balled into fists and headed in my direction.

Then the door behind me opened and a middle-aged woman, looking like a typical potato farmer's wife, walked smiling into the shop. 'Trevor,' she said in a posh Fens accent, 'how lovely to see you again. I'm hoping that you may have just what I need ...'

I took advantage of the opportunity to turn my back on Trevor and exit the shop. Even he wouldn't throw a punch at the back of my head in full view of a regular customer. Once I got outside, I noticed I was trembling. But I was also feeling a degree of satisfaction; I evidently still had some of the investigatory skills that I'd shown in the aftermath of Helen's death during my time at Doveley's. I went home after my customary trip to the bookshop, looking forward to what I had planned for that afternoon.

31

Harriet: e-mails with Simon Fuller

Hi Simon

Alan's away this week (teaching children how to play tennis, ha ha!).

He's nearly finished drafting the agreement with Ian Davey's company. Can I just check that you've given him all the information he asked for? That way, I'm sure he'll be able to put the final touches to the agreement just as soon as he gets back.

Btw, I got tagged into some photos that Ian Davey took in Cyprus. Not a clue why, must be those crazy algorithms!!! Lovely villa, I'm very envious. I've been thinking of Cyprus for my next holiday. Forgive me for being cheeky, but did Ian tell you how much the villa cost to hire?

Best
Harriet

*

Hi Harriet

That's fine, thank you. Alan has all he needs, so I look forward to receiving the agreement early next week.

Sorry, no idea re the villa. I didn't even know Ian had gone to Cyprus.

Kind regards
Simon

Hi Simon

I'll crack the whip as soon as Alan gets back!

No worries re the villa. Funnily enough, I did think I'd seen you in one of Ian's photos, but I must have had too much to drink that night, ha ha ha!

Best
Harriet

Harriet: file notes to self (Re: Simon Fuller/Ian Davey)

Photograph of Simon Fuller at Ian Davey's villa in Cyprus subsequently deleted from Facebook. Good job I'd taken a screenshot! It was definitely him.

Spoke to Simon's PA. General chit-chat. Said I was thinking of going to Cyprus next summer. She said I should speak to Simon as he went there this summer. Hmmm!

Did some online searches into Ian Davey's company. Found some interesting gossip on an obscure forum for investors. Whispers of the company being bought for A LOT of money. The new wearable technology apparently making all the difference to the price. Due to call at School of Engineering tomorrow, so maybe try to arrange an accidental bump into Simon and drop some hints about what I've seen on the forum? Looks like the University's technology is worth A LOT more than what Ian's company is paying for it. All very intriguing ... Alan is obviously itching for there to be something dodgy going on, and it seems he may be right!

Harriet: file notes to self (Re: Amanda Middleton/Landlord Relax)

Discovered via LinkedIn that Amanda was at the same university at the same time as the two Landlord Relax founders. Different courses and a big university, but still! Need to find out if they all knew each other there.

Ta-da! Joined various online alumni groups from the university, using made-up details. Was worried they might check my details against their list of graduates, but evidently not. Saw that Amanda and the two founders all attended the same 'Year of X' reunion dinner last autumn. Got a list of attendees and did some Facebook/SM digging. Found a photo of Amanda at a table with the two founders on either side of her!!!

Was brave today! Ended up walking back to Senate House with Amanda after a meeting. Said a friend had mentioned seeing her and the two founders at the reunion dinner. Said it must be great for her that the two friends were doing so well. Then quickly changed the subject so it looked like I wasn't reading any significance into it. Amanda went a bit quiet though! Alan will be delighted if there is something here as well!!

*

Harriet: file notes to self (Re: procurement of Doveley's)

Looked into whether procurement rules were followed re the appointment of Doveley's as University solicitors. Alan thinks they weren't, or perhaps (ha ha!) he hopes they weren't. He doesn't seem to like Doveley's or in particular Jeff Parker! I'd love to know the real reason he left the firm. Bet there was a woman involved somewhere. Probably one who turned him down!! But all seems above board. There was some wining and dining of Amanda and Lewis, but this was declared and I don't think anyone seriously expects Doveley's to have done anything underhand. I'll need to find the right time to tell Alan, though. He is going to be so disappointed!!!

*

I'd spent the whole of the Saturday afternoon going through Harriet's e-mails and file notes, and I suppose I should have been pleased with what she'd uncovered. I'd been right; there was something fishy about both the Landlord Relax spin-out and the sale of the wearable technology to Ian Davey's company. No definite proof of wrongdoing in either case, but enough prima facie evidence to justify further investigation.

What rankled, however, were some of the remarks that Harriet had made about me. Anyone reading her file notes would have got the impression that she thought I was some kind of obsessive, trying to settle old scores by uncovering wrongdoing by people I'd fallen out with. There was no recognition that I was doing my professional duty as a solicitor and University employee. I was particularly annoyed by what she said about my reason for leaving Doveley's. I'd never talked to her about Helen's death, or its aftermath, even though I could have done so in a way which showed me in a very good light indeed. There can't be many solicitors in Cambridge who have flushed out and captured a dangerous killer. I found it unbelievable, and upsetting, that Harriet could think I left Doveley's because a woman rejected me. All right, in the literal sense, Helen had rejected me, and if she hadn't rejected me, then I would probably still be at the firm. But Harriet's wording made it look like I was a man who would take it personally if a woman chose not to go out with me.

I had done such a lot for Harriet and there was almost nothing that I wouldn't have done for her. So I don't mind admitting that I now felt somewhat betrayed. And if she was prepared to put these kinds of things in writing on a work computer, what might she have said about me in private after a few drinks? What, God forbid, might she even have said to Jeff Parker, and what might he have told her in return?

No good deed goes unpunished; how true that saying was. Nevertheless, I would rise above this, and I would try my hardest to find out how and why Harriet died. And if that meant pissing off any or all of Amanda, Deborah, Lewis, Ruth, Richard, Hugh, Mehak, Simon, or even bloody Jeff 'Nosey' Parker ... well, that would just be a necessary consequence of my having done my duty.

32

I hadn't been back to my tennis club since the business over the half-term junior camp.

Other members must have known what had happened, but no one had bothered to message me to express their sympathy for how I'd been treated by Tony. I noticed on the club's Facebook pages that he'd posted some photographs from the camp showing the usual happy, smiling faces of children, but I didn't appear in any of those taken on the first day when I was there. Examining the photographs closely, it looked like I'd been airbrushed out of some of them.

Since then, Tony had been busy promoting his coaching services on Facebook, often posting photographs of him alongside his female clients, most of whom were on the wrong side of middle age judging by their leathery faces. None of these women were actually much good at tennis and – call me cynical – I doubted that many of them would have paid for lessons with Tony if he wasn't so young and athletic-looking. I'd mulled over creating a fake Facebook account so that I could post some anonymous comments, hinting at improper behaviour by Tony, but after the fall-out from my anonymous e-mail to Ruth I concluded that discretion was the better part of valour.

For some time after waking up on Sunday morning, I toyed with the idea of going down to the club's social tennis session. I wouldn't have to ask anyone for a game because pairings were determined by a random draw every thirty minutes. I hadn't forgotten how I'd been cold-shouldered after the training session for men's team players. But in the end, I decided not to go. I couldn't honestly say there was a single member who I thought would be pleased to see me, and I did still have some pride.

Instead, I spent the morning doing household jobs, and then I lay on my sofa browsing through social media videos and stroking my cat as she purred away on my chest. She wasn't a particularly intelligent creature, but she always seemed content to have me around, and for that I was grateful. Subconsciously, I guess, I was putting off when I'd have to make plans for what I was going to investigate at work next week.

For that reason, it was a relief when my mobile phone rang. Even if it was a scam caller, I could have some fun playing them along for a few minutes. But my relief evaporated the moment I saw who was calling.

'Alan, mate, how are you doing? Sorry to phone you on a Sunday, but it wouldn't have felt right to phone you at work. It was terrible news about Harriet. I just wanted to check that you are OK?'

'Hello, Jeff,' I said. 'Yes, I'm OK, thank you. It's kind of you to call.'

We'd swapped personal mobile numbers earlier in the year, after the death of Helen, when Jeff had invited me to contact him if I ever wanted to talk. It was typical of the insensitivity of the man that he'd thought I might want to use his shoulder to cry on, especially when he had to bear a share of the responsibility for what had happened to her. Now here he was again – the man who'd spent the last night of Harriet's life hoping to get inside her knickers. Did he ever stop to think, even for a moment, what effect his behaviour had on me?

'No problem at all,' he said. 'I thought of you immediately because you must have got to know Harriet pretty well during your time at the University.'

Yes, I had. But not in the same way he had. I'd never had a romantic meal out with Harriet. She'd almost certainly never complained to anyone about my failure to make a move on her.

I said, 'Yes, I got to know her well, thank you. She was very bright. She'd have made a good solicitor.'

'She spoke highly of you, Alan. She was glad to have you as her line manager.'

But not glad enough, I thought, to want to move our relationship to another level. 'How did you hear about what happened?' I asked. I noticed how we were both avoiding using the words 'dead' or 'death'.

'I had a phone call on Tuesday morning. From Kat, Harriet's housemate.'

I guessed Jeff didn't know how much I knew about him and Harriet. Harriet had told me she was meeting him on Monday evening, but I had no inkling of whether she'd told Jeff that she'd told me. And if she hadn't told him, then he might, understandably, not want to mention that they'd been on a date.

I said, 'I'm aware you were meeting Harriet for a meal on Monday evening. She confided in me, as she often did. So presumably Kat knew who you were and how to contact you?'

'Sort of. She knew my first name and that I worked at Doveley's. She phoned the switchboard on Tuesday morning and ended up getting put through to me. God, you've no idea what a shock it was to me.'

Actually, I had. I hadn't forgotten Lucy describing how white Jeff's face went earlier that year when he read Sam Snape's e-mail notifying the firm about Helen's death. Not, of course, that Jeff's affection for Helen had prevented him from sticking his tongue down Lucy's throat when she was still my bloody trainee. I wanted to ask Jeff if he'd told Harriet about everything that happened at Doveley's, but I didn't have the balls.

I said, 'I suppose you've spoken to the police? About what you knew of Harriet's whereabouts that night?'

I had to be careful. I daren't let on that I'd been watching Jeff and Harriet that Monday night. It would make me look like a stalker. But Jeff knew that I knew what his reputation with women was like, so I wasn't going to make a fool of myself by appearing to presume that they'd kissed each other chastely good night and gone their separate ways. A man like Jeff Parker would take it for granted that a romantic meal with a woman would probably end with them spending the night together. I tried to imagine how he must have felt when, for whatever reason, Harriet had indicated that wasn't going to happen. I bloody well hoped he'd been pissed off.

'Yes,' he said, 'I spoke to P.C. Dawn Smith. The same officer who came to see us at Doveley's earlier this year. I'd been at a client's offices on the Monday afternoon, over your neck of the woods. Funnily enough, the client's doing a deal with the University at the moment, but we're conflicted so wouldn't be able to act for either side. The client knew Harriet, as it happens. Her name came up when I was leaving to meet her. Anyway, Harriet and I said our goodnights after our meal, as she'd promised to drop in on a friend who owns a narrowboat nearby. She wouldn't let me walk her along the bank as far as her friend's boat, although I've since found out that I could have gone that way back to the car park just as easily. Perhaps she wanted a few minutes on her own before meeting her friend. In any event, I was home and in bed within the hour. I know the police have to check everything in these circumstances, so I made it easy for Dawn by volunteering that my apartment block has CCTV everywhere so they could confirm what time I got home.'

And no doubt 'Dawn' took it all on trust, I thought. 'It sounds like Harriet had drunk too much,' I said. 'I suppose you were pouring drink down her throat all evening?'

There was a long silence which I deliberately didn't break.

Then Jeff said, 'Alan, I know we've had our differences. But Harriet and I went out for a meal and a bit of a laugh, that's all. Remember that I was driving, so I had a pint at the pub and then we shared a bottle of white at the restaurant. Probably more than I should have had, to be honest, but Harriet drank no more than me. So, yes, she was a bit merry, but she certainly wasn't drunk when we said our goodbyes.' There was a brief silence before he went on. 'My guess is that she had a skinful afterwards with her friend. You know what these boaties can be like. And it was only a short walk home for her afterwards. Or, at least, it would have been if ...'

To my surprise, I heard a break in his voice.

'I'm sorry,' I said. For once, even if only momentarily, I meant it. I hadn't seriously believed that Jeff had anything to do with Harriet's death. I just needed someone to blame. And Jeff was the easy target: a man I despised, even though there were times – in my darkest moments – when I admitted to myself that in some ways I wished I was more like him. He had women throwing himself at him. He never seemed to get stressed at work. He found life so easy, basically.

'No worries, Alan,' he said. 'I know you're finding it tough. I was thinking about you when we e-mailed each other about Landlord Relax. I wish I hadn't left it until the weekend to call you. I apologise, mate.'

Jeff had given me the opening I was looking for, so I decided to sound conciliatory. 'That's OK,' I replied. 'As I said in my e-mail, your paperwork is fine. I'm still puzzled, though, as to why the University is so keen on this investment. It's hardly the world's most innovative product. There's also the question of how the founders – who are supposed to be full-time academics – are going to find the time to support the platform. I don't understand why the University doesn't just license the software to a business which has the experience of supporting this sort of thing. That way, the University gets a guaranteed revenue stream without the financial risk.'

Again, there was a silence. I had the impression that Jeff knew what he wanted to say but was working out the best way to say it.

'Off the record,' he said presently, 'I was a bit surprised by them going down the spin-out route. I've worked on a lot of these types of investments for universities. If I was being asked to give my opinion on the best route to market for this particular product, I'd have suggested the licensing model too. But I've not been asked for an opinion. My instructions were simply to implement it.' There was another pause. 'What you've got to remember,' he went on, 'is that Doveley's have waited a long time to get this account. You don't have a big in-house legal team, so if only half of the University's investment projects take off, there will still be lots of work for us. I wouldn't get thanked by anyone at Doveley's if I were to give, unasked, a second opinion on a decision that the University has already made. If anyone legal is going to do that, it has to be you as the in-house lawyer. But then you've got to think of your position too, Alan. Piss them off and they can make life very difficult for you. You're not an academic, doing ground-breaking research that is going to bring in millions. You're a cost centre – a here today, gone tomorrow lawyer.'

That was quite a speech from Jeff. I remembered the time, back at Doveley's in the aftermath of Helen's death, when he'd opened up to me about the hurt he was experiencing, and I'd pondered for a short time whether perhaps he wasn't a complete shit. For a few seconds, I had the same thoughts again. There was no benefit to him personally in saying he shared my reservations about the spin-out model, and if I'd been sharp enough to record this conversation (I was kicking myself already for not having done so) I might even have been able to use his admission as leverage over him in the future.

After we ended our conversation shortly afterwards, I was too agitated to settle down to anything serious. I had clear evidence now that Amanda was doing something she shouldn't, most probably as some kind of favour to the two men with whom she'd been at university and with whom she was apparently still friends. Or maybe more than just friends. Even someone as hard-nosed and work-focused as Amanda must have sexual interests. And Amanda had known that Harriet had found all this out. Even so, why would Amanda choose to follow Harriet that night down by the riverside? And perhaps even more critical, how would she have known that Harriet was going to be down there in the first place? She and Harriet were hardly bosom pals.

After a while, I tried to put myself in Amanda's position. She might be the Secretary and Registrar, but she must also have human emotions and failings. Imagine that she'd done something wrong. And imagine that Harriet had let her know she knew, on their walk back together to Senate House while I was away. Amanda would have been worried. It was the kind of thing she could lose her job over. Then imagine that Amanda heard Harriet had a date down by the riverside with one of the University's solicitors. Harriet was quite open about things like that, and she could easily have mentioned it to someone who then mentioned it to someone else, and so on. Amanda might have been worried that Harriet would tell Jeff, a solicitor, what she'd found out, and that he might tell her how wrong it was.

So I could see how Amanda might have ended up down by the riverside that Monday night. If I'd been in Amanda's shoes, I would undoubtedly have been down there.

And then, imagine Amanda seeing a very drunken Harriet, on her own, tottering across the plank between the boat and the riverbank. Had she confronted Harriet and had there been a row, leading to a terrible accident, with Amanda then making herself scarce through fear of being blamed? Or had Amanda even – and I hardly dared think it – been tempted just for a moment to give Harriet a push, to silence her for ever?

33

Throughout my time at the University, I'd never felt entirely comfortable going down to see people on the first floor of Senate House. Part of this was because I didn't have a high opinion of most of those who worked there. But the main reason was undoubtedly because of the associations with Hugh.

Hugh had been going out with Harriet when I started at the University, and until I helped her to realise that he wasn't suitable for her, I had to watch her scamper up and down the staircase between the two floors like a teenager with her first boyfriend. And I had to put up with him smirking around Senate House like a lad who's shagged his best mate's mother. After Harriet broke things off with him, I was always slightly wary as to what he might say or do to me. I wasn't sure if she'd relayed to him the things I'd said about him.

I'd enjoyed my early morning coffees with Mehak on the first floor, but these had usually been before anyone else was around. Once I realised that she'd been taking advantage of me, to get her International work prioritised, I was even more reluctant to go down there in case she was secretly laughing at me.

When, therefore, on Monday morning I left the comparative quiet of the second floor to go to see Hugh, I'm not embarrassed to admit that I was nervous. On the last occasion I'd braved him in his 'lair', as he termed it in his nauseating e-mail to Harriet, he'd dropped the bombshell that she'd previously been involved with Lewis – a revelation that I was still struggling to come to terms with.

As usual, Hugh was at his pod in the far corner with the rest of his cabal. None of them, as far as I could see, was actually doing any work. The two men with their backs to me were together peering at one of their phones, no doubt watching some scurrilous video on social media. The third man, who sat next to Hugh facing the door, was talking across the aisle to one of the business development managers on another pod, most likely discussing anything other than business development. And Hugh himself was lounging back magnificently in his chair, his hair as carefully tousled as ever and the top two buttons of his open-necked shirt undone. He looked like a bloody male model in the smart casual pages of an upmarket menswear catalogue. Why women fell for those superficial attractions, I would never understand. He clearly wasn't having sleepless nights over Harriet. He clocked me while I was still some distance from him, but his face gave nothing away as I approached.

I hadn't spoken to Hugh since Harriet's death, so we began with the usual exchanges about how terrible it all was, both of us – as when Jeff had called me – carefully avoiding the words 'dead' and 'death'.

I then said, 'I'm taking over Harriet's work on your KTPs. I see you've had the contract signed with the company on the Business Park. That's all fine. But I want to check a few things about the associate you've lined up for your latest KTP.'

The so-called KTP associate would be the lynchpin of the project: a suitably qualified graduate recruited jointly by the University and the participating company but employed by the University. Their job would be to help 'transfer' knowledge between the University and the company. I had my own thoughts about the value of much of this sort of stuff, but in my relatively short time at the University I'd learnt to walk the walk and talk the talk. So although the recruitment of the KTP associate wasn't really something for Legal, I was able to ask Hugh enough sensible-sounding questions to make the reason for my visit seem plausible.

'It feels strange,' I concluded, 'discussing Harriet's work when she's no longer around. I wish I'd known, the last time I spoke to her, that I wasn't ever going to speak to her again. That was on the Monday she had her accident. You must feel the same. When did you last speak to her?'

Hugh shrugged. 'On the Monday morning. She came down to discuss the new KTP. We privately messaged a bit in the afternoon too.'

It was no surprise that they were still privately messaging. I remembered those e-mails from before their affair started, when Harriet told him how much she enjoyed being led astray. She'd never said anything like that to me. I looked at Hugh's fresh, immaculately groomed face and felt a sudden urge to punch him as hard as I could.

Instead, I said, 'So you didn't see her again after the Monday morning?'

'No. Why?'

I took a deep breath. 'She mentioned, after you met her, that you'd not been happy about her going out with that solicitor from Doveley's. Jeff Parker is his name, I believe. I'm not sure why you felt like that, as you'd stopped seeing each other quite a while ago. I was wondering if you'd perhaps seen her again later on Monday and said something unpleasant?'

'What the fuck are you getting at, Alan?'

'Just that if she'd been upset by anything you said, she might not have been concentrating later that night when she was going home in the dark. The riverside would have been slippery after all the rain. It would have been easy for her to lose her footing if her mind was on other things. So are you sure you didn't see her again on Monday, either at work or in the evening?' Hugh just looked at me, his eyes hard. I bet he didn't look at women that way, I thought. 'Harriet also told me on Monday that her car had been keyed,' I went on. 'Someone singled it out in the car park here at the University and scratched it all the way down the side. She was very upset. Did she mention that to you?'

Hugh looked puzzled, then disbelieving. 'Are you seriously suggesting I might have keyed her car?'

'I wasn't suggesting that at all, Hugh. I was just asking if she'd mentioned it to you. Someone here at the University must have borne her a massive grudge to do something like that. I thought you might have an idea who was responsible. Given that you two were always private messaging.'

Hugh shook his head and sighed. 'Alan,' he said. 'I'm not a fool even though, because I'm not a lawyer, you probably think I am. I know exactly what you're getting at. You think I keyed her car. You also think I had some sort of row with her on Monday because she was going out with someone else. Jesus Christ, what sort of man are you? No, there's no need to tell me, I already know. Ever since you arrived, you were trying to get Harriet to break things off with me. All that crap you gave her about how she shouldn't let herself be distracted from her legal career by a second-rate BDM. Those things you dropped casually into conversation with her about seeing me out and about with a random female. The truth is, you were jealous as hell. Here you were, the great lawyer parachuted in from a top Cambridge law firm to save us from ourselves, and yet the girl working for you was shagging someone on the first floor rather than you.'

'That's not true,' I said. 'I supervised Harriet. It wouldn't have been right for us to—'

'Bollocks,' he snapped, no longer bothering to keep his voice down.

I glanced around and noticed that everyone in earshot was staring very hard at their computer screens – a clear sign they were listening to every word.

Hugh went on, 'You're so far up your own arse that you won't admit, probably not even to yourself, what you wanted. You couldn't handle the fact that Harriet came to you for every bit of supervision she needed at work, but outside work she wouldn't give you the time of day.'

I could feel my face was already red, and now there was a wetness of tears in the corner of my eyes. 'No,' I said, 'we were friends.'

'I'll tell you what I think,' he said. 'I think that if someone here in Senate House keyed Harriet's car, the person they should look for is someone who was jealous of her. Someone who wanted something she wasn't prepared to give. Someone who is obsessive. Someone who hadn't the balls to tell her what, deep down, he wanted. Does that sound like anyone you might know, Alan?'

He stopped, and there was a moment's complete silence. I half-expected a round of applause from everyone around us. But they were still all looking at their screens and pretending not to be listening. I really didn't know what to do or say. After the way this lothario had sounded off, people were going to think it was me who keyed Harriet's car even though I'd been on leave at the time. How I wished I had the guts to punch him or the spontaneous ability to say something cutting in reply. I couldn't even find the courage to tell him to fuck off.

Instead, I turned on my heels and walked as quickly as I could towards the exit. On the way, I spotted Mehak busy at her desk. She must have seen me talking to Hugh, but our voices wouldn't have carried that far. I was full of anger and wanted to take it out on someone. I hadn't forgotten Harriet's report about what Mehak had been up to with the overseas agents.

'Mehak, are you free this afternoon?'

She looked startled, also slightly wary. 'Why, Alan?'

'Harriet mentioned some stuff before she died. About certain things that have been going on in International which worried her legally. She was going to tell me more but, well, she never got the chance. So I need to ask you some questions. Shall we say two o'clock in one of the meeting rooms?'

I saw her swallow. Normally, people made a show of checking their schedules when I asked them for a meeting, to underline how important they were and how lucky I would be if they could find me a window. But now Mehak just nodded a yes.

'No need to bring anything with you,' I said. 'I'll book a room and see you there.'

My heart was still thudding as I walked up the stairs to the second floor. I took some deep breaths to calm myself down before going through the door. I needed to make sure I was in the right frame of mind for dealing with Mehak later on.

34

I spent the rest of the morning and the lunch hour undisturbed at my desk. Richard and Tom didn't need help with anything, and Lewis didn't venture once out of his office. I hadn't seen Amanda or Deborah all day, but I wasn't bothered because I wanted time to prepare for what I was proposing to say to them. Otherwise, the second floor chugged along as steadily as it normally did, with the finance, procurement and insurance teams tapping away at their keyboards like an army of outsized woodpeckers.

I was upset and angry with Hugh. Upset, because he was now the second person, after P.C. Dawn Smith, to ask if I'd keyed Harriet's car. I couldn't understand why people thought so badly of me. And I was angry at how I'd been humiliated in front of so many people on the first floor. How could I expect them to heed my legal advice now they'd seen what Hugh could get away with?

I have to be honest and say that I would happily have gone out and keyed Hugh's car there and then if I could have been sure of avoiding repercussions. I don't like to think of myself as someone who bears grudges, but I would certainly have been willing to make an exception in this case. It would only be a matter of time before Hugh charmed his way into another woman's knickers. However, I could perhaps then cause some mischief by sending her an anonymous e-mail, letting her know the sort of duplicitous bastard he was. Even better, if he got involved with two women at the same time, which wouldn't surprise me, I could send anonymous e-mails to them both, tipping them off about each other. These thoughts provided some comfort over lunch while I mulled over what I was going to say to Mehak.

*

'I still can't believe it,' Mehak said as soon as we'd taken our places.

We were in the same meeting room in Senate House that I'd last used with Harriet. I was also in the same chair, at the head of the table, and Mehak was in Harriet's chair, immediately to my left. She was dressed as immaculately as ever, in black jeans and a white blouse which was sufficiently unbuttoned at the top to reveal her cleavage. I could see the outline of a black bra beneath the blouse. Her long dark hair hung onto her shoulders and she was even more carefully made-up than usual. I got a whiff of the scent I remembered from our regular early morning one-on-ones.

'I don't think any of us can believe it,' I said.

Neither of us had mentioned Harriet's name, but we both knew who we were referring to. I was careful not to look directly at Mehak's cleavage; from experience, I knew this tended to irritate women.

'I think about her every day,' Mehak went on. 'Such a tragedy. And it must have been a real blow to you, Alan.'

That was true, of course, and it was perceptive of her to appreciate this. But I wasn't here to swap condolences. 'I cope as best I can,' I said. 'One thing I'm trying to do, for Harriet's sake, is to complete all the tasks she was working on. I'm sure it would give her some comfort to know they were being looked after.'

Mehak looked as if she wasn't entirely sure how serious my last remark was. I had the impression that if I were to follow up with a wry smile, she was ready to give me one back.

'That's why I called this meeting,' I continued. 'I'd like to finish off what Harriet was doing regarding her International work.' I deliberately avoided referring to work that Harriet was doing *for*

Mehak. I wondered if Mehak would spot the significance in my choice of words.

'I'm very happy with the contracts she was doing, Alan,' she said. 'Honestly, you've no need to worry. There's nothing that can't wait.'

Mehak leant forward as she spoke and her eyes looked deep into mine. For a moment, I half-expected her to reach out with one of her beautifully manicured hands and gently touch my knee. On the previous occasions she'd done this, I'd never quite known how to respond. Sometimes I'd tried to imagine her reaction if I were to place one of my hands on hers, but I'd never had the courage to do this.

'It isn't actually to do with a contract,' I said. 'It's to do with your commission arrangements with overseas agents.'

I don't know how much was wishful thinking on my part, but I could have sworn that Mehak suddenly went very still.

She said, 'We discussed this, Alan. You'll remember I explained why we had to pay higher than usual rates of commission. If we didn't, the agents would send students to other more prestigious universities than us.'

'I remember,' I said. 'But Harriet was still puzzled and you know what she could be like. She did some asking around.'

Mehak made a show of pulling a puzzled face. 'What did she say to you?'

'She said that a particular agent had made allegations which – how can I put this – didn't reflect well on the University. She told me this on the Monday of her death. She was going to speak to you about it as soon as possible in case you had a simple explanation. But she can't have done so before I left the office at around four-thirty or else she would have told me. I don't know if you both stayed late and discussed it then, or if you bumped into her somewhere else later that evening?'

I was pleased with the way I managed to raise a query as to Mehak's whereabouts on the night of Harriet's death.

'No,' she said, 'we didn't unfortunately get a chance to have that discussion. I so wish we had because I'm sure I could have reassured her. But I went out for a drink with Hugh straight after work and, well, one drink turned into another ...'

I couldn't believe what I was hearing. It took me a second or two to pull myself together and decide on my response. 'I'm surprised your boyfriend wasn't bothered,' I said. 'The boyfriend who gets jealous if you go out with another man.' Clearly, she'd forgotten using that line on me. Was I really that insignificant to her?

'He's no longer on the scene,' she said, after an awkward pause.

I toyed with the idea of revealing that I'd read her e-mail to Harriet. The e-mail in which she admitted she'd invented the jealous boyfriend as a reason for turning down a date with me. But I decided it was better not to overplay my hand too soon. I said, 'What you do with Hugh is your affair, of course. My concern is what Harriet found out from someone who used to work in International.'

'Who was that?'

'It's not for me to say at this stage.' I wasn't going to admit that I didn't know the name of Harriet's friend.

'What did this person say?'

'This person knows one of your agents in Malaysia very well. The agent said that you, personally, have been getting so-called "reward money" in return for paying the agent inflated commission. A kind of cash-back, you could say. Apparently, it's not only happening in Malaysia. I gather it's a common practice with a lot of your agents. What do you have to say to that?'

I did wonder if Mehak was going to ask me for the name of the agent. I could probably find it out from the information that Harriet had given me, but I hadn't had time to do so.

Instead, she said, 'Who have you repeated this too, Alan?'

'No one, so far.'

For a second or two, I feared I'd made a horrible mistake. If this was a second-rate thriller and Mehak had been responsible for Harriet's death, I would surely have sealed my fate by letting her know she could ensure her safety by silencing me. Then common sense prevailed. She was hardly going to produce a pistol and shoot me dead or strangle me with her bare hands in a meeting room at Senate House. Even the University wouldn't be able to cover that up.

'Obviously, it's all rubbish,' she said. 'Agents are always claiming to be hard done by. They don't like to admit that they're on to a very good thing. Invariably, the odd agent is going to say they don't get to keep all their commission, so as not to make themselves look too greedy. It's a bit like farmers complaining that they've had a poor year with their crops.'

'It will still have to be investigated,' I said. 'I can't ignore allegations of this nature, even if they turn out to be spurious.'

'But I'm going to get blamed, Alan. You know what they say about there being no smoke without fire. Can't we find a way around this?'

She looked beseechingly at me. I wasn't quite sure what she was suggesting. Was she proposing to cut me in on whatever she was getting? Or was she – I hardly dared even think about it – offering me sexual favours in return for my silence? It goes without saying that I wouldn't have dreamt of accepting sexual favours. But for a few moments, I allowed my mind to explore how such an offer might be put into practice, were I to be so unprofessional as to accept. Would Mehak – God forbid – pull her knickers down on the spot in this meeting room at Senate House and tell me to get on with it and please to hurry up? Or would she

—

'Alan?' Mehak's voice interrupted my thoughts.

'What do you mean by "find a way around this"?' I asked, pulling myself together.

She shrugged. 'What do you want?'

Two could play at that game. 'What are you suggesting?' I asked. I deliberately avoided using the word 'offering'.

'Something which sorts this out without the need to involve anyone else?'

It felt a bit like the opening moves of a chess game: each player waiting to see where their opponent placed their pieces before choosing their own formation.

'I hope you're not suggesting something improper?' I asked. Then I realised this could be interpreted in more than one way. 'I don't mean money,' I went on quickly. 'I mean, I hope you're not suggesting that we do something together that, er, then means we don't have to take these allegations further?'

In isolation, my words were vague, but I felt it was pretty clear what I meant. I was expecting one of two responses. Either for Mehak to say (in effect) yes, that's that I meant, what about it? Or for her to plead with me not to insist on that reprehensible way out. Either way, I would have the confirmation I needed of her wrongdoing, and I would then have to decide how to respond. It was difficult to read any expression on her face; certainly, there was no sign of tears or obvious distress. I guessed she was thinking hard.

Then she said, 'Fucking hell, Alan, what are you suggesting? How dare you!'

'What—?'

'How fucking dare you say that you will ignore these so-called allegations if I go to bed with you.'

I was completely thrown. 'But I haven't. I haven't said anything like that. I wouldn't—'

'Yes, you have. And everyone knows what you're like. Perving over women, first me and then Harriet. No one will be surprised. No one will believe anything you say.'

I could feel the blood rushing to my cheeks. This was so unfair. I was scrupulous about not saying or doing anything inappropriate in the workplace. I mentally kicked myself for not having set up my phone to record this meeting. I would certainly have done so if I'd had any idea that this was how it would turn out, and then I would have had cast iron evidence that Mehak was lying about what I'd said. I looked for some sign of weakening on her face, but her eyes were cold and unblinking.

'Mehak, you're making this up. I've never said anything like that to you or anyone else, and I never would.'

'It's no good denying it, Alan. Lots of people have heard me and Harriet talk about things you've said.'

I remembered the e-mail exchange between Harriet and Mehak. Taken out of context, I could see how it might suggest I had problems with women and couldn't handle rejection. That wasn't true, needless to say. If women were fair to me, I was fair back to them. But no one would believe my side of the story. I remembered, too, the warning I'd had from Lewis over my behaviour towards Mehak. He wouldn't be surprised, or at least he would claim not to be surprised, by what she was now alleging.

'Mehak,' I said, 'you're lying. We both know you're lying.'

She shrugged again. Then she stood up and walked to the door. She turned as she grasped the handle. 'It's up to you now, Alan. As things stand, I won't make a formal complaint about your behaviour. I wouldn't want to see you lose your job. But if you repeat any of these allegations to anyone, I'm afraid I will have no choice. Think about that.'

And then she was gone.

I sat alone in the meeting room for a long time afterwards. I would like to say that I was analysing my options objectively; the truth was that I didn't have the courage to leave, maybe to have to face yet another person who seemed to have it in for me. My legs were like jelly. I couldn't believe the ruthlessness with which Mehak had acted. I had no doubts now that she was on the take. But I also had no doubts that she would make a formal complaint about me if I was to breathe a word about it. I sank tortoise-like even further into my chair as I imagined having to justify, in isolation, certain things I'd done or said over the last few months. I pictured her new friend, Hugh, backing her up, and perhaps other people too with whom I'd fallen out.

What to do? What the hell to do?

In the end, I decided that the only thing I could do was to intensify my efforts to find out the truth about Harriet's death. If what Mehak had said about her Monday evening was right, neither she nor Hugh could realistically have been the secret watcher down by the riverside. They'd probably had their tongues down each other's throats at the time that Harriet was

215

drowning. And if they hadn't been involved in Harriet's death, perhaps I could overlook Mehak's little peccadillo regarding agents. Strictly speaking, it wasn't something which had formally come to my attention, and so, arguably, I didn't have a duty to investigate. Ultimately, it might be a job for the police to check their alibis, but for now I would continue my investigation in other directions.

That evening, before I went home, I e-mailed Professor Fuller and said I'd drop in on him the following morning for a final run-through of the draft agreement I'd sent him. He replied with a simple 'OK'.

35

Heading towards the School of Engineering the next morning, I couldn't help reminiscing about the last time I'd gone to meet Simon Fuller, when I had enjoyed being seen walking across campus in the company of Harriet. Today, almost everyone else on the walkway was in a group of two or more, and although no one paid me the slightest attention, I still felt self-conscious and alone.

The foyer of the School of Engineering was almost empty. Experience had taught me that if the students – and indeed the staff – weren't in a lecture or seminar, they mostly had better uses for their time than to hang around the building. There was a low table surrounded by soft chairs where presumably visitors were supposed to wait. As I walked past, I saw a photograph of Simon Fuller on the cover of a glossy magazine. The star professor was continuing to generate publicity.

Once outside Simon's office on the first floor, I paused and looked up and down the corridor. No one was around, so I placed my ear against the door to see if I could catch any conversation from inside. Silence. After a few more seconds, I knocked.

'Yes.'

The peremptoriness of the response irritated me. He must have known who it was, but he wasn't going to invite me politely to come in.

'Good morning, Simon,' I said as I went in.

He gestured me towards the chair facing him across his desk. At least today I wasn't being put in the small plastic chair I'd had to use on my previous visit. It was the first time I'd seen him since Harriet's death, so we exchanged the usual expressions of sympathy.

'A tragic loss for the Legal team,' he said.

I waited for him to say that it must also be a tragic loss for me personally, but this didn't come. So I asked him when and how he'd heard of her death.

'Deborah told me,' he said. 'I was in Cambridge with her the night it happened. A networking event on the Science Park, followed by dinner with some potential business angels. Deborah was driving, so she dropped me off at my house in Stretham on the way back up the A10. It must have been just after midnight. Hard to believe that by then Harriet was already dead. Deborah heard the news the next day and telephoned me straightaway.'

The mention of the networking event brought back uncomfortable memories of the event I'd attended on the Science Park with Lucy earlier that year, shortly before Helen's death.

'Anyway,' Simon continued, 'very sad though it all is, I suppose we should move on to business. I've read the draft agreement you sent me. Seems very straightforward. I'm just surprised it took you so long.'

Simon seemed to be revelling in the role of the insensitive stock Yorkshireman. With his bullet-shaped, almost bald head, I could easily envisage him at the centre of a pub fight. I supposed I should be grateful that he hadn't said that life must go on.

'The drafting wasn't too demanding,' I said. 'But I had to be sure I was describing the technology correctly. Too narrowly defined, and Ian Davey wouldn't be happy. Too widely, and the University would be giving too much away.'

Simon waved a hand as if to say that he wasn't interested in such minor technicalities. I was feeling nervous about what I was going to say next, but I had no alternative if I was to get to the bottom of Harriet's death.

'The main reason for the delay was something else,' I went on. 'As you know, I've previously expressed concern about the price being paid for the technology. It seems remarkably low for something which, if it takes off, could be worth millions.'

'We've been there before, Alan. I've explained why this deal is good for the University. Deborah agrees with me. So please let's get it signed off with no further delays.'

'It wasn't just me who had concerns,' I said. 'Harriet shared them too. In fact, she took the initiative and looked into the background a bit more deeply than I had done.' This was my plan. I was going to relay what Harriet had discovered, without saying that I'd put her up to it. This way, if someone ended up getting blamed for poking their nose into things, it would hopefully be her more than me.

'What background? You know it all already. So did she.'

'Well, Harriet did spot something which struck her as odd. She said she'd come across some photographs on Facebook of Ian Davey enjoying a holiday in Cyprus. She said that you appeared in one of them. She wondered if you'd gone out there together to discuss the deal in a bit more detail.'

The tone of my last sentence could have been sarcastic, but I tried to keep it as neutral as possible, as if I was merely passing on what Harriet had told me without necessarily giving it any credence. Simon fell briefly silent. I guessed he was deciding what line to take.

Then he said, 'Yes, we did meet up in Cyprus. I was going out there anyway for a holiday. A chance for some sunshine and peace and quiet while I finished a book.'

I resisted the temptation to ask him, in cheeky schoolboy fashion, what he had been reading.

'Ian has a villa out there,' he went on, 'and when he heard I was going, he kindly invited me over for an afternoon. That's all there was to it. I don't know what Harriet was reading into it.'

I could have asked him why the Facebook photograph of him and Ian had been deleted, but I knew he would only shrug his shoulders and say it had nothing to do with him. So I said, 'The other thing Harriet told me was that Ian's company is being sold for a huge amount of money. People are very excited about some new technology which is due to come into the company soon.'

Simon waved a hand dismissively. 'I know nothing about that. I'm only an academic inventor. I'm not sure what you're getting at.'

'It was Harriet who was getting at something,' I said, still careful to shield myself behind her. 'I'll be blunt, Simon. She thought you were selling the technology too cheaply. Much too cheaply. And you can see how it looked to her, can't you? You enjoy some hospitality out in Cyprus from a man who seems to be a good friend of yours. The same man who stands to make a killing if the sale goes through at the price you've agreed. Harriet wasn't suggesting you've done anything underhand. But, she felt, you wouldn't be human if you didn't find it easier to go along with what Ian wanted. And I wouldn't be doing my job properly if I didn't put Harriet's concerns to you.' I was trying to avoid accusing him too obviously of having had the wool pulled over his eyes. 'I have to ask you one direct question,' I went on. 'Did Harriet discuss any of this with you when I was away?' I knew from Harriet's file note that she'd planned to engineer a meeting with Simon and drop a few hints about the rumoured sale of Ian Davey's company.

'I haven't seen her since you both came over,' he said. 'We exchanged e-mails when you were on leave and she may have mentioned the Facebook photograph then, but that's all.'

'You definitely didn't see her again here at the School of Engineering?'

'No.'

Infuriatingly, I had no way of telling if Simon was speaking the truth. Harriet had said nothing about having had another meeting with Simon, but knowing how thorough she was I could see how she might have wanted to build a complete case against him before telling me about it.

I took a deep breath and said, 'Well, I'm sorry, Simon, but I don't think I can allow the agreement to go forward for signature in view of what Harriet told me. I will have to recommend to senior management that the technology is valued independently before its sale to Ian's company can go ahead.'

Simon remained silent. Then he stood up and walked around his desk. For a moment, I was alarmed in case he was going to come and nut me with his hard boxer's head. Instead, he went over to the door and opened it. 'Thank you for coming, Alan,' he said. Then he just stood there, not even doing me the courtesy of looking at me.

As I passed him, I very much wanted to warn him not to say anything to Ian Davey about what we'd discussed. But I knew he would probably just ignore me, and I was conscious of being uncomfortably close to that head of his.

I felt on a high as I walked back to Senate House. I was convinced Harriet had been onto something. Simon appeared to have a rock-solid alibi for the time of her death, but that didn't mean he wasn't still up to his neck in dodgy dealings. It would be a feather in my cap if I could expose him – although, naturally, I would make sure that Harriet's assistance wasn't forgotten.

36

My plan had been to go straight to Deborah's office, to explain what had come to light about Simon Fuller and Ian Davey and to get her support for an independent valuation of the technology. Simon had clearly duped her, but once she knew the truth she was bound to be on my side, notwithstanding the fact that – according to Harriet – Simon was a favourite of hers. Simon would face a disciplinary at the very least, and possibly even dismissal for gross misconduct. Going up the stairs at Senate House, I found myself rubbing my hands together in anticipation.

It was, therefore, a disappointment to discover that Deborah's office was empty.

'Tom, have you seen Deborah?' Richard was in a meeting at the School of Social Sciences, but Tom was at his desk working on a non-disclosure agreement.

'She went out with Amanda just after you left to see Professor Fuller. Are you looking for her?'

That was a typical damn fool question from the man. Why would I ask if he'd seen her if I wasn't looking for her? I bit back an irritated reply. I would keep my powder dry for when I saw the mess he was undoubtedly going to make of his non-disclosure agreement.

I walked over to Lewis's office. 'Sorry to bother you, Lewis, but do you know where Deborah's gone?' I had avoided speaking to Lewis since he'd had a go at me on the previous Friday. I'd been trying not to think about what he and Ruth must have subsequently been saying about me.

'No, Alan, I don't know.' Lewis's voice was calm, but he made no pretence of being pleased to see me. He barely even turned his eyes from his computer screen.

Looking at Lewis with his silvery hair, I wondered once again what on earth Harriet had ever seen in him. He was a lot older than her and never, as far as I was aware, played any sort of sport. Yet she had willingly jumped into bed with him. And not just once – anyone can make a mistake – but numerous times. It made me furious just thinking about him in Harriet's bed during their lunchtime assignations and visualising what she'd done to him and him to her. It wasn't right that he should get away with it. I'd had no luck with the anonymous e-mail I'd previously sent to Ruth, but it occurred to me I could have another go in the hope that Lewis and Ruth would turn on each other. Perhaps I could reveal some details of what went on between Lewis and Harriet; perhaps I could even include some screenshots of their flirty e-mails with each other …

However, I just said, 'Not to worry, Lewis, and thank you.'

I doubt he even heard me; he'd already turned back to his screen.

I spent the next couple of hours at my desk, working on an exchange agreement between the University and an overseas institution. The idea was for each institution to accept the other's students onto its courses for specified periods of time, with the credits gained counting towards the students' overall award. It had occurred to me that maybe the overseas institution was mistakenly contracting with us rather than with one of the better-known Cambridgeshire universities, but I'd learnt from experience that comments – even jokes – on these lines never went down well at the University of East Cambridgeshire.

Richard came back just before lunchtime, looking as shifty as ever. I was mildly curious about what the School of Social Sciences was up to that might require legal involvement. They didn't invent anything or, as far as I could tell, even do much else of any worth. But I knew Richard would tell me at a time that suited him rather than me.

I had my usual lunch at my desk, reading and replying to various e-mails. Amanda came back on her own just after lunch, popping her head into Lewis's office to give him a cheery hello but ignoring me completely. I recalled her comment in the e-mail chain that had been accidentally forwarded to Harriet – about me being 'better than nothing' when they were recruiting for my position. How I would love to wipe that smile off her face. And perhaps, as a result of Harriet's investigations into Landlord Relax, I would have a chance. But I was psyched up to speak to Deborah and I decided to leave Amanda alone for now.

Finally, at about 3 p.m., Deborah came through the door and headed straight for her office. To my amusement, she bobbed her head up and down as she walked, like a thoroughbred being led to the gallops in nearby Newmarket. I was out of my seat and making an exaggerated mime of knocking politely on her open door by the time she'd sat down at her desk.

'Hello, Deborah. I'm sorry to trouble you, but do you have a few minutes?'

'Come in, Alan,' she said, 'and please shut the door.'

Her response surprised me because normally Deborah was too busy to want to spare me any time. I hovered by the chair opposite her across the desk, waiting in vain for an invitation to sit down.

'I need to speak to you, Alan.'

'That's good,' I said, 'because I want to talk to you about Simon Fuller. Can we talk about him first?'

'It's Simon I need to speak to you about.'

'If it's about the contract, then don't worry, because I've finished the drafting. The thing is, though, that I don't think it should be signed. I've found out that—'

'Alan.' Not only was there a note of real exasperation in her voice, but she also held up her hand as if I were a child in primary school being made to shut up. 'I've just had Simon bending my ear for half an hour. He's furious, absolutely bloody furious. And I don't blame him. He said you went to see him this morning and effectively accused him of selling the University's technology too cheaply in return for an invitation to spend time with Ian Davey at his villa. Are you mad?'

'There's more to it than that, Deborah. Harriet did some digging around while I was on leave, and she was convinced that Simon got a free holiday – and who knows what else – from Ian Davey. Once Simon knew what she'd found out, they tried to delete the evidence.'

'What evidence?'

'There was a photograph on Facebook.'

'Have you never taken down a photograph from Facebook?'

I didn't put photographs on Facebook, but I guessed her question was rhetorical. 'There's more to it than that,' I said. 'Apparently, Ian Davey's company is lined up to be sold for a huge amount of money. And the only reason the sale price is so high is because of the University's wearable technology which we're supposed to be transferring into the company first.'

'*Apparently*. Where did you hear about this?'

'Er, Harriet did, not me.'

'Yes, but where did she hear about it?'

'I don't know exactly. Some obscure website where investors chat. She said—'

'Come on. Are you seriously expecting me to pay attention to gossip on an obscure website whose address you don't know and which you haven't even seen yourself?'

'But—'

'Look, Alan. Professor Fuller is one of the University's most prized academics. Do you have any idea how much income he generates for the University, both directly and indirectly? I don't normally like to talk of stars, but he really is one of the University's biggest. And he's also very loyal. The night that Harriet died, for example, he gave up a whole evening to support me at a networking event and later over dinner with some business angels. We didn't get back until well after midnight. There was nothing in it personally for him. He was doing it for the University. He could double his salary overnight by going to a top university. But no, he stays here because of his commitment to us. And, in return, you expect me to accuse him of being bribed by a respected commercial partner. You must be insane.'

I felt both angry and helpless. Deborah was lecturing me as if I was a kid. And, as I had so often done as a kid when faced with bullies, I caved in.

'I'm sorry, Deborah,' I said. 'I made a wrong call here. I'll try not to do so again.'

I'd hoped for a smile of sympathy, to show that at least she understood the dilemma I was in, but none came. She just sat there, looking at me with cold eyes. I realised she'd been hoping and expecting that I would blow my top and storm out. Then, if that hadn't been enough to persuade me to resign voluntarily, the University could have got rid of me easily enough on some kind of misconduct charge. The woman really was a scheming cow. I would have to tread carefully. But I had my pride, and I certainly wouldn't be giving up on my investigation.

I left her office quietly, saying nothing further. Back at my pod, Tom was still working on his non-disclosure agreement. He hadn't noticed anything was amiss. I was glad that Richard was still at his meeting. He would undoubtedly have noticed something.

37

I hadn't yet figured out the relationship between Amanda and Deborah. Although Amanda, as the Secretary and Registrar, reported to the Vice-Chancellor, the VC was mostly interested in swanning around the country making himself look important. On a day-to-day basis, therefore, Amanda was primarily responsible for the running of the University. Deborah, in contrast, was only one of a gaggle of pro-vice-chancellors and was no higher in the official pecking order than any of them.

However, Amanda seemed to spend more time with Deborah than she did with any other of the pro-vice-chancellors. There was no operational reason for this; Enterprise and Innovation – Deborah's baby – was important, but not that important. Accordingly, I presumed that there was some kind of special friendship between the women. I'd even speculated about whether there was a sexual element to their relationship. Women could, as I'd previously discovered, keep this kind of thing very quiet, and I hadn't heard of either of them having a husband or male partner. And, I have to admit, the idea of the horsey Deborah thrashing around in bed with the pixie-like Amanda had occasioned me with some mild amusement. But the most likely explanation, I accepted, was that the two women were simply friends.

That being so, I shouldn't have been surprised when I received an e-mail from Amanda first thing the following day:

Good morning, Alan

Please can you spare me five minutes this afternoon? Perhaps around

3 p.m.? Deborah mentioned that you'd had an issue with Professor Fuller. I'd like to make sure this is now resolved.

Thank you,
Amanda

Shortly before sending the e-mail, Amanda had walked past my pod on the way to her office, not even bothering to wish me a good morning. She could just as easily have given me the message in person. But no, she evidently wanted to make some kind of point by formalising her request. And, of course, it did have an effect – I spent most of the morning mulling over what she was going to say to me and what I was going to say back. I managed to check and correct Tom's non-disclosure agreement and to review some heads of terms that Richard had produced, but my mind was firmly on the 3 p.m. summons. In the end, I came up with a strategy that I hoped was going to work.

*

'Well, Alan, Deborah tells me you now accept you made a mistake regarding Simon Fuller. Is that correct?'

'I think a mistake was made, Amanda,' I said carefully. 'But, to be completely honest, it wasn't my mistake.'

Unlike with Deborah, I had at least been invited to take a seat in Amanda's office. It felt like she was playing the good cop to the Pro-Vice-Chancellor's bad cop.

'I'm sorry, I don't understand,' she said.

'After Harriet died,' I explained, 'I had the job of going through her e-mails. Not a pleasant task, as it reminded me all the time that she was no longer around. But someone had to do it. Otherwise, we wouldn't know which unfinished tasks needed to be picked up by the rest of the team.'

Amanda was already looking impatient, so I decided to shorten my explanation.

'I found out,' I went on, 'that Harriet had been – in her words – carrying out some kind of investigation. She'd got this idea that

Simon was up to no good. It was the first I'd heard of it, and my initial instinct was, as you would expect, to ignore what she believed she'd uncovered. But then I thought I owed it to Harriet at least to pass on her concerns. Probably from a misguided sense of loyalty on my part, but that's the kind of person I am. I like to stand up for my subordinates.'

Amanda threw me a look as if to say this wasn't the Alan she thought she knew.

'With hindsight, of course,' I continued, 'I should perhaps have told you straightaway what Harriet was thinking and left it entirely up to you how much weight, if any, you attached to it. But I made the mistake – and I accept it was a mistake – of putting her concerns to Simon directly. And then to Deborah.'

'I see.'

Amanda hadn't been expecting that. I knew some people would think I was throwing Harriet under the bus. But I had to be realistic; she was no longer around to face the music whereas I very much was. I was sure Harriet would have understood. My primary concern was that Amanda might ask IT to show her Harriet's e-mails and file notes, in which case my role in Harriet's investigation would come to light. But that was a risk I had to take.

'So that's all Harriet had to go on?' Amanda asked.

'Yes. I told Deborah everything.'

'And you didn't know what Harriet had been investigating? When she was alive, that is.'

Irreverently, I noted that this second sentence was superfluous. Harriet could hardly have been investigating anything when she was dead. 'No, it was news to me,' I said. 'And a real shock. Simon is, after all, one of the most respected figures at the University.' Maybe I was laying it on a little thick. However, now came the bit I'd been planning. I dug my fingers into the flesh of my hands and silently wished myself good luck. 'I'd better tell you, though, Amanda, that Harriet had also been poking around into the background of Landlord Relax. Again, something she'd been doing off her own back.' I deliberately used the word 'poking' to indicate my disapproval.

For the first time, Amanda looked slightly uncomfortable, as if she was no longer going through the formalities of giving a tongue-lashing and now had to be careful. 'Go on,' she said.

'It's all very nebulous, naturally. But, well, what Harriet said was that there was some kind of prior relationship between you and the Landlord Relax founders.'

'What sort of relationship?' Amanda wasn't giving anything away. She first wanted to know what Harriet had been alleging.

'She did some digging around on LinkedIn and on social media generally,' I said. 'She noticed you were at the same university, at the same time, as the Landlord Relax founders. She also said she found a photograph of you at the same table as the founders at a recent alumni dinner. I don't know if she said anything about this to you?'

'No, she didn't.'

Well, well, well. Unless Harriet had been making it up about having mentioned the alumni dinner to Amanda, Amanda was lying. And why would she lie unless she had anything to hide? My hands were below the level of Amanda's desk, so she wouldn't have noticed the way I rubbed them together in satisfaction.

'Speaking as a solicitor,' I said, 'the easiest way to dismiss these allegations is for you to clarify the facts. Harriet probably just got some faces wrong in the photograph. Or, even if you were at the same dinner table as the founders, I'm sure there's a perfectly innocent explanation. But the risk, if you don't clarify the facts, is that tongues will start to wag.'

I was pleased with my boldness. I was still blaming Harriet for initiating her investigation, but I was also putting the allegations on a semi-official footing by reminding Amanda of my professional status. She fell silent and I wondered what she was thinking. Was it, I dared hope, how much longer she would be in post at the University?

'Alan,' she said eventually, 'there is nothing to clarify. Yes, I was at the same table at a dinner as the two founders. But we didn't discuss Landlord Relax. You have to remember that I go to dozens of dinners a year, and I must share a table with hundreds of different people. I'm not sure what more I can say.'

'The point,' I said, 'is that some people – not me, I should stress – might perceive a conflict of interest. They might want the reassurance that you declared the meeting, or the fact that you knew the founders from university, in the University's register of interests.'

'Quite a few people – Deborah, for one – know that I've met the founders on a number of occasions. You're making a mountain out of a molehill.'

'It's not me. It was Harriet who—'

'Alan, I'm not a fool. Let me say something that I wasn't going to say. I am, I'm afraid, disappointed with how your appointment is going. You came from a top Cambridge firm and we were expecting great things. But you seem to have developed an obsession with issues that don't really matter. I know you were upset about Harriet's death. But we all were, and life really does have to go on even though I hate that phrase. As it happens, Deborah spoke recently to one of your former colleagues at a networking event. A partner at Doveley's. He … well, I wasn't going to say this, but since I've started, I might as well. He gave her the strong impression that they were glad you left. She asked him if you would be welcome back, and he didn't make a joke of it as people often do in these circumstances. He just looked at her and said "No".'

My cheeks were already burning, but now I felt tears in my eyes. It was so unfair. I'd effectively been kicked out of Doveley's for having facilitated the arrest of a killer. It wasn't my fault that this had caused some embarrassment – to put it mildly – to the firm. I was in the dark about which partner had bad-mouthed me to Deborah, but he or she had no bloody right doing so. I had negotiated a good reference as part of my severance deal, and that should have been all that any partner at Doveley's said about me.

'Do you understand what I'm saying, Alan? Do you accept that

Harriet's suggestions were ridiculous, or are you going to repeat them?'

How I wished I had the courage to tell Amanda that I very much wanted to repeat the allegations and that I would like to hear how she was going to explain them to the Vice-Chancellor. But the senior management were plainly all going to stick together. Deborah and Amanda had already been talking about me behind my back. I remembered that accidentally forwarded e-mail exchange in which they'd slagged me off before I even started at the University.

I couldn't bring myself to tell Amanda where to stick the job. My heart sank at the prospect of having to leave during my probationary period. I winced at the thought of what my former colleagues at Doveley's would say. I imagined the look of triumph on Richard's face, and on the faces of Hugh, and Mehak, and Simon Fuller, and God knows probably loads more people at the University.

I wouldn't give them the bloody satisfaction.

'Yes, I'm sorry, Amanda,' I said. 'Harriet was very foolish. And I was foolish to give even the slightest credence to what she believed. I've still got a lot to learn about life at the University. Please accept my apologies.'

38

My humiliation was, as they say, complete.

I'd been bollocked within the space of twenty-four hours by both Deborah and Amanda. I had no doubt that they would have been comparing notes afterwards, possibly even giving each other tips on how to trample me further into the ground.

As a result, it was a relief to get back to the sanctuary of my house that evening. I was in desperate need of some kind of distraction. However, I wasn't in the mood to read one of my true crime books. There was a logical order and an inevitability about the police investigations that they described, and neither of these concepts applied to my investigation. It was all too depressing. In the end, I found some solace in a recent purchase of mine from a charity shop: an account of life on the fringes of the professional tennis circuit by a never-has-been-and-never-will-be player who jacked in his job to try to fulfil his dreams. How I wished I had even a small amount of his courage. As I read, I drank a large glass of one of my favourite wines, a Cline Cellars Old Vine Lodi Zinfandel, savouring the taste of the ripe, almost sweet berry fruit. After a while, I cooked myself one of my regular quick dishes: fried calf's liver and onions, flavoured with lemon juice, and served on a pile of boiled rice with a couple of slices of crusty bread on the side. By the time I emptied my plate, I'd got through another couple of glasses of the Zinfandel, at which point it seemed pointless to cork the rest for another day.

While I finished my wine, I sank back into my sofa and put on one of my fallback playlists of 'sad' classical music.

Inevitably, it contained a lot of Chopin, including his *Prelude in E minor* and *Funeral March*. The latter brought home the realisation that I would still have Harriet's funeral to endure. I had received no communication at all about this. I appreciated that Zoe, as Harriet's next-of-kin, would have a lot on, but it showed a certain lack of sensitivity for the feelings of others that she hadn't been keeping me up to date. As with Helen's funeral earlier in the year, I had no doubt that Harriet's funeral would be attended by an army of hangers-on who hadn't really understood or cared for her the way I had.

I ruminated over whether Lewis or Hugh would attend the funeral. Lewis might well feel constrained out of loyalty to Ruth. She wouldn't want him watching the coffin being carried down the aisle and remembering fondly all those lunchtime sex sessions. For similar reasons, Hugh might be reluctant to go if he was already inside Mehak's knickers, especially given that Mehak and Harriet hadn't exactly been on the best of terms when Harriet died. Deep down, I realised I didn't want either of them at the funeral. Although neither of them would be crass enough to say anything to me, I could envisage them crowing silently to themselves about the fact that they'd got something from Harriet that I never had.

How I wished I could pin Harriet's death – whether deliberate murder or some kind of accident following an argument – on Hugh or Lewis. Or even on Ruth; that would certainly mess up Lewis's life, at least until he found a replacement for her. I hadn't forgotten how rude she'd been to me the last time I'd seen her. But could I pin it on any of them?

As far as motives were concerned, I couldn't stand Hugh's oily manner, but he'd been around the block enough times with women not to seek that type of revenge just because he'd been dumped. If he was going to have a go at anyone, I was realistic enough to know that it would have been me. He was just the sort of thug who would enjoy punching me in the face.

There was a similar problem with Lewis. I could see him trying to silence Harriet as a way of stopping their affair from becoming known to Ruth, but that genie was well and truly out of the bottle by the time Harriet died. And if he'd wanted revenge on Harriet – and I was struggling to find a reason why – there were all sorts of more subtle ways for a Director of Legal Services to make life hard for a junior member of his team.

No, in terms of motive, Ruth was the obvious suspect of the three – the scorned wife and all that. I could remember the viciousness in the way she'd hissed 'bitch' at Harriet. If she was responsible, I was uncomfortably aware that it wouldn't have happened without my anonymous e-mail to her. But as a lawyer, I was familiar with the concept of defendants only being liable for reasonably foreseeable damage, and I didn't think I could have been expected to foresee that kind of overreaction by her.

However, the big problem with all three was that they appeared to have alibis. According to Lewis, he and Ruth had had an early night. If so, then realistically neither of them was going to have got dressed when the other was asleep, crept out of the house to do a dastardly deed, and then quietly gone back to bed. And according to Mehak, she and Hugh had spent the evening together getting drunk and then doing God knows what. This wasn't definitive, but I certainly wasn't going to ask Hugh exactly what he'd been doing with Mehak all evening, and until what time.

These thoughts naturally led me on to Mehak herself. Her motive for harming Harriet was even more plausible than that of the other three. She was defrauding the University and potentially facing not just dismissal but also prosecution; even the University couldn't cover up something as big as this. In other circumstances, I would have been delighted to see her fall from grace. However, my nagging fear was that, at the slightest hint of police involvement, she might lash out at anyone whom she could find to blame, which could include accusing me of having demanded sex in return for my silence. Although she had definitely twisted what I'd said, I really didn't want to have to defend myself against those kinds of allegations. But, again, if what she said about her and Hugh being together on that

Monday evening was true, she must surely be out of the frame.

I hadn't forgotten about the keying of Harriet's car. It might have been unconnected with her death, but it seemed unlikely that two people, separately, would have wished harm on her at around the same time. I'd told Harriet that I thought Hugh or Lewis were the most likely suspects, as that was what I would have liked her to believe. Deep down, though, I couldn't see either of them keying her car. And Mehak couldn't have done it, because she didn't know that Harriet was investigating her when the car was keyed and so she wouldn't have had a motive.

Consequently, Ruth was still the obvious suspect for keying the car, and although I was too much of a modern man to believe it myself, I could imagine other, less progressive people saying that this was a typical woman's crime. But even if I was right, it didn't weaken her alibi for the time of Harriet's death.

*

After going around in circles for an hour or so, I started to concentrate on all the other people who might conceivably be responsible for Harriet's death, either intentionally or inadvertently.

What about Simon Fuller, Deborah or Amanda?

I had no particular personal gripe with Simon even though he undoubtedly needed taking down a peg or two. And in terms of motive, he had everything to lose if he thought Harriet was going to expose that he was on the take. But he'd been given a cast-iron alibi by Deborah – attendance at a networking event followed by dinner – and one which could almost certainly be independently verified.

Deborah's alibi was similarly secure. In any event, although I couldn't stand the woman, and was sure that she was turning a Nelsonian blind eye to what Simon was up to, that was hardly sufficient motive to confront and possibly even deliberately kill Harriet.

And the same, surely, was true of Amanda. I'd previously

persuaded myself that she could have killed Harriet to prevent the truth about her connection with the Landlord Relax founders being revealed. And, believe me, there's nothing I would have liked more than to see her being led off in handcuffs from the second floor of Senate House, with everyone else open-mouthed in shock and me firing witty quips from the sidelines. But she was the University's Secretary and Registrar, and deep down I knew people like that didn't commit those sorts of violent crimes unless there was some extra personal motivation such as revenge or jealousy. And Amanda had liked Harriet. I had no idea if Amanda had an alibi for the time of Harriet's death, but I most assuredly wasn't going to knock on her office door, pen and notebook in hand, and ask her what she'd been doing on the Monday evening and who she'd spent the night with.

Who else was there?

Richard couldn't be ruled out completely.

He was just the sort of spiteful shit who would happily have keyed Harriet's car as payback for her having – as he would have regarded it – grassed him up to me. But that would probably be enough for him. He would have no further motivation to confront her the following week down by the riverside, let alone do anything to harm her. And he wouldn't gain from her death either; rather, the opposite, as he'd subsequently had to take on some of her workload. In any event, he'd said he was playing online chess when Harriet died, and this was something which could be easily checked via the account of whichever chess platform he used.

There was also Trevor, the landlord.

He claimed to have been at home in Downham Market with his wife and daughters on the night of Harriet's death. It was only his word, and he might have had a chance to slip over to Ely after his daughters had gone to bed, especially if he and his wife didn't share a bedroom. But it just didn't seem likely to me. I was sure that he could use his fists, but he was also a professional landlord and he would have to be on the verge of insanity to think that killing a tenant was the best way to protect himself against a prosecution for breach of the gas safety laws. No one had died as a result of his shortcuts, so I presumed he was at risk of at worst a fine for a technical breach, whereas if he'd caused Harriet's death, he was facing either a life sentence for murder or at least a good few years inside for manslaughter.

Or could it have been some random stranger?

It wasn't impossible, even in Ely with its reputation for being very safe. But it would be a remarkable coincidence for this to have happened to Harriet at a time when she'd been, to put it bluntly, pissing quite a few people off, albeit at my instigation. And if there had been an attempt to sexually assault her – the most likely motive of a random attacker – surely the police would have picked this up. No, I was sure that whoever had been watching Harriet was someone who knew her.

Before going to bed, I started to draft another anonymous e-mail to the police, listing the people whose names I'd been considering and saying that their alibis needed to be checked. But there was a problem. Some malicious people might think I had a grudge against Harriet and that I might even have done something to harm her. For that reason, if I didn't include my own name on the list of suspects, that might itself raise suspicions as to who the anonymous writer was. But I had no alibi. For all I knew, my expedition to the riverside might have been caught on some CCTV camera. I daren't do anything which might risk drawing the police's attention to myself.

What the hell was I going to do?

*

I woke up in the small hours, as I often did after drinking too much alcohol. I sensed that I'd heard a click. For a few moments, I listened intently in case there was an intruder. As my property was a terraced house without a back garden, the only practical escape route in an emergency was via the front door, so the idea of someone breaking in that way was alarming. My mind flashed back to that encounter in the centre of Cambridge earlier that year when I'd literally had to fight for my life.

But there was only silence. Absolute silence. If there had been a sound anywhere in the house, however faint, I would have heard it.

Then I realised that the click which had awoken me hadn't been an actual sound. Instead, it had been a sudden and shattering recognition of something in my subconscious. I searched my brain for a recollection of what had been going through my mind.

Yes, that was it. I'd been remembering the words of a conversation while I slept. Someone had said something which, although I hadn't picked up on it at the time, was significant. But what had they said, and who had said it?

Then it all came back. And it all made sense.

I was frightened. I had to make a phone call. But at 2 a.m. this wasn't practical. It would have to wait until the morning. I just hoped that the person I had in mind would be there. No one else would give me the information I needed.

As I lay in my bed, I could feel my heart beating high up in my chest, almost in my throat. I understood now what was meant by having one's heart in one's mouth. It took me a long time to calm down. I kept picturing how Harriet might have died and how she might have suffered.

Eventually, I fell asleep. And, remarkably, I didn't dream about the riverside in Ely and about the terrible crime that I was now convinced had been committed down there.

39

'Hello, can I speak to P.C. Dawn Smith, please?'

'Who's calling?'

'Alan Gadd. P.C. Smith knows me.'

There was no sound for a few seconds.

Then I heard some muffled words, as if the person to whom I'd spoken had put their hand imperfectly over the mouthpiece: 'Dawn, there's an Alan Gadd for you?'

The reply was equally muffled: 'For fuck's sake. OK, thanks, I'll speak to him. Put him through.'

Again, there was a brief silence. Then a much clearer voice said, 'Good morning, Alan, how are you?'

'I'm OK, thank you, Dawn. Still coming to terms with what happened, of course. Harriet's death has left a big hole in my team. I'm sorry to trouble you so early, but there's something I want to ask you. I learnt from Kat and Zoe, Harriet's housemate and sister, that Harriet fell into the water just before midnight. Have you made that information public?'

'Why do you ask?'

'Er, I was just wondering.' No reply. I continued, 'Someone mentioned the time of her death to me, and I was surprised that they knew. So I thought you might have released that information somewhere?'

'We've said nothing at all about the time of death.' A pause. 'Alan, I hope you aren't making a mountain out of a molehill?'

'What do you mean?'

'You know very well what I mean. I realise you feel very proud of yourself for what you did earlier this year. But this death is quite different. Tragic, but not being treated as suspicious.'

Not for the first time, I had the distinct feeling that Dawn Smith didn't like me. I noted with irritation the way she downplayed my role in catching a killer. Whether this was professional jealousy of what I had achieved, it was impossible to tell. Anyway, it didn't matter, because I had the answer I was looking for.

*

'I'm sorry to trouble you again, Deborah, but may I have a word, please?'

It might only have been my imagination, but I thought I saw her lips also say a 'For fuck's sake' to herself.

Or perhaps, I thought with a flicker of amusement, she was just mentally chewing a cut of hay. She seemed to have made an effort with her appearance this morning: brighter lipstick and less lanky hair than usual. But, if anything, it made her look even more equine. Not that I was going to tell her that, of course.

It was just after 9.30 a.m. I'd driven straight to work after ending my call with P.C. Dawn Smith, and for once I'd been lucky enough to find Deborah alone in her office. I hadn't even stopped to log on or to say good morning to Richard and Tom.

'Yes, Alan, what is it?'

'It's about Simon Fuller.' Deborah took in a deep breath. 'I know what you said on Tuesday,' I went on quickly, 'but I've found something out which is really important. You have to hear me out.'

Deborah was quiet for a few seconds. Then she said, 'OK, Alan. I'll listen to you. But I'm warning you, it had better be good.'

'When I last saw Simon,' I said, 'he said that you dropped him off in Stretham just after midnight on the night that Harriet died.'

'I did.'

'He also said that by then Harriet was dead.'

'So?' Deborah was looking impatient, as if waiting for the

moment when she could legitimately order me out of her office.

'Well, how did he know Harriet was already dead?'

'You tell me,' she said with a shrug. 'It must have been reported somewhere.'

'But that's the point. It wasn't. I've checked with the police. They didn't release that information. The only people who knew were Harriet's friend on the boat, her housemate, and her sister. And me, of course. I've not mentioned the time of Harriet's death to Simon, and I'm pretty sure he doesn't even know any of the others.'

'I still don't understand the significance.'

'I should have phrased it better. As well as the people I've just mentioned, there was one other person who knew what time Harriet died. The person who was on the spot when she went into the water. The person who might have pushed her in.'

I let my words sink in. Deborah must have realised that I was waiting for her to speak. She said, 'I'm not sure what you're getting at. But if you're suggesting that Simon was down by the riverside, that is absolutely impossible. He was with me in my car. Unless you're suggesting that I'm not telling the truth?'

I was ready for this. 'I'm not suggesting that at all. I have no doubt that Simon was with you. I'm sure it even suited his purposes to be with you. But if what I'm saying about him is right, it's not just him we have to consider. He's not been acting alone in trying to sell the University's technology too cheaply. There's the person who has presumably been rewarding him. The person who will benefit the most from the sale.'

I paused, like a teacher giving a pupil the chance to shine by producing the correct answer.

'You mean Ian Davey?'

'Precisely. Assuming what I've said about the proposed sale of his company is right, and I'm sure it is, then he has the most to gain from the sale going through. And the most to lose if something stops it from happening. I've heard nothing about Ian's whereabouts that night, but if he was down by the riverside, he would know exactly when – and how – Harriet died.

And if he's in cahoots with Simon, it's only natural that he would have mentioned the time of death to him. There's no other way Simon could have found out this information.'

'So, just to get this clear, are you saying that Ian Davey killed Harriet?'

'I can't be certain. But it's the most likely explanation. God only knows what the financial consequences for him will be if the sale of the University's technology to his company doesn't take place, or only takes place at a proper market value. I reckon he was following Harriet that night and challenged her when she left her friend's narrowboat. Maybe he'd initially planned nothing more than to have things out with her if an opportunity arose, perhaps just to dissuade her from pursuing her investigation. But then he spotted his chance and, on the spur of the moment, pushed her in. He knew she couldn't swim. I was there when she told him.'

'You have no evidence of this, Alan. No evidence that Ian, or anyone else, was even following Harriet.'

'But I do. That's the point. I was, um, down by the riverside that night, and I saw someone following us, um, I mean following Harriet.'

'You were there?' Deborah looked stunned. 'What for?'

'I was meeting someone,' I lied. 'And I saw Harriet. And then I saw someone following her.'

'Was it Ian?'

I had to be careful. If I lied again, and it later turned out that I was wrong about Ian, I would have Deborah all over me. I said, 'It certainly looked like him. I can't be completely sure, but he is a very distinctive shape and size.'

As I spoke, I realised I wasn't saying anything that wasn't true. The figure I'd seen in the dark, and which I now forced my mind to picture again, had been fairly large and fairly round: a plausible match for a man who looked like nothing so much as an oversized egg.

'Have you told anyone else what you've told me?' Deborah asked.

'No, not yet. But I think we have to tell the police. Let them investigate and see if I'm right about Ian. Let them also find out if Simon is involved as well. In Harriet's death, I mean. He's clearly involved in the deal to sell the University's technology to Ian's company at an undervalue.'

Deborah said nothing. I could understand her dilemma. She must be itching to tell me to get lost, but the consequences for her, and for the University, would be horrendous if it subsequently turned out that I was right. On the other hand, calling in the police to investigate both one of the University's star academics and one of their most important commercial clients was a big step to take. If that went wrong, it wouldn't only be me for the chop.

'I agree that we may have to involve the police, Alan,' she said eventually. 'But not yet. I'll take you into my confidence. Simon has a big job offer from a Russell Group university on the table, and we're fighting hard to keep him. We're also at risk of losing a couple of other leading academics who bring in a lot of commercial business. The University isn't in great shape, basically. So if we have to call in the police, the University's reputation is going to take a dive whatever happens. No one's job will be safe. Not yours, not mine.'

She paused, but I didn't have the impression that I was being encouraged to speak.

'What we need to do,' she went on, 'is speak to Ian Davey ourselves. Not necessarily to accuse him, but just to find out where he was that night. If he had what the police would call an alibi, then it couldn't have been him.'

To be honest, I was relieved. After hearing Dawn Smith's reaction this morning when she knew I was on the phone, I'd been dreading having to contact her again with my suspicions about Ian Davey. If I'd been easily able to get hold of Ian myself, I would have found a way of asking him where he'd been on the night of Harriet's death, as I'd done with the others I suspected. But I'd only met the man once, so I could hardly cold-call him at his company HQ out in the wildness of the Fens north of Ely.

I said, 'That sounds a good idea, Deborah. But how do we go about that?'

'We go out and see him,' she said. 'I've been promising to visit him again, so let's go together.'

*

Deborah's use of the word 'we' had boosted my confidence. Now that I had her on board, things might be looking up for me.

Back at my desk, I began to see her in a new light. It was perhaps understandable that she should have had her doubts about me when I started the job, coming as I did from a background in a very different type of business. She must have been worried that I would want to do things differently, just for the sake of being different. And maybe I hadn't always handled things to perfection. But now, if we could bring our joint investigation – as I was starting to see it – to a successful conclusion, I might have a promising future at the University. The fact that she was on such good terms with Amanda might help too. Perhaps I could persuade Deborah to use her influence to help get rid of Lewis, and maybe also Richard. Even Tom's position would have to be looked at closely.

I started to picture how I could build up my legal team from scratch once the dead wood had been cleared out. Some of the trainee solicitors at Doveley's were very talented, and some of the women amongst them were – although they were careful to whom they admitted this – already looking for an in-house role where they could hope to work flexibly and perhaps even part-time within a year or two. There was no way, I hasten to say, that I would discriminate between male and female candidates, but there were certainly a couple of young female trainees at Doveley's who had always been polite and eager to please. I could envisage them now, sitting at my pod, nicely dressed and well-groomed, and listening earnestly to what I had to say—

'Half-past six this evening, Alan.' I hadn't even heard Deborah's approach. 'Ian's working late so I said we would arrive then. Is that convenient?'

'Er, yes,' I said, not sure if she was going to offer me a lift or if I should offer one to her.

'We might as well go in our own separate cars, so I can drive straight home afterwards. But let's travel in convoy. I'll meet you in the car park outside Senate House at six o'clock. Have a think about what you are going to say to him. You want to get the information we need without arousing his suspicion. You seem to have a knack for that sort of thing, so I'll leave that bit to you. See you later.'

I wished that Tom and Richard had been there to hear me and Deborah talking as equals, with her complimenting me on my investigative skills. But both men had gone off for the rest of the day to a training course run by HR on equality, diversity and inclusion. The University seemed to take these kinds of things seriously, rather than paying lip service to them in the Doveley's way to which I was more accustomed.

Still, today was only Thursday, and if we got the result we wanted tonight, it wasn't impossible that I could be regaling Richard and Tom with my triumph before the weekend.

40

Deborah had said to meet her in the car park, but I'd been hoping we could walk down the stairs and out of Senate House together. Even though there would be hardly anyone around to see us, I felt it would underline my new standing at the University as a trusted adviser and not just an employed lawyer.

However, Deborah left the second floor shortly after lunch and I didn't see her again during the afternoon. By 5.45 p.m., I was the only person left on the floor. Although I had plenty of work to catch up on, my heart wasn't really in it; I was already thinking ahead to the meeting with Ian Davey. It would be easy enough to ask him what he'd been doing on the night of Harriet's death, but he wasn't going to admit to having been down by the riverside, and there was no natural follow-up question. The best we could hope for was for him to come up with some random alibi off the top of his head, which we – or, more realistically, the police – could later check and break. Only someone with something to hide would lie about where they had been.

There was only a handful of cars left in the darkened car park when I arrived at 6 p.m., and Deborah made it easy for me to spot her by flashing the headlights on her Land Rover Discovery.

'This gives the post code, Alan,' she said, passing me Ian Davey's business card through her half-open driver side window. 'You lead. I'll follow. That way, you won't get left behind.'

*

I set the route on my phone with Google Maps and sent it wirelessly to my car display screen so I could put my phone back in my inside jacket pocket. The journey was predicted to take less than thirty minutes. Normally, I would turn right out of the car park to go home, but now I was turning left and heading down the main road towards Littleport.

I was a bit surprised Deborah had asked me to go in front, given that she'd been to Ian's company HQ before and must know the way. I was uncomfortably aware that I was only driving a 1.0-litre engine car, whereas hers was probably a 3.0-litre. I didn't want her to think that I was incapable of handling something more powerful, so I drove faster than I was used to doing.

The roads were fairly quiet at this time of the early evening, but at one point, soon after we'd gone past Littleport, we came up behind one of the slow-moving tractors that were so common in this area of Cambridgeshire. One of my regular peeves was that tractor drivers would seldom pull into a lay-by to let car drivers pass; it was as if they considered their time and tasks more important than anyone else's. In order to impress Deborah with my driving skills, I tried to overtake the tractor and, for a few seconds, felt a flutter of panic as the tractor appeared to increase its speed and my car didn't accelerate as quickly as I would have liked. I would have felt humiliated if I'd had to give up and fall back behind the tractor again, but there were fortunately no headlights coming towards us on the other side of the road and I was slowly able to continue my manoeuvre. In my rearview mirror, I saw the headlights of Deborah's Discovery swoop past the tractor in a matter of seconds and tuck back in behind me.

Despite the attention that I was paying to the road, part of my mind must still have been on my investigation. Something which Richard had said was niggling away at me. He'd claimed not to have heard about Harriet's car being keyed – not surprisingly, given that she'd been too embarrassed to tell anyone at work. But something still wasn't right.

Then, I got it. Richard had expressed astonishment that her car had been keyed in the University car park. He'd said he thought it would be safe there. How the hell had he known that the car had been keyed in the car park? I certainly hadn't told him. The only way he could have known would be if he'd keyed it himself, presumably in retaliation for Harriet having landed him in hot water with me.

But, shit, I'd just told Deborah that Ian Davey had probably killed Harriet. We were on our way to try to find out if Ian was the guilty man. Were Harriet's death and the keying of her car unconnected events, therefore, or had I made a complete and utter fool of myself? My ball sack tightened at the thought of me and Deborah falsely accusing one of the University's most important commercial partners of murder.

But no, I thought, I must still be right about Ian. Simon had known the time of Harriet's death, and this was information which the police hadn't released. And since Simon had been in a car with Deborah when Harriet was drowning, he could only have found out the time of her death from the person responsible. From Ian. The keying of the car and the killing of Harriet must be unconnected. That was the only logical conclusion. Thank God for that.

Not surprisingly, I was sweating. I was pretty sure that I'd also been muttering away to myself. It was a good thing I wasn't giving Deborah a lift or she would have supposed she was being driven by a madman. I glanced at the display screen in front of me and saw that we would arrive at Ian's company HQ in around five minutes. We were now on a long stretch of an unlit minor road which comprised a single lane in each direction. As was often the case in the Fens, the road gently undulated most of the time because of the marshy land on which it was laid, making me feel slightly queasy. There were also potholes all over the place, meaning that I had to keep swerving to avoid them at the last minute as they loomed up out of the dark. A river, gleaming black in my headlights, ran along the left-hand side of the road, only a few yards away from the line of my nearside wheels.

I glanced in my rearview mirror to see if Deborah was also dodging the potholes. For a moment, I couldn't see her, and I was worried that I'd taken a wrong turn while mulling over the keying of Harriet's car. It would be embarrassing if I turned up late at Ian's company HQ and had to admit that I'd got lost. Then I looked in my driver side mirror and saw Deborah's Discovery on my right and only a few yards behind me. My initial reaction was to feel irritation that she was overtaking me after I'd done all the hard navigational work so that she would be the first to arrive. There was nothing I could do about that, however, so I gently touched my brake so she could complete her manoeuvre more quickly. To my surprise, though, the relative position of our cars didn't change, meaning that she too must have braked slightly. I looked ahead to see if Deborah had seen the headlights of a car coming, causing her to abandon her attempt to overtake. But no, the road in front beyond my headlights was almost completely dark.

All of a sudden, the Discovery surged forward so that it was exactly level with my Aygo. Then it swung leftwards, looking like a massive black rock. There was a terrifying instant, which I will never forget, when a collision became inevitable but before the two cars touched. A great chill flooded my body and I braced myself.

Then the sides of the cars met.

I had expected some kind of huge bang, but it was the force of the impact that startled me. It felt as if an invisible hand was trying to push my Aygo to my left. My first instinctive reaction was to fight the pressure by turning my steering wheel to the right. For probably only a second, the two cars pressed up against each other and I heard a combined squealing and crunching sound as metal rubbed against metal. Then the pressure eased and Deborah's car moved a foot or two away to the right. I wondered if she had swerved into me either by mistake or because of a temporary loss of control of her car. But then her Discovery swung back against my car with noticeably more force. It was as if the first collision had been a practice run and now she was doing it for real.

This time, the impact and the noise were greater. Remarkably,

I had time to remind myself that the weight of my Aygo must only be a fraction of that of the Discovery and that the leftwards momentum of the latter would make it impossible for my car to resist. My car moved sideways, towards the river, and I started to panic. Whether it would have made any difference if I had braked so that I fell behind the Discovery, I will never know. I wasn't capable of rational analysis.

There was only a narrow grass verge between the road and the river. Without thinking of the consequences, I saw the verge as a possible sanctuary and turned my steering wheel to the left. I had to get my car away from Deborah's. My nearside wheels were now on the grass, which felt slightly bumpy but otherwise solid. I looked to my right and saw the Discovery moving towards me for a third attack. Turning to face forward again, I spotted a black line crossing the grass just ahead of me. I realised too late that it must be one of the narrow drainage ditches that are often cut into verges in this area of the Fens.

There was a hell of a bang as my front nearside wheel went into the ditch. My car swung to the left, towards the river. For a moment, I feared it was going to turn over. I spun my steering wheel to the left too, in the direction of the swing of the car, to try to keep the car the right way up. And then, without warning, there was no longer any sound of wheels on the ground. I had gone right over the grass verge and the car was in the air. In front of me, a few feet lower down, the river was black and even, like oil.

I heard a scream. It only occurred to me later that the scream must have been mine.

There was a massive impact. Far greater than the impact of Deborah's car hitting mine. If that had felt like an invisible hand pushing my car sideways, this felt like a punch from a giant heavyweight boxer. I was thrown forward in my seat, but was then immediately restrained by the seat belt and by what I later realised was the airbag. All air was forced from my lungs. My only thought was to pray for the car not to turn over in the water.

I don't know how long it all took: from when Deborah's car first hit mine through to when I hit the water. Maybe only a few seconds. But suddenly, after all the noise and the movement, there was complete silence and stillness. Not even the engine was running.

41

It took me a few seconds properly to understand where I was.

My heart was pounding, almost audibly, in the centre of my chest. I was panting hard, but struggling to draw enough air into my lungs. In front of me, the airbag was already deflating. It was like a light-bulb moment for me; airbags must be designed that way so people can get quickly out of their car after an accident.

The most frightening thing was how the car was pointing downwards. The weight of the engine had quickly dragged the front underwater. Much of the windscreen was also already below the surface of the river. I'm not ashamed to admit that I froze completely. I didn't have a clue what to do.

At some point, though, probably still less than half a minute after the car had gone into the river, my panic subsided enough for me to comprehend that I had to escape. I pressed the button to release the seat belt. To my relief, it worked. My next thought was to open the door and get out that way before the car sank completely. But when I tugged the handle and tried to push the door open, nothing happened. I tried again. Still no movement. At first, I couldn't understand why because I could see the lighter shade of darkness, which was the sky and freedom, from the side window. Then it registered that there was already too much water pressing on the door from outside for me to open it from inside.

Christ, I was trapped.

Then I remembered the window. I pressed the button to open it electrically. Nothing happened. I pressed again. Still nothing. Of course, the engine had gone off almost as soon as I'd hit the water. The electrical circuit must be shorted. Or maybe the mechanism had just broken in the impact. It hardly mattered which. I leant to my left and tried the passenger side window with the same result. I turned round in my seat, remembering that the rear passenger windows opened manually. But I'd forgotten that these were hinged and only opened a few inches; even a cat would struggle to escape that way.

I banged my fist against the driver side window so hard that I gasped with pain. It seemed odd that I should be bothered by that kind of pain when fighting for my life. However, even then, I was reminded of a description from a book in my true crime collection – written, I believe, by George Orwell – of a judicial hanging many years ago in colonial Burma, in which a condemned man being marched to the gallows had, purely through instinct, side-stepped a puddle in order to keep his feet dry. Within a few minutes, he was dead and the dryness of his feet no longer mattered.

Again I tried breaking the window with the flat of my hand and then with my elbow, but to no avail.

I almost gave up. I couldn't open the doors. I couldn't open or break the windows. I couldn't do anything. The river was presumably used by boats, so it wouldn't be so shallow that the car would reach the bottom before being completely submerged. Already, the water was rising up the outside of the side windows as the car sank lower into the river. I could also hear water pouring into the car from God knows where.

I was going to drown. I would become one of those bodies that, on a regular basis in the Fens, are recovered from cars that have come off the road into a river.

Think, think, think.

I actually heard myself uttering these words. I was an educated and well-read man. I must at some point in my life have read or watched what to do in these circumstances. There was something familiar at the back of my mind, but I couldn't initially place it. Then I remembered. I'd watched a programme a long time ago on how to escape from a car which has gone into water. There had been a demonstration in a swimming pool. The first thing it told you to do was not to panic. Well, that was a load of fucking good, I thought. The tossers who made the programme had been in a submerged car all right. But they had an emergency supply of underwater breathing gear with them inside the car and a team of frogmen rescuers in the pool outside the car. No fucking need for them not to panic then.

The water outside the car had now completely covered the windscreen and the front side windows. Inside, the water had reached my balls. It was so bloody cold.

But I was remembering more of the programme I had watched. They said that, in theory, you should be able to open the car door when the inside of the car had filled with water, once the pressure outside equalised with the pressure inside. Then you could get out and swim to the surface. Thank God, I thought. I can survive this. I just need to wait until the water reaches my mouth, take a deep gulp of air and hold my breath a few seconds – and Bob's your uncle.

Then I also remembered the result of the demonstration. The pressure hadn't equalised until well after the car completely filled with water. The know-alls inside had to use their emergency supply of oxygen while they waited. It wasn't always so simple, in other words.

I was stuffed. I would probably soon be dead after all. If the door didn't open while I was holding my breath, I would die an agonising, suffocating death, just a few feet away from safety. It was so unfair. Why did it have to be me? Why not one of the many shits at the University or at Doveley's? Funnily enough, I was so wrapped up in my own predicament that I didn't give a moment's thought to why Deborah had forced me into the river.

In utter desperation, I racked my brain for anything in the car which I could use to break a window. Of all the crap that I put into my car, there was absolutely nothing which would do the job. My tennis bag was in the boot, but even if I could reach it, I didn't think it contained anything that I could use.

Then I recalled something. When I'd bought my car, I'd been

amused by the emergency escape tool mounted in the driver's footwell. I'd joked with the salesman about the minuscule likelihood of it being used by the elderly couple who owned the car before me. I don't think I'd even touched the tool, but it was still there. But would it work? Well, surely that's what it was for, to break a car window in an emergency. Could I smash the driver side window and then climb out? I was almost too scared to try. It's the hope that kills you. But I had no choice. If I didn't try, I could be dead within a minute or two.

The water was now up to my chest. It felt like liquid ice. I took a deep breath, put my head below the surface and reached for the tool. It was attached to the side of the footwell, but I gave it a big wrench and it came free. Holding the tool in my right hand, I lifted my whole arm high and as far away from the driver side window as I could, and then I swung my arm across the front of my face and hit the glass with as much force as I could muster. I don't know whether the glass cracked, or shattered, or what. All I know is that there was a rush of freezing water all over my face and shoulders. Luckily, I'd taken a deep breath just before it hit me. Then the rush of water stopped, and I was holding my breath with my eyes tightly shut in relatively still water, with what I knew to be an open window next to me.

I shoved my head and shoulders through the window frame and pushed with my feet against the passenger door on the other side of the car. I'd lost all sense of direction, which way up I was, and where the surface was. My only thought was to get out of that fucking car without my legs or my body being caught up in something. I felt my body rushing through the water and kept my mouth and my eyes shut.

Then, much quicker than I dared hope for, my head broke water. I opened my eyes and took in a deep breath of air. It was the sweetest air I have ever tasted. I drew it into my lungs with the same sort of pleasure as if I were a hardened smoker enjoying my first cigarette of the day.

I was alive. I had got out of the car. Now I had to get to solid ground.

The river wasn't very wide, and I could make out the deeper blackness of the two banks in the darkness. Fortunately, I hadn't lost my glasses. Instinctively, I swam a breaststroke towards the bank furthest away from the road. Looking back at it afterwards, I don't know if subconsciously I was afraid that Deborah may have hung around for long enough to make sure I hadn't survived.

I'm a strong swimmer, and the ten or so yards to the bank should have been dead easy for me. But my clothes were weighing me down as if they were full of stones, and I was feeling exhausted now that my initial adrenalin rush had passed. If I'd had any great distance to cover, I don't think I would have made it. As it was, I got to the bank, panting as if I'd swum the English Channel, and found a place where I could get a sufficiently firm grip on some vegetation to pull myself out.

Then I collapsed onto the ground, face down, focussing on my breathing and trying to get enough air into my lungs to recover.

I still hadn't given a thought to Deborah.

*

I don't know how long I remained lying there in the long grass. I was freezing cold. My teeth were chattering and my body was shaking. I desperately needed something to warm me up. I was about to roll onto my back and then try to get up when, for the first time, I gave proper consideration to what had happened.

Deborah Jones, a pro-vice-chancellor at the University of East Cambridgeshire, had tried to kill me. She had deliberately driven me off the road.

And, fuck please no, had she then got out of her car to make sure I was dead or if necessary to finish me off? I felt a strange prickling sensation at the back of my neck. Was she now standing behind me, knife or stick in hand, ready to stab or hit me? I didn't know whether to roll over and find out or to stay face down in the ostrich-like hope that this would mean she couldn't be there.

But why had she tried to kill me? I had believed that we were now on the same side. Was she trying to protect herself, or someone else?

In the end, I had no choice. I couldn't lie there for ever or I would die of exposure. I gritted my teeth and did a quick roll to my left, ready to fight for my life if Deborah was there.

But I was alone. Deborah must have assumed that I was at the bottom of the river with my car. I wondered if she'd gone on to see Ian Davey or if the entire visit was a charade.

I needed to get help. I scanned the darkness for the lights of a house, but the nearest ones on this side of the river were a frightening distance away. I wouldn't have the strength to walk that far. Hell, what was I going to do?

Of course. My phone. My Samsung phone was supposed to be water resistant, although I'd never put it to the test. I took it out of the inside pocket of my jacket. Thank God, I hadn't left it on the front passenger seat or else it would now be at the bottom of the river. Not only was the phone still switched on, but it had over eighty per cent charge. With trembling fingers, I dialled a number which I'd last dialled as recently as that morning ...

42

'Yes?' The voice sounded both weary and exasperated.

'Dawn, it's me. Alan Gadd.'

'So I gathered. I'm off duty, Alan. Why did you insist on being put through to me at home? Why didn't you call 999 if there's an emergency?'

'Because Deborah Jones has just tried to kill me. The PVC at the University.'

There was a brief silence. I guess if anyone else had said this to P.C. Dawn Smith, she'd have thought them mad. But whatever else Dawn may have thought about me, she knew I wasn't that.

She said, 'Where are you, Alan?'

'On the way to Ian Davey's company HQ. I was driving there with Deborah. In separate cars. She rammed me off the road and into the river. I nearly drowned. I'm on the riverbank miles away from anywhere. Deborah's gone, but—'

'Can you drop me a PIN of your location?'

I could. I was still in Google Maps. Dawn must have read my number because the next moment I received a text message from an unfamiliar number. I quickly shared where I was.

'Stay where you are, Alan. I'll have people out to you straightaway.' She paused. 'But this had better be good. If it's not, you can expect to be charged with wasting police time.'

*

In different circumstances, I would have bitterly resented Dawn's last comment. After all I'd done to help the police earlier in the year, it showed a distinct lack of gratitude on her part.

But Dawn held all the cards now. I'd reached the end of my tether. There was no one left whom I could trust. I don't mind admitting that I was scared. Scared of Deborah, but also scared of everyone else who might have been involved in any way in Harriet's death. Deborah surely couldn't have been acting alone.

Physically, I was also feeling awful: shivering non-stop and finding it increasingly hard to breathe. Every time I tried to draw air into my lungs, something seemed to obstruct the flow.

Everywhere was black, and a typical fenland wind was blowing across the fields, chilling me to the bone. My sodden clothes were making things worse, but I could hardly take them off.

Although my first instinct was to roll up in a ball to retain some heat, I decided I had to keep active. I walked up and down the bank, short lengths of about twenty yards. I alternately waved my arms in the air and banged them against my sides. I kept looking at my watch. It was now thirty minutes since I'd spoken to Dawn and there was still no fucking sign of her.

Another fifteen minutes passed. And then another fifteen. I couldn't last much longer.

Finally, I saw a flashing blue light on the horizon, on the other side of the river. Then a second blue light. The lights were moving along the road which I'd been driving on. At first, they'd been moving quickly but now they slowed down. They must be searching for me. My car had completely disappeared beneath the surface of the river, and there would have been no indication on the road of where I'd been forced into the water. I was racking my brain as to how to make sure that they found me when my phone rang.

'Alan, it's Dawn. Switch your phone light on and wave it towards the road.'

Of course. I did as she said. The blue lights were now moving very slowly along the road, and then they stopped, more or less opposite to where I was. It looked like there was a police car and an ambulance. Doors opened and interior lights came on to provide some illumination. I saw some figures climb out and cross the verge to the riverside. They stopped on the opposite bank, about twenty yards away from me.

'Alan, is that you?' I recognised Dawn's voice. They must have picked her up on the way.

I bit back an angry response. Now was not the time. 'Yes,' I said.

'Are you OK?'

'Well, I'm alive.' I resisted the temptation to add a 'No thanks to you'.

'Where's your car?'

'In the river. At the bottom.'

'Was anyone else in it?'

'No.'

'Can you get back across the river?'

What the fuck? Was that bloody policewoman expecting me to swim back across the river? Why not ask me to go out and catch Deborah while I was at it? And maybe also solve all of Cambridgeshire's unsolved murders before bedtime? I wanted to say all these things to her.

Instead, I shouted, 'No, I can't get back across. I nearly drowned. I need someone to come over and get me.'

I was half-expecting her to say they hadn't been trained to swim across rivers, in which case, notwithstanding my desperation, I would have given her a piece of my mind.

However, she replied, 'Don't worry. You stay there. There's a road bridge over the river a few minutes further on. The ambulance will come round. We'll stay here to make sure you're OK. You're safe now and soon you'll be warm.'

I have little recollection of the next ten or fifteen minutes. My shivering increased, and I was becoming alarmed at my inability to breathe. I remembered an asthma attack which I'd had as a small child on a day trip to London, aged perhaps ten or eleven. It was the first time something of that nature had ever happened to me and I'd thought I was suffocating. I was feeling a bit like that now.

At some point, the ambulance arrived and the paramedics

wrapped some kind of foil blanket around me. They helped me into the back of the ambulance and laid me down inside, asking me all sorts of questions about how I was feeling, checking my pulse, and so on.

I must have fainted because the next thing I remember was Dawn sitting by my side in the back of the moving ambulance. I could tell that the ambulance was travelling quickly, and from time to time I would hear the siren sounding and then the surge of the engine as the driver presumably overtook some car.

'Alan, it's Dawn. Don't speak unless you feel up to it.'

'I'm OK.'

I opened my eyes and saw her studying my face closely. I'd previously only seen her in uniform, wearing little or no make-up, but now she was made up as if for a night out. Her blonde hair, normally tied up behind her head, fell loose around her shoulders. For a moment, I so much wanted to reach out and hold her hand, not for any sexual reason but purely for the benefit of the human contact. But I didn't dare. It would have killed me if she'd rejected my touch.

'Can you tell me exactly what happened?'

I closed my eyes again and tried to explain it all logically, even though there seemed little logic to me in what had happened.

Then Dawn asked me a series of specific questions.

'Do you know the registration number of Deborah's car?'

'No, sorry. But it's her own car. She comes to the University in it every day. It's a black Land Rover Discovery.'

'Are you sure she drove her car into yours twice?'

'Yes. The second time was even more deliberate than the first.'

'Does your car have a dash cam?'

'Yes, front and back.'

'You said that Harriet had made notes of what she'd found out before she died. Have you printed them off?'

'No. But you can get access to them the same way I did.' A chilling thought occurred to me. 'But don't ask Lewis, or Amanda ... or any of the people whose names I've mentioned. Ask for the head of IT. And make sure you supervise him until you have full access to everything you need.'

*

The blue light must have done its trick because we arrived at the hospital – they told me it was Addenbrooke's, in Cambridge – much sooner than I expected. I was carried into A&E and asked all the same kinds of questions and given the same kinds of tests as I'd had at the scene of the accident, but this time by a doctor.

My breathing had slowed down to something like normal and I was feeling pleasantly warm, almost as if I was in bed with an electric blanket beneath me. I heard someone say that I was in shock, although not in any danger, but would need to be admitted overnight. There seemed to be a discussion – slightly testy but not quite an argument – between the doctor and one of the police officers who had come with Dawn. I gathered that the doctor wanted me to be allowed to rest, whereas the police wanted to breathalyse me and to ask me some more questions. I heard the phrase 'attempted murder' used at one point by the police officer, and he added something about needing to ensure that evidence was preserved.

I suppose the police must have won because once I'd taken a breath test and been put in a bed – in a room on my own, I was pleased to note – Dawn sat at my bedside and asked me yet more questions. The other police officer, a young man, sat behind her but within earshot. All I wanted to do was hold Dawn's hand and go to sleep, but I could tell that she wouldn't give up until she had what she wanted.

'There's something I don't understand, Alan,' she said, after I'd told her everything I could remember about my and Harriet's investigations at the University. 'What made you think that Harriet's death wasn't an accident?'

'I was down by the river shortly before she died.'

That was the one bit of information that so far I'd held back. Dawn's eyes opened wide. The police officer behind her leant forward.

263

'Doing what exactly?' she asked.

I was too tired to think up any kind of explanation that would show me in a good light. I also probably only had the one chance to get the police on my side. I said, 'I was following her. She'd been on a date with Jeff Parker from Doveley's. They then went their different ways, and I followed Harriet as far as the narrowboat where, it turned out, she was visiting a friend. Next thing, I spotted someone who'd been following me. Or, as it later turned out, following Harriet. But I thought it was Jeff, so I ran off.'

'Why were you following her?'

'I was upset. I couldn't stand the idea of her being with Jeff. You remember the history of him and Helen at Doveley's?'

'Yes, I do. What were you planning to do when you followed her along the riverside?'

'I honestly don't know.' That was true as well, of course. 'I suppose I just wanted to see what she was up to. To make sure that she was going home on her own and not with that bastard.'

Dawn's expression stayed neutral, but the police officer behind her gave me a look as if to ask which rock had I crawled out from under. I felt like bursting into tears. I hadn't behaved perfectly throughout, I knew that, but I had been trying to root out a wrong-doer.

She said, 'You can't be sure it was Ian Davey following you?'

'No. But, thinking back, it was definitely a man and someone of his rough shape and size. At the time, obviously, it hadn't occurred to me that it might be him.'

'Is there anything else you need to tell me? Anything you might have done because of how you felt about Harriet?'

It was too late to hold anything back. I told her about the anonymous e-mail I'd sent to Ruth, tipping her off about Harriet's past affair with her husband. And about what this had led on to.

'Can I ask why you sent the e-mail?'

'I ... I was annoyed.'

'With Harriet?'

'No, with Lewis. It wasn't right that he'd done what he did and got away with it. I thought Ruth had a right to know.'

'Even though she then took it out on Harriet?'

'Yes, I know. I hadn't thought it through. I guess—'

'You were just jealous, weren't you? You couldn't care less about Lewis having been unfaithful. It was because he'd been unfaithful with Harriet, wasn't it? You wished it had been you having sex with her?'

Normally, I would have retorted that my relationship with Harriet had been purely professional and that it would have been improper for me even to consider crossing the line with her. But my heart wasn't in it. I realised, perhaps properly for the first time, that what Dawn was saying was right. Oh, I was such a fucking shit. I deserved everything that had happened to me.

Dawn was now saying something about having to check my whereabouts at the time when Harriet was believed to have died. She asked a few more questions, and then she and the other police officer got up from their chairs.

Just before going out of the door, with the other officer already in the corridor outside, she turned and gave me what looked like a genuinely sympathetic smile. The first such smile she'd ever given me.

She said, 'Alan, once this is over, I think you need to get some help. For your own sake. I really do. Now, get some sleep, and we'll speak again soon.'

43

I don't know how long the hospital had originally planned to keep me in, but I was sure that whatever plans might have existed went out of the window pretty quickly. I'd been admitted on Thursday evening and, not unexpectedly, didn't sleep well that night. I was told that I woke up screaming in the early hours of Friday morning. I'd had a nightmare in which I was at the bottom of the river in my car. This time, I couldn't break a window to escape, and as I sat in the driver's seat with my air running out I saw outside the car, looking in and laughing at me, all the people at the University with whom I'd crossed swords. There was Deborah, naturally, but also Simon Fuller, Ian Davey, Amanda, Lewis, Ruth, Hugh, Mehak, Richard and Tom. In the background, I even spotted Trevor, Harriet's landlord. None of them had oxygen masks on, but it didn't occur to me to question how they could breathe underwater.

When I woke up from the nightmare, there was a young black female nurse holding my hand and reassuring me I was safe. I told her I was too frightened to go back to sleep. Some time later, a doctor arrived and I think I was given an injection. I did then sleep, but I felt completely exhausted when I woke up in the morning. I had no interest in the food they brought me and I burst into tears when a nurse said that some breakfast would make me feel better. All I wanted was to crawl under the sheets and make everything go away. I didn't want to make decisions about anything ever again.

Another doctor came to see me during the day. He didn't seem interested in sticking things into me, or getting food down me, or taking things out of me. He was more interested in how I was feeling. He was a young man, with his whole life in front of him, and he seemed shocked when I said that I might have been better off not escaping from the car. When he asked me why, I started crying again and saying that only Helen would have understood. He asked who Helen was, and I told him, and I told him about Helen's death and how I'd caught the person responsible and how nobody had ever thanked me properly for doing so. I then told him how Harriet had made my life worth living again, but now she was dead and no one other than me seemed to care, and no one had even bothered to contact me to let me know when Harriet's funeral was taking place.

After that, the nurses would come in regularly to check how I was. I've never been that keen on medics, but I have to say that the staff in the hospital did me proud. I knew that major decisions in hospitals were not usually taken at weekends, because senior clinicians were not around, so I wasn't particularly surprised when I was told that I should just have a good rest on Saturday and Sunday and we'd all see how I felt on Monday.

*

I had, therefore, definitely been expecting visitors on Monday. But I hadn't expected to see the two people who came into my room at around 10 a.m.

'Good morning, Alan. How are you? This is Detective Inspector Edwards from CID.'

I nodded a hello to the tall, serious-looking man who was being introduced by P.C. Dawn Smith.

They sat down in the same chairs that Dawn and her other colleague had used on Thursday, but this time they sat side by side rather than one behind the other. I wondered for a moment if there was trouble in store for me. However, their body language seemed to show that they were in a conversational, rather than an interrogative, mood.

'We thought you'd like an update on what's been happening,' the Detective Inspector said. 'If it's all too soon, though, please say. We can always come back. We'll need to ask you for a formal witness statement on another occasion anyway. And you'll probably be called upon to give evidence at trial in due course.'

'Trial? Whose trial?'

'I'll let P.C. Smith explain. I understand that you two know each other from earlier this year. You did well there, by the way.'

That was the first piece of unqualified praise I think I'd ever had from the police. The cynical side of me said that they were probably keeping me sweet for something.

Dawn took over. 'As the DI said, Alan, do interrupt me if I'm saying too much, or if anything upsets you. The doctors have said that you aren't very well.'

'I'm not great,' I said. 'But you don't need to sugarcoat anything. What's happened regarding Deborah?'

'Deborah Jones was arrested on Friday morning. She'd booked her car in for a repair and respray at a body shop, but we got there first. We've also recovered your car from the river, and the memory card for your dash cams was still working. So we've got footage from the rear dash cam which confirms your account of events.'

Ever the police officer, I thought, not believing what I told her unless she had independent confirmation. 'But why did she try to kill me?' I asked.

'She denies trying to kill you.'

'What?'

'At first, she said it was a complete accident. She said she was overtaking you when she hit a pothole and lost control of her car. She said she was horrified when she collided with you and saw you go into the river.'

'That's crap.'

'Yes, we know. We showed her and the duty solicitor the dash cam footage. The rear camera caught enough of what she did to make her change her story. She then said that when she was overtaking you, she had what she called a "moment of madness".

She wanted to prevent the meeting with Ian Davey from taking place, for reasons which she said she would explain, and she thought she could do this by nudging your car off the road. She says she didn't know the river was there and believed you'd just have to stop on the verge.'

'That's crap, too,' I said. 'She's been to Ian's place before, so she definitely knew the river was there. It was my first time on that road and I could see the bloody river clearly enough in my headlights. Anyway, why did she say she wanted to stop the meeting?'

'She says to protect Professor Simon Fuller.'

'What?' My head was starting to spin, and I don't think it was just the medication.

'She says she wanted to protect him because they were in a relationship.'

'Are you serious? Deborah Jones and Simon Fuller?'

'Yes. They've both confirmed it. Didn't it seem odd to you that they, a pro-vice-chancellor and an academic, had gone to a networking event and a dinner in Cambridge together? Just the two of them?'

But Deborah looks like a bloody horse. I didn't say that, of course. Women such as Dawn generally didn't like those types of comments being made about other women. They were all bloody at it at the University, I thought. First Harriet and Lewis. Then Harriet and Hugh. Then Mehak with God knows who, but probably including Hugh. Now Deborah and Simon. I was amazed that any of them had time to do any work with all their shagging around.

'But why?' I asked. 'I don't mean why were they in a relationship. I mean why would she need to protect him?'

'She was worried that Simon Fuller was going to get the blame for what, according to the two of them, Ian Davey did.'

'You mean to Harriet?'

'Yes. We now have CCTV footage which shows that Ian Davey was in the riverside area of Ely when Harriet died. We hope the forensic evidence we've recently obtained will confirm that he was responsible for her death. We're now treating Harriet's death as a case of murder. Thanks to you, obviously.'

That was twice now that I'd been praised. The police must really need my help with this one. Without my evidence, I guessed they might struggle to build a case.

'Why did Ian Davey kill Harriet?' I asked.

'We think it was to stop her from telling you what she'd found out. Basically, that Ian Davey stood to become a multi-millionaire overnight from the sale of his company. But only if his company could first get ownership of the University's wearable technology. Ian was worried that you might still be able to put a spoke in the wheel if Harriet passed on what she knew. He found out where she was going the night she died and, well, he seized his opportunity.'

'But how could he have found out where Harriet was going? He'd only met her once, and that was before ... before she made arrangements to go down to the riverside.' Even now, I couldn't bring myself to mention Jeff's name, let alone refer to him having a date with Harriet.

'That was pure bad luck, I'm afraid. Your old firm, Doveley's, acts for Ian Davey's company, as well as being the University's solicitors. This means, incidentally, that they couldn't act for either party in relation to the sale of the technology to Mr Davey's company. They had a conflict of interest.'

Christ, that rang a bell. Jeff's phone call on the Sunday after Harriet died.

'Jeff Parker?' I asked.

'Yes. Mr Parker had been at Mr Davey's company HQ on the afternoon that Harriet died. Her name came up in conversation and Mr Parker mentioned where he was having dinner with her that night.' Dawn paused and looked slightly uncomfortable. 'He also mentioned that Harriet was going on to see a friend on a narrowboat afterwards.'

It wasn't just people at the University who were conspiring to destroy me, I thought. Jeff Parker was at it too. 'In other words,' I said, 'if Parker had kept his mouth shut, Harriet would still be alive?'

'As I said, it was pure bad luck that Harriet's name came up.'

I wanted to ask why they weren't charging Jeff with something too. Anything. He was as responsible as anyone for Harriet's death. Everyone must see that, surely. But I knew I would get nowhere.

Instead, I said, 'So it was Ian Davey following me and Harriet?'

'Yes.'

'And then he pushed her into the water?'

'We believe so.'

I remembered something else. 'He knew Harriet couldn't swim. She told him that when we met him and Simon. So he pushed her in when she was drunk, and he knew she wouldn't be able to save herself.'

DI Edwards was scribbling away next to Dawn. That's something else they would no doubt need me to testify about.

I went on, 'You said that Deborah wanted to protect Simon. They both must have known what happened that night, then. Were they there as well?'

Dawn shook her head. 'We've checked their whereabouts, and they definitely weren't down by the riverside when Harriet was pushed into the water. It wouldn't have been possible for them to get there in time after their dinner in Cambridge. But we think Ian Davey told Simon Fuller what had happened, perhaps saying that it was some sort of accident, but not knowing that Professor Fuller was in a relationship with Ms Jones and that he would then tell her.'

'But if Ian said anything at all to Simon, that must mean the two of them were in it together. In selling off the University's technology too cheaply, I mean.'

'Yes. We're pretty sure that Simon Fuller stood to benefit financially as well as Ian Davey, although perhaps by not so much. Ms Jones probably got involved at a later stage, as a result of her relationship with Professor Fuller.'

'But it was Deborah who arranged the meeting with Ian. She must have done that to try to silence me. She's as involved as any of them.'

So far, Dawn had been doing all the talking, but now DI Edwards took over. 'There's a difference, Alan, between what we know – in other words, what we can prove – and what we believe but can't yet prove. For what it's worth, we believe all three were equally involved in the attempt to defraud the University by selling its technology at an undervalue. We suspect, though, that Ian Davey was the only one who planned or was involved in Harriet's death. The other two are now going to throw as much blame on him as possible, both for the murder and for the sale of the technology. No doubt Mr Davey, in return, will do the same to them. It's what we call a cut-throat defence.'

The logic was inescapable, but I still found it hard to believe that all this had been going on under the University's roof. Things like this just didn't happen in English universities.

'Have Simon and Ian been arrested too?' I asked.

'Yes,' DI Edwards said. 'They were both arrested and interviewed under caution, and they have been released under further investigation.'

'You mean that they and Deborah are free to walk the streets?'

'Yes, for now. But you won't see them at the University, and they aren't to contact you. We expect a charging decision to be made very soon.'

'What about me?'

'In what sense?'

'Do I just go back to work as normal?'

Dawn took over again. 'That's for you and the University to decide, Alan. But yes, once you're well enough, you can continue as best you can. We'll arrange for you to make a formal witness statement. We may also need your help from time to time once a decision has been made regarding the charges to be brought against Deborah, Simon and Ian. As the DI said, you can also expect to have to give evidence at their trial. In the meantime, try to rebuild your life as best you can. And as I said to you last week, do please take whatever help is offered.'

And that was that. Dawn and her DI Edwards left as

unobtrusively as they had arrived. I wondered if they'd been asked by the nursing staff not to upset me. They hadn't brought up the reason for my presence by the riverside the night that Harriet had died, but I could anticipate being questioned about that at trial. How was I going to explain the fact that I'd been following Harriet and Jeff? The more I described the kind of person that Jeff was, the more I would risk looking obsessive and unhinged. No one would understand how I felt. I could envisage the media headlines and the looks on people's faces at the University. I didn't know if I would be brave enough to cope with that.

44

Hi Lewis

Good news, I'm ready to come back to work. I was discharged from hospital this morning. I'll see you tomorrow!

Best wishes
Alan

I'd decided to swallow my pride and not let my resentment of Lewis show. I wasn't going to let bygones be bygones, but I would be careful about when and how I got my own back on him.

The hospital had said I could go home the morning after the visit by the two police officers. They urged me to see my GP as soon as possible, to discuss the medication they were putting me on, and there was a recommendation that I also see someone to talk through my issues, as they charmingly put it.

I asked one of the nurses if anyone from the University had been in touch to check on my welfare. She did well to hide her embarrassment at having to say no.

I'd e-mailed Lewis as soon as I got home. I had a reply within ten minutes:

Hi Alan

Great to hear that you are feeling better. There's no rush to come back, though. Someone from the University will call at your house tomorrow morning to talk things through if that's OK. Stay at home and get some rest until then.

Regards
Lewis

I did as I was told, though I had to wait until nearly 12 p.m. the next day for the visit. I spent the first part of the morning looking repeatedly out of my downstairs window for whoever was coming, but eventually I gave up and plumped myself down on my sofa with my phone to see if there were any media reports about what had happened to me. I found some references to a car having gone into the river and then being subsequently retrieved, but I got the impression that the reporters had lost interest once it was clear that a body hadn't been recovered. I found nothing about any arrests having been made.

It was a relief when the doorbell rang. I had no idea who was coming to see me, but I was startled to see Amanda, looking as much of a pixie as ever, standing on the doorstep with a young, po-faced woman whom I vaguely recognised from Senate House.

'Hello, Alan, I hope you're feeling better?' Amanda said with the kind of tight smile that normally gets described as polite. 'You probably recognise Kate, from HR. May we come in, please?'

We sat ourselves down in the lounge area of my downstairs space. I only had one sofa, and although it was designed for three people, we could hardly have a proper conversation sitting three in a row like birds on a fence. I therefore gave them the sofa and perched in front of them on one of the tall, three-legged stools from my breakfast bar, feeling slightly ridiculous. Amanda and Kate both politely declined my offer of coffee.

Amanda began with the sort of stuff I expected: checking on my well-being, saying what a terrible shock the whole thing must have been for me, observing what courage I had shown, and so on. It sounded like a prepared speech, if I'm honest. Kate sat there primly with a notebook and pen in her hand, with her legs pressed tightly together as if she thought I was the type of person who would try to peer at her knickers given half a chance.

I hadn't forgotten what Amanda had been up to regarding Landlord Relax, but I'd decided as soon as I saw her that it was better to get my feet back under the table at Senate House before I brought this up again. When she paused, I wondered if she was going to give me a reward for what I'd uncovered and gone through. I wasn't expecting her to produce a gallantry medal and pin it to my chest, but I thought she might propose some kind of financial bonus or a more prestigious job title, or at the very least a vice-chancellor's award.

Instead, she said, 'Do you have any questions so far, Alan?'

Well, if she wasn't going to mention a reward, I wasn't going to make a fool of myself by bringing the subject up. 'I'm just keen to get back to work, Amanda,' I said. 'I've got a lot on at the moment, as you'd expect with Harriet, um, no longer being around. I won't come in this afternoon if that's OK, but I'll be at my desk first thing tomorrow.'

It was only when the silence extended beyond a couple of seconds that I realised I might have misread the situation. Amanda and Kate exchanged looks, and I could swear that Kate gave her colleague a slight nod.

Amanda said, 'We'd love to be able to say come back straightaway. Unfortunately, things aren't that simple.'

'If you think I'm worried about Deborah and Simon being around, there's no need to be concerned. The police told me that, after their arrests, they aren't allowed back on campus. That's correct, isn't it?'

'Yes, it is. And, needless to say, we're grateful to you for having exposed the things which led to their arrests.'

Amanda was probably exaggerating her gratitude, I thought, given that she and Deborah were friends, but no matter.

'The thing is, Alan,' she went on, 'certain things have come to light while you've been away.'

'Regarding what?'

'Well, there has been an allegation of bullying.'

'Bullying? What do you mean?'

'Richard has made a formal complaint to HR that you have

been bullying him. He says that Tom will back him up in this. As you know, we have to take this kind of thing very seriously.'

'But that's ridiculous. I've never bullied anyone. Richard's work has been sub-standard and I've had to pick him up on this. But that's my job. Lewis will tell you what Richard's work can be like. He's simply not – if I'm honest – good enough.'

'Lewis says that Richard is an excellent worker and a valued member of the Legal team.'

So that's how that sod Lewis is going to get his own back at me, I thought. He's not man enough to have a go at me face-to-face; he has to go behind my back. Well, I'd show him, once I'd got Richard sorted.

I said, 'But Richard keyed Harriet's car. I can prove it. He knew it had been keyed in the car park at the University, and Harriet hadn't told anyone where it happened.'

Amanda continued as if I hadn't spoken: 'And there are other things, unfortunately. Ruth – Lewis's wife – received an anonymous e-mail making certain personal allegations about Lewis. We've spoken to Hugh, and he says he told you something private that was the subject matter of these allegations shortly before the e-mail was sent. He says you are the only person he told, and that he's sure no one else knows about the subject matter.'

I noted the careful way in which she avoided saying that Lewis, married to a University employee, had been shagging another junior University employee during University hours. 'Lewis and Hugh both bear a grudge against me,' I said.

'I notice you aren't denying sending the e-mail, Alan. The point, anyway, is that, according to Kate, sending the e-mail was potentially an offence under malicious communications legislation. We will have to discuss with Ruth whether she wants the police involved.'

I was kicking myself now for having told P.C. Dawn Smith about the e-mail. Otherwise, there was no way they could prove it came from me. This was the reward I got for being too honest. Anyway, if Lewis hadn't been shagging Harriet behind his wife's back, there would have been no need for me to send the e-mail. So it was really Lewis's fault and, I suppose, Harriet's as well; it certainly wasn't mine. I didn't say any of this, of course.

'And there's something else,' Amanda went on. 'I've received a very troubling allegation from Mehak in International. She says that you tried to blackmail her into giving you sexual favours.'

What the fuck. Mehak had offered me a deal. I wasn't proud of myself for going along with it, but I'd kept my side of the bargain. I could see Amanda and Kate watching my reaction very carefully. 'That's rubbish,' I said. 'I don't know what she's talking about.'

'She says that you accused her of taking bribes from overseas agents. And that you then offered not to report her if she slept with you. When she expressed her shock, you told her to take some time to think further about your offer and said that you wouldn't report her in the meantime. Is it true that you accused her of taking bribes?'

'Yes. Because she was.'

'So why didn't you report it to me straightaway?'

'Because … well, because she threatened to make these allegations about me if I did.'

'So, just to get this clear. You – a senior lawyer at the University – accused an employee of taking bribes. Then, when they threatened to make up a story about you, you chose not to act on what you had found out. Seriously?'

It didn't sound great, put that way. But Amanda didn't understand the position I'd been in.

She went on, 'We've spoken to the agents, and I can say now that there is no truth whatsoever in what you were accusing Mehak of. Some agents were paid higher rates of commission than normal, but that was to incentivise them and reward them for going the extra mile. There was no personal benefit to Mehak.'

So that was it. Mehak had used our 'deal' to buy herself time to cover up any incriminating evidence. It wouldn't be in the interests of any agents to admit what they'd been doing. And it sounded like the University had decided, for whatever reason, to accept her version of events rather than mine.

'She's lying,' I said simply. How I wished I'd recorded that conversation with Mehak.

Amanda ignored me. 'All things considered,' she said, 'it's difficult to see how you can remain at the University. You are still within your probationary period and, regrettably, we are not going to be able to make your position permanent. However, we wouldn't want to prejudice your future elsewhere. So, if you were to agree that your role at the University hasn't worked out, I'm sure we could provide a reference that other employers would find satisfactory.'

So that was it. The old tactic of go quietly and get a good reference. Well, sod that.

I said, 'I'm sorry, Amanda, but I don't think you are in a position to pass judgment. I've already told you what I uncovered about your relationship with the Landlord Relax founders. How they are personal friends of yours. How you are favouring them with the University's money without disclosing your relationship. That's corruption in anyone's book.'

Amanda's face creased in a complacent smile. She turned towards Kate and made an exaggerated gesture with her hands as if inviting her to speak.

Kate said, 'Amanda has, naturally, informed the Vice-Chancellor of the fact that she was at the same university as the founders, at the same time although on a different course, and that she has seen them occasionally over the years since they all graduated. The Vice-Chancellor agreed that there was no conflict, and he congratulated Amanda on the way the funding decisions for Landlord Relax were taken by the whole Enterprise Board, of which Amanda is just one member. Amanda also informed the Enterprise Board members individually of the relevant facts. I'm sorry, Alan, but making wild allegations of corruption against the Secretary and Registrar is just more proof of why your position hasn't worked out.'

It hadn't passed me by unnoticed that Kate had avoided

saying when exactly Amanda had informed the Vice-Chancellor and the individual Enterprise Board members about her own relationship with the founders. She certainly hadn't informed me. I had no doubt whatsoever that she'd only done so after I raised the issue with her. But the nails had already been hammered down into the lid of my coffin and nothing I could say was going to make a difference. The University wasn't going to suspend and investigate its Secretary and Registrar for corruption shortly after a pro-vice-chancellor and a star academic had been arrested in relation to a murder. How on earth would the Vice-Chancellor explain that away over the glasses of port at the next national get-together of university big swinging dicks?

Amanda and Kate left less than ten minutes later. The deal they were offering was crystal clear. If I resigned now and didn't work my notice period, they would give me the reference I needed and would pay up my salary for the rest of my probationary period. Kate said that I needn't trouble Amanda again and that if I gave her a call when I'd reached my decision, she could sort out all the paperwork very quickly.

*

I sat on my sofa for a long time after Amanda and Kate had gone, staring through the window which overlooked the communal garden at the front of my house. The University had gone full speed into damage limitation mode. I had, in my exit from Doveley's, found out how ruthless a private practice firm of solicitors could be. But it was clear that a university – for all its preaching about mission statements and core values – could be just as bad. It seemed that you could shag or bribe who you wanted as long as your face fitted and you didn't upset the apple cart.

Everything was so unfair.

I thought about my last year.

I'd loved Helen, and she'd been taken from me. I'd

subsequently found Harriet, but she too had been taken from me. Worst of all, Harriet had been taken from me before we'd even had the chance to get to know each other properly.

Work-wise, I'd lost my job at Doveley's after giving them years of service. And all because I'd done the right thing in bringing a killer to justice. I was now losing my job at the University for doing much the same thing. Where was I going wrong? I laughed bitterly at the recollection that I'd even lost my 'job' as an unpaid volunteer at a children's tennis camp.

Everything I touched seemed to end in disaster. I had no real friends, not even any acquaintances whom I could casually refer to as friends. The only person who seemed to show me any respect was that shit Jeff Parker, the man who'd shagged Helen and who'd been doing his damnedest to shag Harriet too. No doubt he would have his eyes on any other woman to whom I might get close in the future. Not that there was much prospect of that, if the e-mails which Harriet and Mehak had exchanged were any reflection of what most women thought of me.

My cat liked me, I supposed. And, ironically, all I'd ever done for my cat was to provide her with food and somewhere warm to sleep and to give her a stroke from time to time. But that was never going to be enough for me.

*

Towards tea time, I heated up a Charlie Bigham meal: a Thai Red Chicken Curry. I washed it down with a couple of bottles of Singha beer, then drank another couple of bottles afterwards. I had always tried to moderate my drinking, but recently that had gone out of the window.

Afterwards, I sought comfort, lying on my sofa, in some of my collection of true crime books. I found myself drawn to some accounts of people awaiting execution in English prisons, mostly from the 1940s through to the early 1960s. I'd often mulled over what it must have been like, sitting in a condemned cell in perfect health but knowing to the minute when you were going to die. I'd assumed that it would have been terrifying. But perhaps, I now thought, there was a certain comfort in knowing that this awful thing was going to happen to you and that nothing you said or did was going to make any difference.

Maybe that was why most men – and women – had gone quietly and uncomplainingly to their deaths.

I read some final letters from condemned men, written in their last hours of life, which contained references to the rising sun throwing light through the barred windows of their cells. There was no self-pity in their letters. They wanted to say a dignified goodbye to those who had loved them regardless of what they had done.

One young man, still a teenager, asked his family to make sure that his bicycle was handed down to his younger brother. Another man shook the hand of the prison governor as he and the hangman came into the condemned cell to take him to the execution chamber. He thanked the governor for the consideration that the prison staff had shown him during his final confinement.

My God, these murderers had done terrible things. But they'd also known how to die like men. In the manner of their deaths, they reclaimed their dignity and would be remembered – rightly or wrongly – for the courage they showed in their final moments.

It must have been well into the small hours when I fell asleep on my sofa. The beer had had the same effect on me as the sleeping draught often given to condemned men on their final night.

When I woke up and looked at my watch, it was 7.30 a.m. Wryly, I noted that most executions in England had taken place at 8 a.m. If I was a condemned man about to be hanged, I would already have had my breakfast and got dressed in the civilian clothes in which I was to die. I would have had the doctor's tot of brandy to steady my nerves. I would probably now be sitting at the table in my cell, flanked by two prison officers who – working in eight-hour shifts – would have been with me for every minute of my time in the condemned cell. By now, we would surely have run out of things to say to each other. The officers, if they were experienced, might have tried to make sure that my back was turned towards the door, so that when the hangman and his assistant came in they could, as I automatically stood up, more easily take hold of my arms and pinion them behind my back without panicking me.

In a little while, I put a big bowl of cat food and a bowl of fresh water down in my kitchen area. I wrote a short note to my next-door neighbours, asking them to look after my cat if they didn't see me around, and put it through their letterbox. I went up to my bedroom and removed the belt from my dressing gown.

I went onto the landing and reached up to push the loft lid into the loft. I took the landlord's stepladder out of the cupboard at the top of the stairs, and I used it to climb into the loft, carrying the belt with me.

I tied one end of the belt around a rafter directly over the open loft hatch. I tied the other end around my neck, standing right on the edge of the hatch. I couldn't create the kind of noose that had been used on condemned men, intended to break their necks rather than strangle them to death, but no one else was going to be affected by that.

It was now 7.55 a.m. English hangmen had always prided themselves on minimising the stress to their clients. They were never left to stand, hooded and noosed, on the trapdoor of the gallows for more than a few seconds before the lever was pushed. I was five minutes early. I would have to wait until 8 a.m. in order to do it properly. It would give me the chance to show the same bravery as others had shown before me. Perhaps I would be remembered for that, at least.

It was just such a shame that neither Helen nor Harriet could be here to watch.

AFTERWORD

In the afterword to *Biding My Time*, the first book in this series, I cautioned against reading too much into the fact that Alan Gadd lived and practised as a lawyer in Cambridge just because I also once lived and practised as a lawyer in Cambridge. In this sequel, Alan is now living in the beautiful cathedral city of Ely, twenty miles north of Cambridge, and working as an in-house lawyer at a university. Coincidentally, I too now live in Ely and I have also worked as an in-house lawyer at two universities. I would therefore like to stress that the University of East Cambridgeshire, and the characters who work there, and all the other characters and businesses in this novel, are entirely fictitious, as is the story itself.

Notwithstanding this disclaimer, some readers may be curious about my experiences of the English higher education sector. After all, the University of East Cambridgeshire, as seen through the prism of Alan's jaundiced eyes, surely deserves its reputation as one of the worst universities in the country, staffed as it apparently is by crooks, reprobates, time-servers and intellectual Lilliputians. I would therefore hasten to declare that my years as an in-house university lawyer were amongst my happiest in legal practice. I have fond memories of the people I worked with, including ('without limitation', as Alan would undoubtedly say) other lawyers, business development officers, academic inventors and even pro-vice-chancellors.

As with *Biding My Time*, it will be perfectly possible for the diligent reader to track down some of the places that Alan visits in *Drowning My Sorrows*, including the area around the River

Great Ouse where – tormented by jealousy – he follows Harriet on the last night of her life. However, I have invented some other places, so do not blame yourselves too harshly when you are not able – for example – to identify the club where Alan plays tennis, or the shop in which Alan confronts Harriet's landlord, or indeed the campus of the University of East Cambridgeshire.

When doing my final proof-read, I did wonder how realistic it was to portray a university world where so many people still work traditional nine-to-five hours on campus. Solicitor friends in private legal practice tell me they are getting back to something like 'normal' after the pandemic (e.g. three days in the office, more if junior or senior). However, friends who are university in-house lawyers report that they still work mostly remotely. In the interests of preserving these latter friendships, I refrain from an Alan Gadd-style riposte, recognising that they – and their managers – know better than me what works for them and their university. And by the time you read this, it is of course possible that most universities are also back to 'normal' … but if not, please treat this aspect of the book as part of my authorial licence.

I would like to add my customary thanks to those who read and commented on drafts of this novel at various stages, including in particular Keith Aggett (whose own first novel, *Mixed Messages,* a thriller set partly in Cambridge, originally inspired me to write *Biding My Time*).

If you enjoyed this book, I would be grateful if you would consider leaving a rating (and ideally a review) on Amazon. It's not easy for new, independent authors to publicise their work, and reviews are very helpful in this respect and therefore much appreciated.

Finally, if you are interested in further information about the background to this book (and to *Biding My Time*), please also visit my author's Facebook page at https://www.facebook.com/MartynGoodgerBooks.

Printed in Great Britain
by Amazon

38165266R00169